MW01232348

The Fat Lady Sings

ALSO BY DAVID SCOTT MILTON
NOVELS:

The Quarterback
Paradise Road
Kabbalah
Skyline

PLAYS:

Duet
Skin

The Fat Lady Sings

David Scott Milton

iUniverse.com, Inc.
San Jose New York Lincoln Shanghai

For Kyle and Abby, the treasures of my life.

The Fat Lady Sings

All Rights Reserved © 2001 by David Scott Milton

No part of this book may be reproduced or transmitted in any form or by any means, graphic, electronic, or mechanical, including photocopying, recording, taping, or by any information storage or retrieval system, without the permission in writing from the publisher.

Published by iUniverse.com, Inc.

For information address:
iUniverse.com, Inc.
5220 S 16th, Ste. 200
Lincoln, NE 68512
www.iuniverse.com

ISBN: 0-595-14748-8

Printed in the United States of America

Chapter One

I was running through fog. I could see nothing. Thick brush slapped at my face. The ground was a marsh beneath me and I stumbled as I ran. The air was crisp with early morning chill. Muck and water filled my shoes and it was cold. Gunfire cracked the air, growing more insistent. I'm dead, I thought. Wake up. Wake up. Wake up!

I opened my eyes. I was sitting in a chair at my desk. My reflection in the window opposite stared back at me. I glanced at my watch. It was still early night, not yet eight. I had nodded off for less than a minute.

A wide, white river of fog poured through the valley. I could see the lights of the prison below floating in and out. It felt as though I were on the shore of fast rushing waters, which parted from time to time to reveal a ghost city.

I sat trembling, chilled. I had been here for hours, drinking, staring at the sea of fog below, trying to figure out what I would do with my life. At some point, a curtain had fallen behind my eyes. And a nightmare had then come to me, as it did every night.

It was a horrendous period in my life. I felt as if I would never come out of it whole. I realized I must examine all that I had done in my life and live with it or cast it away.

A year before, my wife had come to me to announce that our marriage was over. She shrugged, no big deal. Not your fault, not mine. I'm just out of here.

,o kids and I was alone in a mountaintop
out lacerate myself with all the stupidity and
ced my life for as long as I could remember. I
er everything I had done and said, or not done,
not ⌐   on regrets. I was judge and jury, prosecutor and
defense a⌐   nd the verdict was always the same. No one ever got
off in that cou⌐ . And I would watch television, drink, and stare at the
prison lights.

After she broke the news, it took a few weeks for her to get everything together to go. I thought I could salvage the marriage. We would
sit at dinner and I would look at her and she was a stranger; and she
behaved toward me as though I were a stranger. We had been together
eleven years and suddenly we did not know each other. In those tense
days before she left, I would tell stupid, self-serving stories to this
woman I no longer knew, desperately trying to impress her. She was no
longer impressed, not by my stories, not by anything I had done in my
life. I no longer existed for her. Nothing I could say would move her.
Just as when someone dies and the body no longer seems to be that
person, so it was with our love. It was foreign, strange, an object. We
were objects to each other.

And now, night after night I would sit in the dark, drink Irish
whiskey, and stare at the prison lights.

After my wife left, I talked to my friend, Phil Kleinmutz, a local
lawyer with contacts at the prison about teaching a class there. I would
encourage the prisoners to tell the stories of their lives. They must have
interesting tales to tell, I reasoned. I wanted to get to know them and
learn what it's like to have your freedom bounded by real walls instead
of the walls inside your head.

I'm a writer: that is I'd been paid for my stuff, even if I had done it
only fitfully in recent times. I had had one or two things to say and I had
said them and now I was a kind of glorified con man, pitching tales for
anyone who could come up with some bucks for me. It was a dog and

pony show. I was hustling for my next payday, a man who cared for nothing, who believed in nothing.

I had begun to despise myself, the things I said, the same empty phrases, tired stories, not just in my work but in my life as well. What at one time had been original and promising and deeply felt was now flaccid and boring. I was an old pitchman weary of my own bullshit.

My days had a sameness to them that was brutal. I would rise late, then call my agent in Los Angeles. He wouldn't take the call. I knew he wouldn't, but hoped that before the day was over he'd get back to me. While shaving, I'd watch the end of the Kathy Lee and Regis television show; then with "The Price Is Right" on, I'd have my first cup of coffee of the day. I'd move to my desk and try to write.

You may know my first book, "Funhouse Mirrors." It had respectable sales and they made a godawful movie from it, "Call for Heroes." The film brought me out to California. Every year or so I would sell a film script and the money was good, but the films never were made, and the novels I wrote after "Funhouse Mirrors" sold poorly and so it was a matter of churning the things out for increasingly less money and satisfaction.

"Mirrors" had been written out of my experiences in Vietnam. I had gone into the war as a young man. I had fought with a Special Forces unit. In late 1967 I was involved in a singularly vicious and bloody incident in Kien Hoa Province, the Plain of Reeds. We had been working with a group of peasants in the area around Moc Hoa to locate and eliminate a Viet Cong regiment. The V.C. found out what we were up to and swept into the town and wiped out everyone.

They arranged to make it look as though it had been our doing—they had captured American weapons and used them in the attack and scattered around other captured items and spread the word through the region that we had perpetrated the atrocity.

I was the captain who ran the operation and there was a great deal of publicity growing out of the whole thing—the American media jumped on the story like a raven on a road kill and I spent a good deal of effort trying to get the thing straight. There was an inquiry and our unit was exonerated but the accusation stuck in popular memory.

I hadn't been able to tell everything, not out of mendacity, but ignorance. Flashes of memory would come back at odd times, catch me when I shaved or showered or watched television, rise up in my dreams, stuff I had either blocked out, misunderstood, or hadn't fully known. The bad dreams had started then and they never really stopped.

I came out of the army in '72, drifted, drank, walked a thin line of sanity. Then one day I sat down and began to write about what had happened, wrote it as honestly as I could, and the book was published as "Funhouse Mirrors." I thought my dreams would end. They didn't.

The movie occasionally comes on television, usually in the middle of the night. In the T.V. Guide it gets two stars. I only watch it when I'm very drunk.

But I had a profession now, a writer, and I went at it with more diligence than talent or inspiration. As I said, I had had one story to tell and I had told it and if I had any deep moral center I would have given up writing at that point. But Hollywood kept throwing money at me and I took the easy way out. I earned a good living. I married. I was nearly forty by then. We built a house in the mountains where I thought I'd write a great book. We had two kids.

My wife, who had been a model before our marriage, took a part-time job selling real estate. She met a Fedex driver on the job who looked like a road show Elvis and they had an affair and she suddenly decided that the brooding gaze with which I fixed the world was not as interesting as the smoldering looks the truck driver radiated and one day she informed me she no longer wanted to be married; she took our two kids, a boy four years old and a girl of six, and moved with Elvis to Bakersfield, the largest city near our town, Tehachapi. Roval was his name, actually, a large man with tattoos who favored sleeveless undershirts, chain-smoked Camels, and drank malt liquor by the quart.

It was something I never could have imagined. But I had learned long ago in war to take nothing for granted, not your next day, not your next hour.

Life was a wildcat poised to leap in your face.

I stayed in the house we had built on the mountain just outside Tehachapi, the house that was supposed to feed my inspiration. I promised myself I'd only write books that wound and stab, axes for the frozen sea inside all of us.

I took to drinking a lot of Bushmill's thinking about that. Halfway into the bottle, television seemed pretty good, a lot of good things being done there. I watched much television, news mainly. I'd watch it ten, twelve hours a day, the same stories over and over. In one month I learned more about what was going on in the world than my grandfather had been exposed to in his whole life. And the more I saw, the less real knowledge I possessed. It was a geometric progression. I knew more and more about less and less.

I suffered for my kids. I saw them every other weekend or so and it wasn't enough. How did they get along when I wasn't there? Were they treated well? When you're only marginally in their lives, everything related to them becomes magnified. You're an outsider who messes up the rhythm of their lives. You show up and the boyfriend hides and their mother is nasty and you feel like a stranger with your own kids. It takes you most of the time they're with you to get them to warm up to you and then its time to return them.

It's been said that a parent is a hostage to fate. I had heard this as a young man. I hadn't understood it, then, but I knew it now, the helplessness you feel in the face of all that can visit a child in this world.

They were so needy, clinging: "Hold me, daddy. Tell me a story. Sleep here with me. Leave the light on, daddy. I'm afraid."

After taking them back to my wife, (beer-bellied, tattooed Roval bolting at my arrival, secreting himself among the bougainvillea in the backyard) I would travel out to a baseball batting range near Sam Lynn ballpark, home of the Double A Bakersfield Blaze, and hit baseballs by the hour. I became quite good and prided myself on being the oldest batter in the cages who could belt out an eighty mile an hour fastball.

I spent great chunks of time imagining my life as a screenplay where I could go back and re-write the second act. I would go over and over it, from the end of the war in Vietnam to the day when my wife walked out on me, polishing it, perfecting it, erasing stupidities, wasted opportunities, harsh words. I promised myself that I would go over it until I got the damn thing right.

I had starting off writing consumed by what I had to say. I lived to write. Now I wrote so that I wouldn't die.

I would go round and round in my head about the whole thing, not only the writing, but my career. Why had I taken this job, why had I dealt with that producer? How had I allowed myself to fall into such a sinkhole of mediocrity? And then I turned that back on myself and began to attack the very act of writing for a living: why was I worried about fiction when life was so oppressive? What did it matter to me what 'characters' did? What stories did I have to tell? *Life was eating me up and there was no room for fiction.*

I knew I was now very drunk. I would end up getting sick. I would throw up.

I thought of the fatuous producers whose only real interest in the project was the bottom line—how much money would it earn for them; the mendacity, the viciousness, where everybody went to bed with a single prayer: that those doing well have their lives shattered before morning. It wasn't just that they wanted what you had. They wanted that, yes, but more: they didn't want you to have it. They didn't just want you to fail: they wanted you to die. No one rooted for you unless they *knew* you were dying. And only then if they had seen the lab reports.

There was the story about the agent who was visited by the Devil. He was told that he would guarantee him Sylvester Stallone, Jack Nicholson, and Tom Cruise as clients. But the agent must sacrifice his wife and children forever to him. The agent eyed Satan narrowly. "What's the catch?"

Staring past my reflection now, I gazed inward, a spectator at my own existence. I was thinking: life is godawful. And anything else is a lie. Stories are lies. I'm not interested in that anymore.

I was overcome by an awful realization: my mind had stopped absorbing the new. It refused to retain anything it didn't once already know. And so I knew that I was doomed to writing what I'd already written, only doing it more proficiently, cleanly, without guts and blood and soul. I was lost.

There was a manuscript on my desk, a novel I had been working on for years, another novel about war. In it I had tried, without success, to come to terms with what had really happened in Moc Hoa. The events in the gunfire, chaos, fog, death, formed a mystery, mute, impenetrable, a body frozen beneath ice, staring up at me. I could not reach it or bring it alive.

I spread the manuscript out on the desk. A paragraph caught my eye: "My men knew well how to kill. And the bodies were piled high that afternoon piled in a huge pyre, children, old people. And it was set on fire."

I took a pen and pressed as hard as I could on it and ripped the paragraph and crossed it out. I tore the paper with the pen. I phoned up Kleinmutz. We talked every evening, sometimes two or three times, two drunks with lousy, lost lives. His marriage had recently gone into the crapper, also, and he was taking it hard.

He had handled my divorce and at that time seemed to be the most happy of husbands. A year after my break-up, he, too, was visited by the devil of deceit: returning from a business trip, he discovered his wife and a refrigerator mechanic from Keene, a town down the road, passionately practicing the beast with two backs in his marriage bed. Desperate, humiliated soul, he had spied out the deed by scaling a tree outside the bedroom window.

As things transpired, while he was gone, wifie had brought the mechanic in to fix the Kelvinator. The man never left. All the house locks had been changed, their bank account gutted, and Kleinmutz' motorhome spirited away.

He confronted her at the local diner, The Mountain Inn, and she threw a fork at him; it stuck in his cheek; he belted her; she got an injunction against him.

Kleinmutz called me to try to help him figure it out. "We never even had an argument," he said, blubbering. By then he knew all the details and was frantically trying to bury assets and an old Judge from up near Fresno had offered him advice. "He said to me, 'I understand exactly Phil. But don't jump to conclusions because the conclusion you jump to just might be your own. This woman is disturbed. She has a fine husband in you. And she has a chemical imbalance in her brain now that prevents her from realizing this. You have to get your dauber up."

"What's a dauber?" I had asked.

"Who the fuck knows? Dauber. Some nautical thing. 'Don't let this get under your skin,' he said. 'In a month or so her illness will pass and she's going to come crawling back to you because she knows deep down that she has a great home with you, you're a good provider and a kind man and she'll realize what she's done and come back beggin' your forgiveness.'"

Kleinmutz, in telling me this obvious fiction, was creating what he really wanted to see happen.

At one time he had been in the D.A's office in Bakersfield. He couldn't take the politics. "You could be kissing the wrong ass for months," he once told me. "Everybody's nightmare who works in that office is to ride the wrong political horse. One fart and they call you stinky the rest of your life."

He transferred out of prosecuting into defense work; he built a successful small-town practice; he now had a lot to lose and was frantically trying to salvage what was rapidly turning into a nightmare. His wife was after blood and Kleinmutz was falling apart.

She was living in the house with the mechanic and the two of them had recently vacationed in Big Sur in the motorhome. He had taken to downing a fifth of Scotch every night. In addition, he would polish off a large pizza and a quart of beer. He had gained forty pounds and he was not small to begin with.

He answered the phone and his voice was thick and I could tell he was deep into the bottle. When he was in his cups he would babble for hours about love and the human condition and his divorce and the state of his bowels. (I once pointed out his alimentary looniness, the energy spent on fecal movement; he replied that since his life had turned to shit, why not?)

I could either hang up or wait him out. "You know the stages of the decline of a relationship? First romantic love, that idiotic interlude between when you think she's beautiful and when she begins to look like a mackerel. Then you're living together. Then you marry. Next kids. Now she's disgusted with you cause you watch television all the time. Next comes separation so she can hump whomever, grease monkey, I don't know. Then divorce. Then the real woman, the real revelation. Now you really get to know her. You've known nothing. You know nothing about a woman until you meet her in court."

"Did you set up my appointment?"

"Your appointment's set up," he slurred. "I have the fucking time somewhere…" I could hear heavy breathing. "Eleven. Do not wear denim. The prisoners wear denim and if you come in with denim you might not get out. We have to talk first."

"Okay."

"Breakfast at the Inn. Did you know Doug Filiberti?"

"Yes."

"A prince. Died, you know? Pancreatic cancer."

"Yes."

"Keeps banging around in my head: the Cat, Death, will one day decide to have fun with the Mouse, us. Thinking about Doug. Dead."

"Yes."

"He was on his way out." When drinking, Kleinmutz had a magical way with voices. He would switch back and forth between them and you'd swear there were two or three other people in the room. He now spoke in Doug Filiberti's voice, hoarse, New York Italian: " 'I gotta tussle with this thing, fuck it in the ass, go into the medical history books.' " Doug Filiberti! A felon, yes, but never a bore. 'I want to get this cancer here, nearby, so I can deal with it, eat it up before it eats me.' 'Kleinmutz,' he used to say to me, 'two guys, you and me, just trying to make an honest living and all these thieves trying to take it from us.' Remember his brother, Jerry?"

"Auto supply? Up in Tulare?"

"Up in Tulare. Buy all my batteries, tires, that stuff, from him."

"Good price?"

"The best! Anyway, Jerry would say to him, he couldn't understand it, Doug rested back and the money rolled in and Jerry had to work his tail off. 'Things you get away with,' he told him—" This was in Jerry's voice, which was just like Doug's but an octave higher. "—'I'd get an ax in the head for.' Doug said he told him, 'You get an ax in the head, you just pull it out and keep on going.' This was his philosophy, take an ax in the head, keep on going. Couldn't do that with your career."

"No." There was silence on the other end of the line except for Phil's deep breathing. For a moment I thought he had fallen asleep. I realized he was crying softly. "I get emotional," he said at last. "He was a scamp, but I loved him. I miss him. He would say to me, 'I go into a meeting with an honest businessman and he has an AK-47 behind the desk.' He's telling me what business has become. This is all a rationalization for his own larceny." He was back speaking like Doug Filiberti, hushed, confidential, thick Bronx accent: " 'I see it and get up close to him and tell him what a great suit he has on. Can you believe this, Kleinmutz? An

AK-47! And he's supposedly an honest guy and he's going to take it away from you and me with an AK-47! I'll tell you, Kleinmutz, I don't know what the world's coming to! Look, you and me are going to get something really big. I have to make it big now for myself or at least leave something for my family.' He died not long after, and left his wife $750,000 in debt." Kleinmutz didn't speak for a minute. "Vale of tears."

"I think you're right," I said.

"You don't want to hear about business," he said. "You're an artist." He liked to chide me about being a writer.

"I admire businessmen," I said.

"You have disdain for them."

"No," I said. "Businessmen are much maligned. They should receive medals. Is there anything we do in this life more boring than business?"

"You're pulling my woodie."

"Much more fun to be an artist or a revolutionary, a bank robber, an athlete—even a day laborer. Give your businessman a medal, condemning himself to eternal boredom!"

"You have contempt," Phil said. I heard the receiver fall. It banged around for a while. Then he hung it up.

I returned to my Bushmill's and thought about how sad and silly it was for two middle aged men to mourn loves and lives that were probably never what we thought they had been.

There was a guy I hung with years before—this was a time when I did some boxing and we sparred together and in that game things rarely go the way you'd like them to, and he would say, "what you want in this life and what you get don't always come on the same bus," and after all these years I had come to realize how true this was.

I was exhausted but I couldn't bring myself to go to bed because I would dream. Lately it had been about being lost in an unknown city. I didn't remember the name of the street where I lived, or I couldn't find my way home because I was really in some other land. I was lost because the world was meaningless.

And I would awaken in a sweat aware that we lived in chaos with glimmers now and then of some secret order in the universe. And I would think that perhaps after death I'll discover that secret order.

I leaned back in my desk chair and stared at the fog. The wind was blowing now and the fog streamed past the window glass. It was racing. I was being swept along by it. I was drowning in it. The world was fog and illusion and the fog was consuming us all, illusion was consuming us all. And I fell asleep in the chair.

I was with the director of "Call for Heros," a tall, drunken Englishman who always had a starlet or two stashed away in his trailer. He told me a girl working on our film had just mutilated herself in a terrible way. She had been depressed and just as shooting was completed she chopped off both of her hands, then ground the stumps against a stone lathe.

I was on a boulevard and it was thronged with people and I realized it was Tu Do Street, the red light district in Saigon. I saw the girl. I could not be sure that she had only stumps where her hands should have been—she was wearing a long-sleeve jacket, which covered the ends of her arms. But I did see blood dripping there. I attempted to hurry away from her but she wandered after me. She was not following me particularly. She was just wandering aimlessly in despair, but somehow, no matter what I did to try to evade her—I rushed up and down the boulevard, changed directions abruptly, crossed and re-crossed my own path—she was always near me. And then I saw one hand—fingers closed in a fist. So there had been exaggeration—she had not ground both hands to stumps. But what of the other one?

I awoke staring at the fog outside my window, shaken.

I had a headache. I felt nauseated. I forced myself to throw up but that didn't help and I swore I would never drink again which I knew was a lie.

Phil was waiting for me when I arrived at the Mountain Inn Diner. With a piece of sourdough toast, he was slopping up bacon and eggs and hash browns. The whole mess was drowned in ketchup. He was still half in the bag, dribbling egg yolk and ketchup all over himself.

The diner, decorated like a railroad station, with a lot of rough wood and railroad crossing signs and warning lights, was filled with ranch hands, prison guards, and workers at the cement plant just outside of town. They were either going to or coming off work. The air was thick with cigarette smoke.

There was a model train on display that replicated in miniature the Tehachapi Loop, a famous railroad landmark in the area. For a quarter you could watch it chug up and around plaster-of-Paris mountains, through tunnels, switch tracks, back up, blow its horn, chug on back down the loop. The display was tacky and rundown, the landscape crumbling, the glass case that held it littered with candy and chewing gum wrappers.

I slid into the booth opposite Kleinmutz. He looked like hell. I'm sure he had slept in his clothes, black sweat pants and a black knit sweater. He hadn't shaved. "Anyone seeing you, Phil, would have to say, there goes an ex-athlete."

Kleinmutz was pleased. "Really?" He studied his image in the mirror opposite the booth. "What is it, the sweater?"

"Could be the sweater. Just the look—"

"Must be the sweater. Looks like one of those varsity sweaters."

"I was pulling your dick. You look godawful. Keep this up, you're never going to live long enough to look your age."

"What is it?" He studied himself in the mirror. He wiped some egg yolk and ketchup off his chin. "I'm turning a leaf. You'll see how heathy I'm going to be. Going to this woman over on Union. Colonics. They clean you out. All the old shit. I'll take your there sometime. It'll be my treat."

The waitress came to the table and I ordered toast and coffee. Phil returned to the egg mess, scarfing it down with a greed and ferocity that was frightening. We didn't talk for a while.

Suddenly Kleinmutz pushed his plate away. "You're a real asshole," he said, disgusted. "Why do you want to do such a stupid fucking thing as this? These guys are all assholes. They do this, they do that, they lie, cheat. I'm telling you I know these guys."

"They're your clients."

"That's right. Had this thing up in Joshua Crest. Guy's accused of killing—who the fuck knows? Who even wants to touch it?"

"What are you talking about?"

"You know Joshua Crest? Out in the desert. A scorpion's nest. Rotten place. Rotten, corrupt people. Young guy convicted of murder. They want me to handle his appeal. Fuck 'em. Can't get involved out there. God I hate that place! Fuck 'em! Deceiving fucks. I've had it up to my eyeballs with this shit! And you're putting yourself in with them—"

"I just want to learn their stories."

"Asshole."

"Does the prison want me?"

"Department of Corrections've completed a background check on you. They like you."

"That's good."

"Yeah, yeah. They're impressed by the military stuff, the fact that you were a government killer. They like that idea. Feel military people do well working for the Department of Corrections."

He studied himself for a while in the mirror. "I played football in high school," he said after a while. "I was all-Chicago, second team."

"You've told me."

"I'm worried about you. I just don't understand it. Why do you want to get involved with these fucks?"

"These are your clients I'll be teaching."

"That's what I mean. And these are my failures. You ought to meet the ones I get off. And I get most of them off. I'm good."

"We know this."

"I work on this theory: Tell enough people over enough time that a duck is a swan, they'll be someone who'll finally say, 'hey, I heard the swan quack.' Got a real sleaze bag as a witness? You tell the jury, 'When you have a crime that occurs in hell, you're not going to have any angels as witnesses.' This is the way we do these things."

I finished my toast and paid the check. We walked out to Phil's battered '78 Ramcharger. The exhaust was cracked and when he started it up, the truck sounded like a rocket going off. We drove out onto Valley Boulevard and headed west toward Cummings Valley.

The prison is set in the foothills of the Tehachapi Mountains. You drive through a picturesque valley of small ranches and orchards and you come to a row of small houses, which belong to the warden and other of the prison hierarchy. There are neat little lawns in front and rose bushes and it all looks very sweet and pastoral.

A short way beyond the houses is a guard building and a gate. Kleinmutz identified himself to the uniformed officer and we drove through the gate and down a long narrow road to the farthest section of the prison, up against the mountains. We got out of the truck just opposite the personnel office and entered the building. Kleinmutz told me he'd wait here for me. He made a joke about them not letting me out and no one laughed.

The guards were all business. I was put through a search with a metal detector, then passed off to a large muscular Chicano who led me away. I was taken on to the Maximum Security Yard, to the administration building where I met with a middle-aged woman with kinky gray hair and a light moustache whose I.D. tag identified her as "Mrs. Ramos, Program Administrator." She told me how pleased they were to have someone of my background to work with their long-term prisoners.

"What have they done?" I asked.

"Most are murderers," she said. "Life sentences with no parole."

"I'll be in a room with them—"

"Alone," Ramos said

"No guard?"

"We call them Correctional Officers," she said. "They're professionals and, well, we just don't call them guards these days. No. We'll give you an electronic alarm, but to be very honest, it won't do you much good if they want to harm you. It's primarily there in case there're problems between the men. Does that bother you? Not everyone is suited for this job. I thought with your background you'd be good at taking care of yourself."

She took me onto the yard to show me where I'd be teaching. In order to get onto the yard proper you had to go through four check points with guards behind bullet-proof glass and heavy metal doors. "You'll be given a permanent badge with your picture on it," Mrs. Ramos said.

Above us were high wire fences, concrete walls, razor-sharp barbed wire, manned towers.

She pointed out the electronic fence that ran along a no-man's land between the double outside fences. "Sometimes you come down here in the morning," Mrs. Ramos said, "And there's a rabbit or a squirrel cooking on the wire there. The electric force just sucks them in."

The library, a concrete-block room about the size of a large living room, was part of a building that housed several cramped offices for the correctional officer brass. There was a thick yellow line, which ran the length of the walk alongside the building. There was a painted warning next to the line: "Out of Bounds".

Several inmates in blue denim were doing work in the prison yard, tending a bed of flowers, sweeping the walks. They looked lumpy and sullen in their heavy denim outfits. There were blacks, Chicanos, whites, and what they mostly seemed to have in common were bad teeth and worse complexions.

At the far end of the yard I could see a weight pit, several handball and basketball courts. The men were heavily muscled and it struck me as peculiar that we take the meanest members of our society, cage them, and then put them to work lifting weights so that they could become ever larger and meaner than they were to begin with.

There was only a handful of guards on the yard and half were women and I was surprised at this. It seemed odd and cruel that prisoners with no likelihood of ever having a life with a woman should be faced with them day in and day out, have to watch them, smell them, be tempted by them.

And I wondered at the women having to ride herd on a group of frustrated, sullen, murdering men.

The women guards on the yard were thick and dikey-looking, but the officer at the library area was attractive, a lithe blonde whose black plastic name tag read "Macklin." "Mr. Dogolov here will be teaching creative writing," Mrs. Ramos said to Macklin.

"Shouldn't someone teach them how to read first?" Macklin said. I laughed, but she did not. I could see she was tough one.

She was not beautiful, but there was something about her that stirred me, a coldness that was sexual. She'd do you. She might count the pattern on the wallpaper while she was at it, but she'd do you good.

At first glance, she reminded me of the women who worked the check-out lines in the local supermarket; in their off hours they helped out at the family ranch, drove thick-tired pick-ups, wore cowboy boots and hats, jeans, flannel shirts: regular shit-kickers who liked nothing better on a Saturday night than to go out Country and Western two-step dancing with their men and get into a good, knock-down fight. But there was something else there, something more complex.

Mrs. Ramos was busying herself with the lieutenant of the yard on some paperwork to do with my class. It was decided the first class would be the next Monday. I'd come in to teach twice a week.

I asked Macklin what most of the men who would be in my class had done.

"You don't want to know." She was staring at me, her light blue eyes like ice. "Don't go down that road," she said. "Don't delve. They'll look to manipulate. Don't tell them anything about yourself."

"My name?"

"I'd rather they called me asshole, than by my name," she said.

I looked from the guard office to the mountains beyond the prison. With a shock I realized that my house was the only view of civilization these men had. I imagined that as I was staring down at them wondering what their lives were, they were gazing up at my house wondering what my life was like.

Now we would both have the chance to find out.

Chapter Two

The day was gray, cold and drizzly, the mountains and valley buried in cloud. I drove the long road out to the maximum security yards feeling uneasy. What would I say to these men? How would I deal with them?

I had never done any teaching. I had written out of my own experience with very little idea of what I was doing. And going face to face with men who had committed horrific crimes stirred up a measure of anxiety within me. How would I react to them? And they to me?

Before I left the house I downed a water glass of Bushmill's. It helped, but not much.

At the administration area I had to go through the metal detector; the buzzer kept going off until I emptied my pockets. The guard, thick-bellied and unsmiling, motioned me to the wall where he performed a rapid hand search, groping up the insides of my legs, jabbing at the crack of my ass, rummaging around my gonads.

At last, he passed me through. I entered the personnel office and was given my I.D. as well as an electronic alarm, a square device smaller than a t.v. remote which I was to wear on my belt.

The guard in the area, a solidly built middle-aged woman with an iron-hard face, warned me about the alarm. "That thing's more sensitive than a sissy in love. Just brush 'er accidentally, you're going to be dick-deep in C.O.'s"

I came to the first bullet-proof glass cage, called into a metal box, "Stairwell!" as I had observed Mrs. Ramos do and was buzzed onto the top landing. The stair area was a creamy white and smelled of fresh paint.

The guard stared at my I.D. He looked back at me, then back to the I.D. He gazed long at me. At last he buzzed me through. I moved down the concrete steps, called out, "Stairwell!" at the bottom, and was buzzed into another hallway where again the guard studied my I.D. for what seemed an interminable time. At last I was buzzed onto the yard.

Macklin sat at a desk in an alcove in front of the library area doing some paper work. She did not look at me.

An inmate was making coffee at a Mr. Coffee in one corner of the concrete-block alcove. "Hey, stupid," Macklin called to him, "where's the list?" The inmate pulled a folded piece of paper from his rear pocket and handed it to her.

"This is Baker," she said, still without looking at me, all business. "He's going to be in your class. What are you going to write, Baker?"

"Love stories."

"Can you write your name?"

"Yes."

Baker was a small man in his late thirties. He had long, graying hair tied in a pony-tail and wore glasses; he had smiling eyes. It was hard to believe he was a killer. "Have you done any writing?" I asked.

"Letters," he said. "I write good smut letters." He smiled and it was a friendly smile and his eyes danced with mirth. "Want some coffee, boss?"

"That'd be good."

"What do you want in it?"

"Milk and sugar."

Baker went off to the Mr. Coffee, drew me a cup, and began to fix it. "Macklin?" I said, reading her tag. "Do you have a first name?"

"Officer," she said, still without looking at me. "You're going to be locked in that room there with them. The only way out will be onto the yard. If there's any trouble—you have the alarm."

She unlocked the room for me and Baker brought my coffee and Macklin went out and I sat there with Baker at a long library table. "She's not too friendly," I said.

I was thinking, I'm sitting here with a killer and in a few minutes I'm going to be here with a room-full of killers. And for these hours in the prison this will be my life.

"Most are like that. Hey, you're dealing with the assholes of the world here so you get bigger assholes to do the job." He took out a small sack of tobacco and Zig-zag paper and rolled himself a cigarette. "I'd offer you one," he said, "but that's against rules. It's a form of bribery. If I give you a hair from my ass that's a form of bribery."

I noticed that a group of men had gathered at the door leading to the yard. "You have to leave them in, boss," Baker said. "That door only opens to the yard. It's locked once you're on the yard."

'And the other door is locked to Macklin's area?"

"Right. Your ass is ours."

"So it's true what they say about prison?"

"Oh, it's true. You got to stand up in here," Baker said. "I've seen the toughest guys from the street come in here and in weeks they're on dick. You see, they could kill a guy with a thirty-ought-six from 500 yards. But up eyeball to eyeball—that takes some guts. I've had one incident in fifteen years. This was up at Old Folsom. They give me a cellie. Guy never says anything. He doesn't read a book, write a letter, listen to the radio. Just lies on his bunk and stares at the wall. That's okay with me. I don't want to have to talk to no one in here if I can help it.

"Finally one night, just after the lights are out, I hear him say in this really quiet voice, 'You want to have sex?' I jumped down off my bunk, put my hand around his throat and said, 'I'm in here for killing three guys. I don't know what you're in here for, but I don't want to hear that talk again.'" Baker laughed softly. The laugh lines around his eyes crinkled up. He was a man who enjoyed life. "He asked to transfer cells the next day. Naw, no one bothers you unless you don't have any heart. I've seen stone cold killers in here and in a week they're sucking pipe. They don't have heart. Did their killing at a distance, drive-bys, car-jacks."

"You killed three men?" I said.

"Yeah. But they deserved it. Sometimes there's people deserve a little killing." He suddenly looked embarrassed, as though he had gone too far in telling me things. "I don't want you to get the wrong idea."

"No."

"I'm not hard-hearted."

"You killed three men?"

"Yes. But I'm actually, not really just a killer." He stood there, uncomfortable. "I feel like I've lost your respect," he said.

"We don't really know each other," I said.

"No, we don't." He stood quietly for a short while. "Why don't you let the men in? That yard's cold, boss."

I opened the door and the group shuffled into the room. I looked across the yard toward the far prison wall. The cloud and drizzle were a blanket pressing in on everything, obliterating the mountains beyond. You could not see my house now through the cloud.

The men glanced at me without interest. There was an almost equal number of whites, blacks, and Chicanos. All were tattooed, several of them elaborately—snakes, daggers, hearts, streaming locks of hair. They handed me paper chits. "Ducats," Baker said. "Their pass to take this."

The men just stood there eyeing me with what seemed dull hostility. "Sit," I said.

"Mind if we smoke?" a small, compact Chicano said.

"What's the rule?"

"Up to you," a white inmate said. He had blond thinning hair and a thick, heavily muscled body. He had dead eyes. "The rules change from motherfucker to motherfucker. You've read Joseph Heller, I'm sure. Well, this is more than Catch-22. It's Catch-We-Have-Your-Ass-Forever…"

I nodded okay and several more of the men took out tobacco sacks and paper and began to roll cigarettes.

One man of the men caught my attention, a young man. I found myself staring at him. There was an aura of aloneness about him. He sat with the other inmates at the table, yet he seemed apart from them. He was handsome, in a graceful, intelligent way. His gaze seemed to be turned inward.

"My name's Paul Dogolov. I'm a writer," I said.

"What nationality's that?" a muscular black inmate said.

"Ukrainian."

"Those are Jews, aren't they?" the black said. He had a vague stammer.

"Not too many."

"I thought all those people were Jews. I've read some books about this," he said. "You ever hear of the Rothchilds?"

"Fucking Rothchilds again," a middle-aged white said. "This guy has two things on his mind. The Jewish conspiracy and the pussy conspiracy."

"I'd say he got one out of two there," an older Chicano, a dumpy man with baleful eyes, said.

"They own the world," the black said.

"If you're talking about pussy, you're right there," the middle-aged white said.

"Let's get off this," I said.

The dumpy Chicano fixed me with a stare. He stared long at me.

"What?" I said.

"I done seventeen years in the hole. Could you do that?"

"Maybe."

"I don't think so."

"Why do you ask?"

"I want to know what you're made out of."

Seventeen years in the hole! What could he have done? "Why not?" I said. "I'd get a lot of writing done."

"I don't think you'd last a week," the Chicano said.

"All that time in the hole. You should have a lot to write about."

"I do," he said. "I could write about how to survive."

"He knows this," an older black said. He had a thick, hoarse voice and his body was severely hunched; his head seemed to grow directly out of his shoulders. "We been in a lot of joints together over the past twenty-five years."

"There was Quentin, Soledad, Old Folsom, Corcoran," the dumpy Chicano said. "Sergeant and I go way back."

"Where do you live, boss?" the middle-aged white said.

"I'm not allowed to tell you that."

"What are they afraid of ?" he said. "We're going to fly over these walls, molest your wife and kids."

"And you don't have to call me boss. Now why don't we go around the table and just tell us a little bit about yourselves."

"What—they—put us in here for?" the black with the stammer said.

"Not your crimes. I'd like to know if you read, have you done any writing? What kind of education you might have? I'm not really a teacher so I'm going to treat you all just like other writers. And we're going to deal with what you're writing and try to make it good."

The black with the stammer made a soft snorting sound. He continued to stare at me with dark, hostile eyes. "You gonna talk on us," he said.

"No."

He laughed knowingly. "Yeah, I believe that." He continued to laugh softly to himself.

I was feeling tired, fed up; there was something gloomy and dead in these men; perhaps I was one of those not suited for this job. "So let's just start over here and learn a little bit about each other."

The man sitting closest to me was a light skinned black, wiry, with a narrow face and darting eyes. His head would swivel from side to side as he constantly checked everything around him. One of his arms was shorter than the other, withered. He spoke with a voice that was flat, toneless. "Maximilian Robinson. My father was an Australian

Aborigine, my mother is from Iran. I like books with complexity that are not easily understood. My favorite writer is Harold Robbins. Do you know who he is?"

"I know him."

"He has complexity."

He sat back, watching me with dark, empty eyes. "Okay," I said. I nodded to the pony-tailed inmate.

"Jeffrey Baker," he said. "I like Harold Robbins. But I prefer Stephen King because he is a master at creating horror."

"Stephen King is a master," Robinson said. "But Harold Robbins excels. Stephen King is a craftsman. Harold Robbins is an artist."

"I like Sidney Sheldon," the older white said.

"What about Jackie Collins?" the black with the stammer said.

"She's good," said Baker. "But I like my books more bloodier. I killed some men—" He paused, gazing around at the men. They avoided his look, staring at the wall or the table. The handsome kid was watching me. "I don't say I didn't do it like so many of you do. I killed the motherfuckers and they had it coming to them. Some bad people in this world."

The large white guy spoke. His voice was soft and intelligent, but his eyes, too, were dead. "We all have felt that in some way or another. It doesn't make what we've done right, however."

"Depends," the middle-aged white said. "There was this guy, on the yard, Dunspaw—" The men nodded at his name; they knew him. "He had killed a ton of men—he was the Chinatown slasher, had a liking for cutting up older guys. They move him up here and what do these goofs do? Give him a *older guy* for a cellie!"

"He chilled old dude that very night," the black with the stammer said.

"I knew Dunspaw," said Robinson. "He had his reasons. Now they wouldn't make sense to you or me. But he had his reasons."

"I know," said the large white. "Fucking step-father beat him—"

"—every day of his young life," the middle-aged white said.

"Molested him," the black with the stammer said.

"He was a cop," said the older white. "Used to take his billy club and jam it up his ass."

"He hated older men," the large white said.

I was looking at the young man. He had paled. His gaze was somber, pained. He stared at the tabletop.

"I told him right out on the yard," the middle-aged white said, "Come near me, I'll kill you. I'd kill the motherfucker. Can you imagine the mentality? Put an older man in the cell with him? I mean, what kind of irresponsibility is that?"

"When they opened this prison, you couldn't find a fry cook in all of Bakersfield," Baker said.

"Dunspaw had his reasons," Robinson said.

"We've all had our reasons," the large white said.

"Sometimes you have to kill to survive," the short Chicano said.

"Maybe we all have murder in us," I said, only partially believing it, but in some way trying to reach these men. They gazed at me as though I had a point. "And in our writing perhaps we'll deal with that. I hope that our writing will help teach us what it means to be human."

"To be human is to kill," said Robinson. "Else why would it be going on since the time of Cain?" He looked at me waiting for an answer. I couldn't think of one.

The young white kid continued to watch me. There was something about him that was moving to me and I didn't know what it was. It was in the eyes, though, sorrow, pain.

The next man around the table was a heavy-set white in his late thirties. His sandy hair was beginning to show flecks of gray. He had a soft voice with a trace of a Southern accent. "Calvin Shea. Temple City, Louisiana. I have a bachelor's degree in business from Tulane and received a master's degree in clinical psychology from Oberlin University in Ohio while in prison. I like books on psychology, psychological novels, books on serial killers, things like that."

The large, muscular white spoke: "Steven McMullin. They call me Big Mick. I'm from Long Beach, California. I like to read the New York Review of Books and I'm interested in philosophy and political theory."

The middle-aged white was next. "Duane Culpepper. Yard name's Shank. I'm County born, State raised—"

"What does that mean?"

"Foster homes, to Youth Authority, to the joint," the older black croaked.

"I've spent thirty-seven years in the joint," Culpepper said. "Since I was fourteen, I've been on the street exactly fifty-two hours. I've been in Folsom, San Quentin, Federal Max Prison in Marion, Illinois. That's a level 6 facility, only one in the U.S. I've read every book in every library in every prison I've been in. I was originally locked up for stealing a car. I learned how to kill in the joint."

"I know this," the older black said, his voice like sandpaper.

"First they take your watch or your shoes. Then they want your asshole," a young, black Latino said.

"You get yourself a shank," the middle-aged white said. "When he goes to fuck you in the ass or shove his cock in your mouth, you cut him wide deep and continuous."

"I know this," said the older black.

The small Chicano said, "Ramon Imperial, born in Albuquerque, New Mexico. I been trying to survive ever since I've been in the motherfucking joint, which has been twenty-five years. Before that I made my way on the streets. I'd run game, gank dudes. I was only twenty and they called me *veterano*. I get me a *rucka* and have her out working for me. I'd run with dudes, do all kind of shit, ratpack guys and shit. I was making my way any way I could. Better believe it. Anything beats a blank. Street success is better than no success."

"You got—that right," the young black with the stammer said.

"I was caught at this drug house," the small Chicano said. "Cops wanted me to draw diagrams on whoever provided the drugs. 'Go with what you got,' I told them. 'You got me. Show me to the cell. I know how to do time. I don't know how to snitch.' Yeah. I like to read books on hot air ballooning so I can get out of this motherfucking place. When I was on the street, they called me 'Fifty-nine'—"

"'Fifty-nine,'" the young black said, laughing. The middle-aged black laughed harder. "That was the motel room Dude here worked out of!"

"You got it," the Chicano said.

"They also called him 'Goldie' or 'Jaguar Goldie,'" Culpepper said. The men all enjoyed this. They laughed and the Chicano looked pleased.

"I was a junkie, a jacker, anything to earn me respect on the street."

"Junkies are scandalous," the middle-aged black said.

"You're right about that," the Chicano said. "They'll turn on a friend. They're turn on their mother. We all know this. And I behaved like this."

"But you were—mainly—a pimp?" the young black said.

"Most of all I was a man who had him a 'ho stroll,'" the diminutive Chicano said.

"Ho track," the middle-aged black said.

"Believe it."

"Section of sidewalk where the girls parade," the middle-aged black said to me.

"And you know it's a lie, you can't hook no *ho*,'" the Chicano said. "The *ho* chooses you."

"You got to pose to be chose," the middle-aged black rasped. "A *ho* chooses you. You don't choose her. But all that's in the past, my little amigo."

"Them days I was suited and booted, ballin' on the town—"

"Past, past."

"—I had prestige, honor, respect. I loved the smell of real leather. I'd go in a new car showroom and say give me one of those, one of those, one of those, blue one, black one, red one. Whoop de whoop de woo. If I liked 'em I'd buy three. Buicks. Cadillacs. All with real leather seats."

He stood now, eyes sparkling, relishing the memory, demonstrating to all of us. " 'How much is it?' Dude tell me, twenty thousand, thirty, whatever it was. 'I'll be back,' I tell him. And I go to the far side of town walk right into a bank or a supermarket or whatever, level that shotgun. Go from register to register, just grab everything. And by the end of the day, I'd have me my cars with leather seats, motherfuckers paid in full."

"These days," the middle-aged black said, "they call him Crow."

"That's right," the Chicano said.

"Someone who—eats roadkill," the young black said. The men laughed quietly. Crow looked glum.

"What do you prefer," Shank said, "the smell of leather or the smell of pussy?"

Crow brightened. "Pussy, man, what do you think!"

"I didn't know." Shank winked at me.

"With pussy, first you smell it. Then you lick it. Then you fuck it."

"Been a while," Big Mick said.

"I hope we're not too crude for you," Shank said to me. "Due to our situation our interests are limited."

"Better pussy than dick," Robinson said.

"Hey, don't say nothing against no fag," Crow said. "Those people are the bravest people in the world. Anyone who can take six inches of dick up the ass, that's a brave person."

The men all laughed. "You're scandalous," the middle-aged black said. We continued around the table. It was his turn. "Roderick Cook, San Jose. I was in the Vietnam War. I was wounded there." He lifted his head. There was a terrible scar at what remained of his throat.

"What unit?"

"I was with a Ranger unit attached to the 175th. We were out of Bien Hoa. They call me Sergeant. I like to read books of a political nature."

The young muscular black with the stammer spoke next, "Eric Platt, South Central Los Angeles. Yard name's Blast. I like to read books about the international financial situation, about Jews, and like that."

"What's your obsession with Jews?" I said.

"They own the world," Blast said.

"That's his stick," Shank said and several of the others chimed in; Blast just sat there grinning, a forced, twisted grin, more like a grimace. "Guys—here don't know—what the world is. Peckerwood motherfuckers," he stammered.

"Either hate the Jews or go on cock," Crow said. "Isn't that right, Blast?"

"You ain't never going to—find me—on pipe," Blast stammered. The men all laughed. "You got to fight for your manhood in here. Sometimes—you see even dudes was so bad outside, killed this one, killed that—and in two weeks—they're on cock."

"They killed at a distance," Big Mick said.

"Got them those rifles," Blast said. "In here there's—a thin line between a—man—and a bitch."

"Man's right on that one," Crow said.

The next man spoke, the young latino. "Hector Arragon. I'm from Ecuador. Call me El Negro." El Negro was perhaps twenty-five, compact, very dark, with a pock mottled face. "I'm doing the Big Bitch."

"That's L-wop," Big Mick said. "Life Without Parole. There's the Little Bitch, life with parole. Most of us in here are doing the Big Bitch."

"Most none of us are ever coming out," the older black said. No one spoke for a while. I nodded at the Chicano who had spent seventeen years in the hole. "Raul Escalante. They call me Joker. I come into the joint thirty years ago and I killed to survive. Like Crow here. We both know how to survive."

"Do you read?"

"I read everything. I've read more than you. I used to read three books a day. Did you ever do that, teacher?"

"No."

"Okay, then," he said.

"You'll discover that murderers are smart people," El Negro said. "When a man is stupid, he usually doesn't kill. When you put ideas in his head, then he has justification to kill. It's a mistake to try to make men better than they are. As long as they're just rotten they remain thieves. Educate them, they become killers."

Big Mick smiled. "He has a point there. Usually murderers are the smartest, best educated of the bunch."

The last inmate was the handsome white kid. Though his features were delicate, his lithe body, like most of the men, was well-muscled; a jungle of finely limned tattoos flowered across the skin of his arms and neck, vines, trees, a woman's face framed in skeins of long, flowing hair. His voice was soft. "My name is Travis Wells. I'm from Joshua Crest. That's out in the desert between Mojave and Barstow. I like to read and write poetry."

"We call him Poet," Culpepper said.

"He can write that shit," Roderick Cook said. "He can make you weep some time. You want to win yourself a woman, don't send her no smut poetry. You get Poet here to write you something."

"You want to get yourself a woman," El Negro said, "you get you one of her pussy hairs and you put it in a coke bottle. And you keep that bottle under your pillow. That's how you get yourself a woman."

"How we gonna get us a pussy hair in here?" said Blast.

"Get Poet to write you a poem, then," El Negro said.

"Hey," Blast said, "I wonder, you know, if Dude's on pipe. Hey, Poet, man, you—not on—pipe, are you?" He laughed but no one else did. Poet stared at him and he stared back.

"You want something?" Blast said.

"Ask him if he's a Jew?" said Shank, laughing.

"What do you want?" Poet said.

"I don't want nothing."

"I thought maybe you wanted to get 'em up."

"If I want to get 'em up, I get 'em up. It's just—you're just so fine looking," Blast said. He and Poet continued to stare at each other. At last

Blast looked away, laughing to himself quietly. "He could be a Jew," he said to no one in particular.

"You have to realize," Big Mick said, "we usually don't have anything to do with each other, blacks, whites, Mexicans."

"This class is the only place you actually inter-act?"

"Just about," he said.

"We all—stay—to ourselves," Platt said. "Oh, some of us might work together in the kitchen or something like that. But that's it."

Crow said, "You want to hear a joke?"

"All right," I said.

"New inmate arrives on the yard and one of the old cons goes up to him and says, 'Do you like tennis?' He says, 'Yes, I love to play tennis!' 'Well, you're really going to like Monday cause that's when we play tennis. How about handball?' 'I like handball.' 'Well, you're going to love Tuesday cause that's when we play handball. Are you straight or gay?' 'I'm straight.' 'Well, you're going to hate Wednesdays.'"

They all laughed except Poet. I gazed at the men for a long moment trying to figure out what I would say next. I hadn't an idea in my head. The palms of my hands were perspiring. I suddenly felt very thirsty. I longed for a tall beer and a shot of Bushmill's.

"As I told you, I'm not a teacher. I'm a writer. Self-taught. I've picked up a few ideas about the craft as I've gone along. I can only tell you what I've done. I know a few things, but not a lot—"

"What the—hell—you doing here, then?" It was Platt and his voice was angry.

The men were all looking at me and I felt foolish, embarrassed, a fraud. What was I doing there? "I have sold some books and scripts and things like that. I've been paid for my writing. And I do know the best things I've written have been the things that I've really cared about, where I was asking a question of myself, of the world."

"What does that mean?" Platt said. He was smiling but it was angry, frozen, a killer's smile I was thinking.

"Why don't you shut the fuck up?" Culpepper said. "You give a fucking woodpecker a headache." Blast glowered at him and the muscles in his jaw tensed up and I moved my hand to the alarm on my belt.

Crow said: "We should be like a turtle and pull into our shell and think about what we did to get here in prison—we were lazy and greedy and wanted this and that, whoop de doo—"

"That's right," said Cook.

"Why do you have an attitude?" Crow said to Blast. "Because you resent this, you have a rage about that—don't remove yourself from the reality of your environment. I want to see you neck deep in your own shit with your hand raised up. We all need a lifeline."

Blast snickered and looked like he was about to speak, but the words wouldn't come out. When they did they exploded in a heavy stammer: "I—want the man—to make clear—what it is he—means."

"You need a question you want answered. It could be: why am I here? And not just in prison. Why was I born? You see so many things in this life—you've seen things. We all have."

"What—does that—have to do—with how I'm going to—write something."

"I'm divorced. I feel badly about it and I wonder why it happened. I might sit down and write a book and the question might be something like, 'What happens when a writer suddenly is informed by his wife that she no longer wants to remain married?' You see? I want you to work on stuff that's really eating at you. And this question that you're asking will inevitably bring up complications. For instance: 'What happens when a writer approaching middle-age comes into a Maximum Security prison to teach?' Complications. How does he even get into the place? He has to be photographed, security check on him; searched. How he relates to these men? Where is he in his life now?"

The men looked dully at me and I felt tired, irritated, foolish. Why had I come there? What was I trying to find, to prove?

"I'd like to do an exercise. We'll go around the table. And each of you come up with a question you could ask in your writing. And some complications that could grow out of that question. Who wants to start?"

No one spoke. It seemed they were all looking at me as though I were crazy and I really wanted to just say, I don't know a thing. Let's call it quits right here.

They sat there for a long time. I could feel perspiration gathering under my shirt. I had no desire to say anything more. I would wait for the in-line announcement and then leave and never come back. At last Robinson spoke. He was staring at me with his narrow, ominous eyes. Aborigine eyes, murderers eyes, I was thinking. "What happens when a man commits murder," he said and his voice was quiet. "And is sentenced to twenty-five years to life?" He remained quiet for a moment.

"Complications?" I said.

He took a sharp breath. "How the victim's family feels about you? How your family feels about you? How you feel about yourself?"

"Good," I said. "That's good. That's a dramatic problem."

Now Arragon, El Negro, spoke: "What happens when a man who is convicted of murder one, gets life with no parole, goes into prison at the age of eighteen? Complications: how does he look at his wife, his little baby? How does he look at himself in the mirror, getting older, the years going by?"

Now they all began to talk, all pouring out their dramatic problems—their life problems—and they were all variations on the same question: what happens when a man commits murder?

"What happens when a man is convicted of Murder One," Shea said, "and is sentenced to death in the gas chamber. Complications: how he deals with the idea of his own death…"

"But you're not on Death Row…" I said.

"…how he deals with getting a new trial. And how he's convicted again. And beats the gas chamber this time."

"What happens when you're convicted on Murder One," Steve McMullin said, "and your first day on the Max Yard dude standing next to you is stabbed to death and the blood spurts all over you. Complications: the fear you feel. The prisoners who want to turn you into a punk. The prison gangs you have to deal with…"

He finished and everyone remained silent. "Any others?" I said. I was thinking, what can I tell them now? Where do I go? My mind was racing, trying to figure out what next to say.

"What happens when a man is accused of murder—" It was Travis Wells, Poet. His voice was barely audible. He was looking directly at me and there was a sadness in his gaze; a veil and behind it pain. "—and he is sentenced to life with no parole? And he didn't do it?" He continued to fix me with his eyes and I was unnerved. "Complications: how do you get through every day without going crazy?"

I waited for him to say something more, but he remained quiet. No one said anything. The other men seemed embarrassed, as though it had been poor form of Poet to cop a plea. They had all admitted their deeds. Why not him?

I was shaken. There had been something simple and resigned in the way the kid had talked; it wasn't as if he were trying to convince me of anything. He was just stating a fact—how do you get through the days when you are innocent?

And the pain in his gaze—I had seen something like it before, once. A man in my unit in war had stepped on a land mine; the lower part of his body had been blown away and his life was pouring out of him and I had held him in my arms and he had asked me if he was going to die and I had said, no, even as I saw him slipping away. And he had had a look in his eyes not unlike what I had seen in this kid's gaze; disbelief, pain beyond pain.

Was it possible? Could he be innocent? Phil Kleinmutz had warned me that most of the murderers I would meet would maintain their innocence, would try to con me. But could someone have faked that look?

Travis Wells had been shatteringly convincing. He had touched me deeply. I could not show this, of course. I forced myself to push it away. He's a con trying to hook me in. He's a con.

"Is that what you meant?" Poet said. "Is that a dramatic question?"

"Yes," I said and I was troubled, uneasy in my own skin.

The day outside had grown dark with cloud. A strong wind blew across the yard, snapping the flag and its rope on the pole just beyond the first perimeter.

Macklin appeared at the door. "Yard recall," she said. "Fog's coming in."

Chapter Three

The men moved away across the yard. The yard was dark now. The yellow lights above the prison walls fought the fog, which had pushed in further on the yard, swallowing up the men as they walked off. The guards in the watchtowers had turned on great floodlights, which they shined from group to group in the yard.

A thick, sleety rain was falling now and it was cold. Poet was moving off toward the cellblocks. "Wells?" I called. He turned. "That problem you spoke of—"

"You'll hear it a lot around here. Everyone's innocent."

"How long have you been in?"

"Six years."

"Write about what happened to you. If you're really innocent—"

"What?" he said. "They gave me life with no parole. They've turned down every appeal I've mounted."

"If you're really innocent, it'll show in the writing," I said.

"And what's that going to do? It'll be artistically true, but it won't change my situation in any way." He was right, of course. He had been convicted. He had exhausted his appeals. The most well written book in the world wouldn't change that. Barring a miracle, he would die in prison.

"Move off!" It was Macklin and she was angry. "Yard recall, asshole!" Poet bowed his head and nodded shyly and started away. He paused to turn to me, smiled apologetically, waved. As his slim, graceful figure disappeared into the fog, he suddenly seemed to me a magician-artist who had, with that small gesture, performed a wondrous vanishing act, slipping from this hell on earth into some anti-matter, other dimension, a limbo-land of gray, eternal gray, eternal nothingness.

"When it's yard recall, you can't be talking like that," Macklin said. She stood there, close to me.

"You have a mouth on you."

"He's an asshole. They're all assholes."

She was staring at me and there was something unsettling in her look. She seemed to be gauging me: What was it? Was it sexual?

These things are fragile. Sometimes because you wish it, you think it is. Who knew what was going on inside her?

It was entirely possible, I told myself, that I was misreading the situation entirely, projecting my desire onto something that had nothing to do with me?

"What did he do?"

"What do you mean?"

"Wells. His crime." She shook her head. "What?"

"I can't say."

"Why not?"

"We don't talk about those things. Not to outside staff."

"He claims he's innocent."

Was she leaning into me, slightly, subtly? Her gaze, deep, unwavering: was she trying to convey something to me? What?

"They all say that. But in his case—" She caught herself and I could feel her withdraw. Whatever she was about to say, she had changed her mind.

"What?"

She remained quiet. "It's possible he's innocent," she said at last. She did not say it easily.

We stood without speaking for a while. She was staring at me. I felt she was trying to think of something to say. She's attracted to me, I was thinking. Is that possible? "You have a husband? Boyfriend?" I said and felt as though I couldn't breath properly and I cursed my ex-wife and divorce and the fact that I was forty-eight years old and trying to flirt with someone nearly half my age and feeling unbearably stupid. What had my life come to?

Her eyes were a very light blue and there was a coolness there: Was it sadness, loneliness? Or—nothing? My imagination? Was I reading more into it than was there? Was it myself I saw in her gaze? "I didn't mean to offend you," I said. "I just thought that maybe some evening we could have dinner. Just a friendly thing." I added: "I'm recently divorced."

"I don't go out with people on the job," she said. She turned from me and walked back into her alcove and I found that I was shaken inside, trembling. Dumb! Dumb! How long would it take me to finally feel at ease again with women?

My wife had walked out on me and it had shattered me in some profound way. I felt inept and old, without skill in even the simplest areas.

And that's what my ex-wife wants, I thought. She wants me destroyed.

I moved to the steel and glass door and called out,

"Stairwell!" The guard leveled an opaque gaze at me and I said fuck you to him inside my head.

How could I continue with this? I was tired, depressed, sick of Macklin and Poet and the whole prison.

I steered my truck through the fog across the valley, speeding home. The fog was thick around the car and I couldn't see more than a few feet along the road, and I told myself to slow down, but I couldn't. Inside I felt as though I were splintering. My nerves were electric throughout my body. It was a feeling that had first come to me in combat: a sense that my body was flying apart, that my soul was fractured.

I had seen so much carnage, men shattered, blown to bits. Every day in the war you woke to a charnel house. You could never get that meaty smell of death out of your nostrils. And now in prison, the

men, questions of guilt and innocence, my feelings toward Macklin—
all of this had set something off in me.

I started up the mountain. The truck bucked up the narrow, winding
road and I skidded several times on the road's drizzle-wet surface and
there was inside me a profound despair.

I built a fire when I got inside and opened a new bottle of Bushmill's
and drank and stared at the blank television screen and watched the
prison lights in the distance move in and out of the fog.

I thought of Macklin and Poet and how shaken I was inside. I called
Phil Kleinmutz. "I don't think I can make it with this job."

"What's the problem?" His speech was thick and I realized it was the
drunk leading the drunk.

"My nerves are not good. I think I'm having some sort of psychological flashback or something. The prisoners—"

"A-holes."

"I met a guard I'd like to fuck."

"Female, I hope," he said. "Let me tell you something about female
guards. These are women who couldn't make it as nurses aides or get on
at the post office. This is a really depraved lot."

"I sensed she might have a thing for me, too."

"Good."

"I don't like my life."

"All right."

"Where is the truth?"

"It's in your colon, and you don't want see that. The answer is in your
shit."

"What I mean—"

"I'll tell you about truth. Truth is a weapon of power. A sword. A can-
non. People hang onto their truth like a lifeline."

"No, you don't understand—"

"In a world where truth has become a function of power and the
most shameless bastards among us preach 'truth' louder than anyone,

ambiguity can be viewed as a triumph. Ideology is not thought. It is the shadow of thought."

What the hell was he talking about? In his youth he had been trained by the Jesuits, then had become a communist, then a kind of super nihilist. He was a first-rate debater with a focused intelligence and a passion for logic. Now he just babbled. His argumentation had deteriorated into a muddy, aggressive loquaciousness that had little to do with anything, a drunk spewing out words like vomit, hoping that something would mean something.

"What difference does it make?" he said. "The Cat, Death—"

"The Cat again."

"—will one day decide to have some fun with the Mouse, us."

"There's a kid in my writing group, terrific-looking kid—"

"Ah, you're flirting with convict sex—"

"He has this look about him, a kind of sensitivity—"

"I'm getting worried."

"This is something that really bothers me."

"What?"

"I think he might be innocent—"

"Please!"

"He comes from this town out in the desert—"

"Joshua Crest?"

"Yes."

"Killed his grandfather or something?"

"Yes."

"I know about this. They called me out there, his family, mother or someone, to see about this. Grandfather? Some other stuff—a couple of people—"

"His grandfather. He's writing about it in my class—"

"It's a scorpion's nest out there. You don't want to know anything about it. They wanted me to look over the case. They want to get the verdict overturned. Something. I ran."

"What? What is it?"

"Their own world out there. Scary. You don't want to mess with it. It's like the people who go over to China to convert them and end becoming Chinamen."

"It bothers me. This kid—"

"Everything bothers you. What you need is a good colonic. And poontang. When you start talking about handsome, sensitive kids in prison, I worry. We'll hit Bakes, the hillbilly bars, scrape the nodules off your prostrate."

"Prostate."

"That's that thing behind your balls. I'm talking about prostrate. You have a prostrate condition. You're lying prostrate on your ass because your wife did you in. My wife did me in. So there we are."

"There we are," I said.

"We'll find us some poony."

"Naw."

"Why not?"

"Don't have the desire, the touch. Maybe this guard—"

"Even a blind squirrel finds nuts," he said. "False hope springs eternal. Look, don't make too much about what goes on in the Big House. These guys are fakes, pussys."

"Really?"

"Yes."

"You think so? Pussys?"

"Listen. Listen to this. I had this client, old mafiosa from Vegas. He hears on the t.v. this mafia killer. He wrote a book and he's talking on t.v. Gubby gets pissed off. 'I was with them,' he says, 'the old Black Hand, from 1936 to 1960. And my father was with them from 1910. These guys today aren't like the guys in the old days, Pittsburgh Phil Straus, 60 hits, Abe Reles, 50 hits, Bugsy Goldstein, 75 hits. These guys today, 10 hits and they're on the t.v.!' This is this generation. Liars, frauds, pussys."

"Everything bothers me," I said. "Over there, you know, in battle, we went into this town."

"I know all about it."

"After, they had a hearing and we were cleared. But it always bothered me."

"What? You mean what happened there?"

"Not only what happened. It was—I didn't know everything."

"No one knows everything."

"I know. You're right. I know."

"You see, this is your trouble. You keep talking about that place over there and everyone is sick of it. You're a caricature."

"Yes."

"Thousands came back from Vietnam and they all had important things happen to them, but when you talk about it to the exclusion of everything else, you turn people off. We're sick of fucking Vietnam and the Vietnamese. It happened to you, it happened to this guy, that guy, it happened to a lot of people."

"You're getting me angry."

"The Cat—"

I hung up. I turned on the television and watched replays of Jerry Springer and Maury Povich. They were the same shows I had seen earlier in the day. Oh, the humanity, the ugly humanity. The flotsam and jetsam of our race, rotted teeth, pitted complexions, lumpy bodies. What hope was there for any of us?

I realized I had just about finished the bottle of Bushmill's.

I lay back on the couch on my loft and the fog streamed past my windows and I felt as though I were moving with the fog, streaming into oblivion.

You couldn't see the prison now. The whole world was fog. I was sunk and drowning in fog viscous as quicksand.

Out of it now Poet appeared, smiling at me, a delicate, shy smile. Magician, I was thinking. And I could see beyond him, the dead children.

And I was aware in the dream that my *life* was a dream and the dead children had only been dreamed by me. I controlled it all. Therefore, if I concentrated hard enough I could wake from the dream of my life (But what would that *mean?* Waking, would I die?), and force myself back to a time *before* the slaughter of the children and re-do the dream of my life, removing the children's killings. Of course, in re-dreaming that part of my life I would lose total memory and knowledge of the original.

I felt as though I could do it—if I just concentrated hard enough. But I was afraid. What else would I be erasing from life? And would I in fact be able to go back to sleep and continue the dream of my life, or would I be dead?

Chapter Four

The weekend came and I picked up the kids in Bakersfield. Roval, who was working in the front yard, bolted like a rabbit as soon as he saw my truck coming down the street.

My wife, as usual, was sour. "I don't know what you think you're doing with these kids. Do you ever say 'no' to them? Do you ever discipline them?" The kids were standing there staring at us and I just wanted to get out of there without a scene. "You bring them back and they're like wild Indians," she said. "They tell me they can get anything from you."

She had this way of tensing her jaw and glowering at me as though I had committed a crime of extraordinary proportion, when I had done nothing. This had all started after our break-up. I put it down to guilt she felt over wrecking our marriage, a marriage which, though affected with a its share of problems, was, I thought, happier than most.

I believed that right up to the day she came to me and asked for the divorce.

I leaned close to her so that I could speak without the kids hearing. "You dare talk to me about discipline? You walk out and the next week you're shacking up with Elvis here—"

"Just watch it, mister."

"These kids went from a house with a father and mother to a shack-up situation and you talk about discipline? You think that's what these kids lack?"

It angered me, how she twisted everything; the egoism, the selfishness. I thought of how things had been when we were married, how indifferent and self-centered she had been. She would spend her time in the car driving from shopping mall to shopping mall; she could kill days shopping and it was never enough just to buy one of something. If an item were on sale, she'd buy a dozen and then tell me how fortunate I was to have saved all this money. Was she that way with Roval? I doubted it. Tattooed, brooding, beer-besotted Roval looked as though he'd knock her on her ass.

She had asked to handle our finances. We nearly went broke behind that: unpaid bills would lie scattered through the house like confetti. Bank statements opened, but not read, would rest on the wet bar. It was a disaster and yet I loved her (or cared for her so deeply that it must have been love) and missed her without exception and would have taken her back in an instant.

The realization that I hadn't known her at all troubled me deeply. It was my obtuseness, I had come to believe, that was at the heart of our break-up. I had been in love with a chimera.

After the divorce she treated her past as if it were an unclean thing, a pariah trailing blood: she deserted not only me but all our friends, her friends, her family, everything that had once been her life. It was eerie how she had fled from it all.

All save our kids. These she clung to with an awesome tenacity. They had been witnesses to perfidy and betrayal. Was she afraid that one day they would break loose and rush through the streets crying out the truth?

Or did I have that all wrong, as I had so much wrong in my life?

I turned and started out. "Let's go, kids." They followed after me and I felt ugly inside. Had they heard what I had said?

What were they feeling?

I was upset that I had lost control, but the situation was so rotten I just had no idea how to handle it. The frustration I felt was immense.

The whole thing about my wife and her boyfriend and my kids depressed me; what was it doing to the kids? What could I do to help?

My ex-wife's face was a mask of anger. She was pale and trembling. "Kiss your mother goodbye," I said and the kids went back to her and I could see she was crying as she hugged them.

In the truck driving over to the baseball batting cages Annie said, "Why was Mommy crying?"

"Because she loves you kids. She misses you."

"It's only for the week-end," Kurt said.

"Did you say something bad to her?" Annie asked.

"I said something I shouldn't have, something harsh."

"What does 'hash' mean?" Kurt said.

"Harsh. It means 'mean.' I was mean."

"Why?" Kurt said.

"When people get divorced there are a lot of bad feelings and some-times people say bad things."

"Mommy says bad things," Annie said.

"About me?"

"About everyone. Sometimes she gets mean and she yells at us and that's not fair because we can't answer back."

"I love Mommy," Kurt said, "but I think deep down, in a corner, I hate her a little bit. Just a little bit."

"We all have little bits of hate inside us," I said. "We don't even know it most of the time." And I thought of the murderers in my writing group and their hate and what they had done with it.

I hit baseballs for an hour or so and the kids hit in the slow-pitch softball cage and at one point Kurt was watching a lazy blooper-style pitch coming in and he just watched it and watched it, right down to his face. It hit him in the eye and he came crying out of the cage.

I held him to me. "Kurtie," I said, "you have to move away when the ball comes in on you like that."

"But, daddy," he said with all the innocence and belief that a child of five possesses. "You told me to keep my eye on the ball."

And I laughed and hugged him to me and felt the softness of him and the love of him. And then my daughter was pressing in against me, pressing for her share of love, and I hugged them both to me. They smelled fresh of soap and a yeasty, new skin smell and I thought there's nothing so sweet in this world as the smell of your kids.

On the drive up to Tehachapi, along Interstate 58, the Tehachapi Mountains rising black and jagged above us to the south, the Sierras to the north, high, dark, brooding, I felt the tension I carried inside me always, suddenly ease off. It was like a soap bubble bursting.

There was a lightness in the center of me and it soared from me into the power and sweep of mountains, and I had a rare time of peace.

The kids began bickering. The radio was off and it was evening now and a great quiet and darkness pressed in on the highway from the surrounding mountains and now Annie wanted to hear music,

"Sibelius!" she said.

"No, Annie! Bruce Springsteen!"

I put in the Sibelius tape, "Finlandia", then Springsteen's "Human Touch" and we exited the highway, skirted the town of Tehachapi, sped along the prison road and started up the mountain to the house. We could see the prison lights across Cummings Valley.

Kurt asked for a story. Annie insisted it was her turn and they argued over this all the way to the house.

With some nagging, I finally got them to brush their teeth and change into their pajamas and then I sat on Annie's bed and began a story that I knew would be acceptable to both of them. It involved a character I called Dr. Miracle—I had lifted him from one of E.T.A. Hoffman's tales, transforming Hoffman's malevolent doctor into a kindly miracle worker who was there to bring good things to Annie and

Kurtie. "So Dr. Miracle came to Annie and Kurt and said, 'Now it's time to leave for Noddy-noddy land—'"

"Hi, Doc," Annie said, joining in on the story.

"Hi, Annie," I said, using Dr. Miracle's voice which was not unlike mine, though heartier. "Are you ready to go to Noddy-noddy land?"

"Yes."

"Me, too, Doc," Kurt chimed in.

"Okay, first thing, we have to get into my miraculous time machine—"

"Dr. Miracle, can I ask you a question?" Annie was looking at me with a sudden serious expression; it was an adult look and she would get it from time to time and it always amazed me that children were kids and babies and adults at the same time. Like a seed that contains the whole tree, our progression from infancy to maturity is within us throughout our lives, not at specific stages. The baby, the child, the adult are with us always, even from the beginning.

"What is it, Annie?"

"Why did my mommy and daddy get divorced?"

She was staring at me with a serious, wise look and I looked at Kurt and his eyes were wide and there was a hint of fearfulness in them. "That's a tough one," I said.

"You can answer that, can't you, Doc?" Kurt said.

The convention of our game was that Dr. Miracle knew everything and could do everything, but I could not answer and we sat in silence for a moment. Kurt said, "Doc?"

"What's that, little munchkin?" There was something tight in my voice and I hoped that the kids wouldn't notice it, though I knew they probably did.

"Can you get mommy to move back up here?"

"I don't think so."

"But you're Doctor Miracle," Annie said. "You can do anything."

I got up from the bed. I could not look at the kids. "Okay, kids, time to sleep." I leaned down and kissed both of them and tucked them into bed and told them I would continue the story the next night.

I went out onto the loft and stared down at the prison, at the lights across the valley. I sat at my desk. I opened the bottom drawer and took out the bottle of Bushmill's. There was only enough for a long swig. I drank it down and I began to think about my life and I got fed up with myself.

A person could wear himself out beating himself up over the way he had lived. Life was like a football game and you're in the locker room at half time, at the board with chalk and pointer showing up all the mistakes your team made in the first half. And you never get around to playing the second half, so numerous are the indiscretions of the first half.

Chapter Five

The day was cool and sunny, a perfect mountain day, crisp and fresh as iceberg lettuce. Class had started and the prisoners were looking at me as though I held the secret to all of existence; they seemed serious, intent on the work, though for all I knew they were calculating the years they had to either release or death.

I could see my house at the top of the mountain and I marveled again at how it was the only element of civilization they could see beyond the prison walls. What would they think if they knew I lived there?

I had heard one of the men on the yard refer to the place as "Star Wars" and at night with the lights on it did appear to be a space-craft hovering among the stars.

I was sure that night after night men lay awake on their steel bunks and stared up at those lights and imagined rocketing the sky, even as my kids did with Dr. Miracle, to find love and family in far corners of the universe.

None of the men had volunteered their work. I prodded them. Poet had brought in something but he told me he didn't want to read it. "Why not?" He shook his head. "Please." He didn't speak.

"I know it's tough to read your work out loud to people. If the work has worth, you're laying bare everything, your most secret thoughts, fears, inadequacies. You're writing in blood, doing an autopsy not only on someone you might love, but cutting open your own heart."

He stared for a long time at the pad in front of him. Then he began. His voice was soft, toneless. You could barely hear him. He was having a difficult time.

Few of the men had access to a typewriter and I could see that he had hand-written his work on sheets of yellow notepaper. The lettering was precise, even ornate, as though this were a medieval scroll.

Through the glass door, I watched Macklin at her desk. She was doing some paper work and from time to time she would look over at me and I felt something watchful in her gaze, as though she had a question for me. Or, again, was I imagining it? Was she really interested in me or just sitting there wondering why I was looking at her?

"'My father had walked out on us just after I was born,'" Poet read. "'My grandfather became the most important person in my life. We lived out in the desert and there weren't many kids around. We would go out in the desert and hunt snakes and rabbits. He would take me on trips.'"

He read in a voice so quiet I had to strain to hear him. I wanted to tell him to speak up, but I didn't want to make him any more self-conscious than he already was. I could see how difficult this was for him and so I said nothing.

"'He taught me about nature, how you hunt not for sport, but to eat. And how you relate to people. When I was a teen-ager my mother re-married and she and her new husband had two more kids, my half brother and sister.'" He took a deep breath. His gaze was focused inward on something unutterably painful, it seemed. He continued with great difficulty. I thought he was going to break down. "'I loved the kids very much. I didn't particularly get along with my step-father. I became even closer with my grandfather. And he took the two little ones under his wing and taught them as he had taught me, how to be better human beings.'"

He stopped again, stared at the paper. "I don't want to read this," he said.

"I know, I know," I said. "It's hard. It's our soul and we're laying it out there naked." He didn't speak. He didn't look at anyone. His stared down at the pages and you could feel the pain radiating from him. It was not forced, it was not done for our benefit; it was delicate and very powerful and I could see that the men in the room felt it and were moved.

It took him a long time to gather himself to continue. When he began again I could hear the pain in his voice, the strain he was feeling. It was soft, very light, almost a child's voice. "'I was at my girl friend's house when the call came. There was a man at the other end of the line. He said my grandfather was in trouble. He lived in a trailer a distance from the town. As soon as I came into the place, I knew something terrible had happened.'" He stopped once more, staring down at the paper.

"'I could smell this odor, like copper. A terrible feeling came over me. I knew something was wrong. It was blood, the smell of blood. There was a pool of blood in the middle of the floor, a trail of blood leading out behind the mobile home. I found him outside.'"

He stopped again, his gaze burning inward. His breathing was rapid. His fingers trembled.

The men in the room were all watching him now with something that seemed like indifference to me, a kind of cool objectivity, and I wondered what they were thinking. His story—was it true? Did they believe it? They had been moved and they had caught themselves, re-grouped, and we're looking at him with skepticism.

It felt true to me. The reluctance, the shyness, the pain. There were details that just seemed right. The coppery smell of blood, the feeling of dread that had come over him.

And why fake it here? Why? Why come into my class with a lie? What could I do for him? He seemed like someone wounded—my boys in war. He had been cut down by Fate's scythe.

Perhaps he was lying to himself. Perhaps he had told the lie so long and so often he believed it.

He continued. His fingers were trembling. He talked in a rush, the words pouring out of him, soft, soft, barely understandable: "'Someone had smashed in his skull. He was covered with blood. Blood was pouring out all over. I cradled him in my arms. I returned to my girlfriend's house. I was covered with blood…'"

He stopped and looked directly at me. His eyes were very blue. "That's as far as I got." He was muscular yet he seemed terribly fragile, so young, so very, very young, just a child. "Writing this is like walking down a dark alley," he said, again so softly I could barely hear him. "And you get to a place where it's just too dark."

He stared down at the table top. He sat there just staring at the table, his head bobbing up and down, a kind of tremor.

"All right," I said. "We'll talk about this story."

I looked over the men. They appeared vastly indifferent. They had been moved earlier, of that I was certain, then had shut it down. What would they do now? How would they would deal with one of their own who insisted he was innocent?

I had to be careful. It was important to me that a writer who had bared himself as completely as Poet not be savaged. I called on the white inmate, Culpepper. He was older, had been in the prison system most of his life. Hopefully, he would be wiser, more understanding than the others.

Culpepper leaned forward on the table and fixed Poet with a serious gaze. He spoke in a matter-of-fact voice. "I'd like to know what kind of case they had against him? From what he's read, I don't see where they made a case. I mean, why did they come to you?"

"There were certain things." Poet spoke so softly that I had to crane forward to hear him. "My grandfather had an attack dog. The dog hadn't done anything—no one had heard it barking or anything. There was no sign that the dog had gone after the intruder and so the police figured it must have been someone the dog knew. Also, my grandfather had been beaten to death with some sort of club. I had a baseball bat, which they tested for blood. They said it contained blood consistent with my grandfather's."

Culpepper turned to me. "I believed it. I believed him and I believed the writing."

Sergeant said, "It was moving. I believed him. But I don't understand why he came back to the girl's house."

"The phone wires were cut," Poet said. He did not look at anyone. He was staring down at the manuscript on the table in front of him.

El Negro shifted in his chair. He leaned forward, tense. "Yeah," he said, "but on the way back to her house—the first phone he came to—why didn't he call? Or go right to the police station? This is a small town, right?"

He seemed angry and I was baffled by this. Poet was one of their own; why wouldn't you give him the benefit of the doubt? They were both young, serving life sentences. Shouldn't El Negro give his fellow murderer the benefit of the doubt?

Was El Negro offended that someone should shop their innocence around? Was it that El Negro, knowing that he, himself, was guilty and had been convicted, felt that everyone convicted must also be guilty?

I interrupted him: "We're not lawyers here fighting Travis' case. Do you believe it as a story?"

Escalante, "Joker", the man who spent seventeen years in the hole, jumped in. He, too, seemed angry with Poet. "I didn't believe it. I mean, you find your grandfather who you love so much. You just let him lie there? You don't try to get a doctor?"

Poet could barely get the words out. "I knew he was dead…"

Crow, also called "Jaguar Goldie" and "Fifty-Nine", the Chicano with an ambition to go hot-air ballooning, was talking now, his voice hoarse with emotion. There were tears in his eyes. He could barely speak. "I believed dude, here. I found it moving." He shook his head. "Very, very moving." He looked as though he wanted to say something more, but instead just shook his head and looked over at me, embarrassed.

The man from Louisiana, Shea said, "I believed him, too. It *felt* like the truth. It was messy like the truth. Usually when people lie, they tend to neaten things up. Everything is nice and tidy. The truth, in my opinion, is not like that. Truth is messy like life."

The rest of the men remained quiet. They were all looking at me, waiting to hear what I had to say and I could only think how remarkable the whole situation was. Here I am, I was thinking, sitting with ten men who have been convicted of murder. One claims he's innocent, and these convicted murderers are dealing with the whole thing as if none of them are murderers. They're students, critics, consultants, people who just happened to drop by.

"It has a ring of truth to it, just like Shea said. It is messy like the truth. But, again, you may be a psychopath."

There was uneasy laughter from the group. Poet remained serious, even doleful, crushed that I would doubt his truthfulness.

"I don't know," I said, "I mean, I don't know, so I don't want to comment on the legalities of the thing. You've been convicted. There's nothing any of us can do about that. But as a story, I believe it and I think that if you really are innocent as you claim, then you owe it to yourself to write this."

I sat there feeling foolish and uncomfortable. I had called a man who very likely was a murderous psychopath, a psychopath, and he had listened to me and even nodded his head slightly at the possibility that he could be a psychopath and nine other possible psychopaths had taken it all in in the most natural way.

I was moved and bewildered and wondering what the hell I was doing there? I didn't like the way I felt inside. "Anybody else bring in something?"

Eric Platt, "Blast", the young black with the stammer, said, "I'm working on an article… about sexual harassment."

"Okay," I said not sure what he was talking about. Sexual harassment in a man's prison?

"How the female guards harass the male inmates," he said. The men around the table shifted in their chairs, laughed uncomfortably.

"Does this happen?" I said. No one spoke.

Blast's words came out in an indignant, stammering, torrent: "You be taking a shower and they're in the bubble up there looking at you. And sometimes... sometimes... they'll search you, you know, in a way, you know that they... that they... want to see... how big your... *dick* is..."

McMullin, the muscular intellectual, said, "It happens. We're all aware of incidents where inmates who have gotten it on with women guards..."

"Does this happen?" I said. No one answered. "How could it happen? Where?"

"There are nooks and crannies," McMullin said. The men snickered.

Blast ran right on, his voice strident: "Plenty of places, kitchen store room, laundry, offices. Library here, the book stacks. We're at their mercy, one of these... one of these... bitches... wants your dick..., your dick... is hers... And some...of them... I wouldn't fuck... with my worst... enemy's dick."

The men laughed and Poet said, "Platt has funny ideas about a lot of things. Isn't it the Jews who are making it with the guards?"

"What...the fuck do you know, faggot?"

"If this is true," I said, "write it as an article. If it's just made up—"

"You buy into this... women's lib shit. You suckered... by this shit, this newspaper shit, always trying to get women, you know everything a woman wants she would get... That's not the way we do it in my... family. In my family, the woman,... she don't mean...shit, she just listens... to what I have to say..."

"Let's get off this," I said. He was getting to me, the relentless, grinding hostility, the arrogance that seemed to be at the core of all he did, the way he thrust his face at me, the challenge in his tone. I even resented his stammer, how it seemed to suck time into quicksand. Words became thick ooze. A simple sentence became an eternity.

Platt's face was contorted with anger now; the vein on his forehed bulged as he fought to get the words out: "I… I… need, a list of… specific techniques… on how to write… this shit…"

"There's no list," I said. I was tired and exasperated. I wanted out of that room. List of techniques? I had no list of specific techniques. I went about the process of writing word by word, paragraph by paragraph, chopping away at it, refining it, trying to do a clean and honest job. It was a grueling process of endless tinkering and I never knew if I was getting it right.

Platt was staring directly at me, his eyes wild. He was yelling now. "I…want…a specific list… on how to write…this!"

"Look," I said. "I told you I don't have a list."

"You a… writer,… ain't you?" Platt shouted. He was still staring right into me and I continued to stare back at him and the anger in his eyes was immense and frightening, yet I would not look away.

"I'm somebody who had things happen to him," I said, "and I got them down on paper. I guess that makes me a writer, but I don't feel like a writer and I don't think of myself as a writer—"

"What… do you… think of yourself as?" Platt demanded.

"I experienced certain things in his life and they haunted me and in order to get rid of these demons I put them down on paper and some people were moved by what I had written. And they started calling me a writer. And they started paying me for it."

Platt, who had been sitting right next to me, leaned very close. His face was damp with perspiration from his anger and the effort it took for him to speak. He was still looking into my eyes and I continued to stare back at him. "State… paying you a whole lot of mmmoney… and you're going to come… come in here… and bull—bullshit us… with… a lot of…shit…" He looked round at the other men. "Dude… here just using us with all this bullshit…"

Poet had gotten out of his seat and had come around the table. "Eric," he said.

"That's my name."

"Simmer down."

Platt leaned back in his chair and shifted his attention to Poet. His hands gripped the edge of the table. "My...man..."

"I'm not your man."

"Okay. Punk. You want to get down?" he said quietly. "Let's get down."

I stood and walked around to Poet, placing myself between him and Platt. "Just take it easy now," I said.

"You have no right taking it out on him," Poet said. He said this quietly, reasonably, but I could see he was ready to fight.

The rest of the men sat there watching. Robinson swiveled his head from side to side, his eyes shifting nervously, checking everything out. Culpepper and McMullin had both moved their chairs back a distance from the table.

Platt pushed hard on the table. "No *right!*" he screamed. "I'll fuck you in your neck! With a shank, I'll fuck you!"

"Sit down," I said to Poet. He hesitated. "Sit." He moved around the table to his chair and sat. I turned to Blast. "I don't know what's bothering you, but we're not going to operate on this level."

"You got to operate on this level," Sergeant said. "This is the level you on."

"We're not prisoners here," I said.

"What are we?" Sergeant demanded. He, too, was shaking with anger.

"Back off," McMullin said to me. "This a black-white thing."

"Not to me. We're not going to get into the color thing. In here we're writers. All of us. You're upset about something, you hate this place, you hate this other guy, you hate me? Write about it."

"This man wants his respect," Sergeant said. "And he has earned that respect. You must respect him. And Poet, here, must respect him."

"He wasn't respecting the teacher," Poet said.

"Maybe he sensed the teacher was disrespecting him," Sergeant said.

"Why do you say that?" Culpepper said. "I didn't see the teacher disrespecting Platt. You mean because he's white and Platt's black?"

"You know, Shank. You been in the system long as me. Youngster here—" He nodded toward Platt. "—was asking the man a question and youngster felt the man was condescending. You know that."

"Disrespect," I said. "That's a big deal out on the yard. That's the way you live out there. That's not the way I live."

"You're in here now," Sergeant said. "Your ass is *here*."

"But my imagination is everywhere. With your imagination, your ideas, you can fly out of these walls. They may have thrown away the key on you, but with writing you can go anywhere."

"Hey, boss, no disrespect, but you don't know fuck-all about what goes down here," Sergeant said. "Them cops out there on the yard and in the towers—they don't like the way you part your hair or the crease in your trousers—they call you out: 'Black motherfucker, kiss my red peckerwood ass! Get your nose way up in there. I'm nothing but an ignorant, loser, asshole with a 65 IQ, but I'm a better man than you. So get down on your knees and kiss my balls. Make sure you get all the shit out of my asshole.' And you suck it up and you take it because you want to visit with your wife or your kid. You want to be able to write a letter. To buy some shampoo in the canteen. You try to tell yourself you're still a man, but you don't want to do seventeen years in the hole like Jaguar Goldie here. You don't want to do your whole life like that."

There was a knock on the glass of the door to the guard's station. Macklin was standing there, signaling to me that time was up.

"That's it for today," I said.

The men got up and moved slowly out of the class. They were subdued, shaken by what had happened. I sensed that my response to it had not been taken well by them. I had let them down in some way.

Through the glass door, I could see Baker talking with Macklin. I was certain he was telling her what had happened.

I walked out onto the yard. Dusk was moving in from the mountains. I could see the lights I had left on in my house. The early autumn day was turning cold.

Travis Wells was waiting for me. Sergeant stood a short distance beyond him. "I just wanted you to know," Wells said, "I'm not writing to prove I'm innocent. I know everyone in here says they're innocent."

"You didn't kill your grandfather? Who did?"

"What difference does it make?"

"If you're innocent—"

He shook his head slowly. "They've taken my life from me." He didn't speak for a while. He stared at me. "I have an idea who did it," he said.

"Okay."

"Belle."

"Someone you know?"

"His second wife. They call her Fat Belle. Not my grandmother. My grandmother died years ago. Fat Belle wanted his money."

"Did they investigate Fat Belle?"

"She had an alibi they couldn't crack."

"Write it all," I said. "If you're telling the truth, it'll come through." What else could I say?

He stared at me and there was something wounded in his eyes, a sadness there. "I don't lie," he said. "Ever. Anyone knows me, knows that."

He moved off across the yard. Sergeant waited for him to disappear into a group heading for the far end of the yard and the cellblocks before coming up to me. "I want to apologize," he said. "I got emotional about Blast. I get crazy sometimes. Don't report me on this. They'll give me a 115. I'll lose my canteen privileges. I was in Vietnam and sometimes I get emotional." He didn't speak for a while. We stood there gazing around at the mountains. There was a tart chill in the air. "You were there, weren't you? In country?" he said.

"How do you know?"

"I just know."

"Where were you?"

"Kien Tuong," he said.

"Plain of Reeds."

"You were there?"

"Moc Hoa."

"That was some mess," he said. "All those women and children were killed there." Of course he would have known about it; had he been in the Plain of Reeds during the late sixties, he would have heard about it.

"It wasn't what they said."

"Well, that's what you hear. Heard we killed a lot of, like I said, innocent people."

"Who said that?"

"I heard that. I heard they set them on fire."

"No." I felt ill inside. I felt as though I might throw up.

"Well. You hear those things." He held out his hand and shook my hand hard and stared at me and nodded his head and there was some attempt in him to forge something between us; or perhaps he felt that something had been forged. We had both fought in the Plain of Reeds. "Lot of peoples killed there," he said quietly. Then he moved off across the yard.

I started toward the stairwell. "Hey, writer!" It was Macklin. She stood in the doorway to the office alcove. One hand was hooked in her belt, the other covering the head of the billy club slung through its leather holder, a tough guy stance. "Heard you had some trouble."

"It'll be all right," I said.

"He'll test you," she said. "You were right not to back down. But watch yourself. Watch your back."

She was staring at me, waiting for me to say something. I felt uneasy in her presence. What did she want from me?

What did I want from her?

"What kind of stuff do you write?" she said.

"Novels."

She smiled. It was the first time I had ever seen her smile. "You going to put me in a book?" she said.

"Maybe."

"Buy me dinner tonight." She said this very quietly. She was watching me, studying me and there was something dark and unnerving in her gaze.

"Where'd you like to go?" There were two or three places in town which could be described as dinner spots.

"How about your house?"

"Okay."

She looked toward the mountains beyond the prison wall. "That's your place?"

"How did you know?"

"We're supposed to know all about you. You're civilian staff. Department of Corrections doesn't trust any of you. I always wondered who lived up there."

"Now you know."

"Bet it's lonely."

"Sometimes."

"Why live there, then?"

"Long story."

"Six o'clock?"

"That'll be good."

"I'll make pasta. It's the one thing I can cook."

"Sounds good."

There was a stir at the far end of the yard. All movement among the men on the yard stopped. A voice came over the squawk box Macklin carried on her belt. She spoke into it. I heard: "Walking her off…" and Macklin snapped the box off hard. She took in a deep breath. Her face had grown very hard; her jaw was clenched.

The guards who were in the building came out on to the yard. From every area of the yard guards suddenly appeared. They stood very still, watching. The prisoners moved back to the wall. Everyone stood still. "What is it?" I said.

Macklin just shook her head. She looked profoundly troubled.

"What?"

A young redheaded female guard was being led across the yard by a Lieutenant and two other guards. She was in handcuffs.

She walked with her head down. I could see tears streaming down her face.

"Ah, Damn," Macklin said. "Damn it to hell."

The redhead walked the whole length of the yard under a gauntlet of stares from both prisoners and guards.

The yard was completely quiet. Suddenly from the rear of a group of prisoners, a shrill, obscene whistle sounded, the sound you'd hear at a strip show. There was nervous laughter and several guards quickly moved toward the area of the yard where the whistle had originated.

Everything was silent again. The female guard reached the end of the yard and the Lieutenant called out, "Stairwell," and the door opened and he and the two other guards and the redhead moved out of view.

The yard remained in silence, stunned. At last the men began to mill about, moving back to their basketball and handball and weight-lifting. "What was that all about?"

"They call that walking you off the yard," Macklin said, still shaken.

"What for?"

"Bad cop. Could have been fooling around. Doping. It was Terry. She knew the okey-doke. You want to play, you gotta pay." She stared for a long time at the door where the girl had exited. "See you tonight," she said without looking at me. She moved back into the office area.

I started for the stairwell, feeling uneasy with myself, disappointed. Why had I said this and not that with Macklin? Why had I done this and not that?

Why was I attacking myself? She was coming to my house. What else could I have done?

Forever I seemed to be accusing myself, questioning myself, questioning everything I did, embarrassed by my place in the world, by what I did in the world.

As best I can tell, it had first become a problem when I returned from war. But I might have always been like that. I didn't remember much of my life before the war.

You'll be seeing her tonight, I told myself. You'll make everything up. You will finally say the right thing.

Platt was standing not far off, helping with some yard work. He looked at me and his face was creased by a large grin. "I…told you," he stammered. "I told…you. Bitch was fucking… an inmate. I… told you!"

I continued on to the steel and glass door at the end of the yard. "Stairwell," I called out and felt a great sense of relief as I was buzzed out of the yard.

Chapter Six

Waiting for Macklin, I watched the great red disc of the sun slide toward the low mountains to the west. I was on my second Bushmill's. It was doing its job. I felt good.

It was one of those spectacular mountain evenings, clear, the sky a deep, velvet blue, the air cool with a snappy breeze blowing from the west. I was thinking: how lucky I am, my life—a miracle. I had known worthier men, braver men, more honest men. And they would never see an evening such as this.

Macklin arrived. The sun was blood red, enormous, and I pulled her to the window to see it slice behind the horizon.

She had bought a large jar of supermarket sauce and some garlic and onions and green peppers and sausage and she began now to chop the whole thing together. She seemed vaguely annoyed. "I've seen the sun," she said.

"That color?"

"Yes."

"It's red."

"I can see that."

She was wearing a light print dress and out of her Correctional Officer khakis she looked small and dowdy. Still, there was a sexiness about her. Her breasts were not large, but nicely shaped. Her body was well-formed, something you could not tell when she was in uniform.

She didn't seem particularly happy to be with me. She chopped up the onions and the garlic, dumping the mess into a pan, going about it as though she were being paid by the hour. "I hope you're not too fussy," she said. I had poured us out a couple of glasses of red wine and she drank hers right down and poured some more.

"You like cooking?" I said just for something to say.

"Not particularly. Oh, I'll cut out a recipe from the paper once in a while. But I never cook them."

"All right."

"I don't cook much. I like recipes, though. I just read this great one for turkey stuffing. This is the way it goes. You take three eggs, slice of bacon, popcorn, raw rice, bell pepper."

"Popcorn?"

"You cook the bird and stuffing at 350 degrees until the popcorn blows the turkey's ass off."

"That's a joke?" I said.

"No."

"Oh, I see. I'll have to try that."

"Me, too," she said. She grew solemn. "I realize I've been cool to you but the prison, that's just the way it is. They don't like outsiders, contract staff. They figure you're a bunch of do-gooders who feel these assholes are somehow human. Well, they're not human, not the things that they've done."

"They're not all the same," I said. "This guy, Wells—"

"He's an asshole, too. Some kind of psychopath."

The water had begun to boil and she took a couple of handfuls of pasta and dumped them into the water. Then she added more garlic to the sauce, which had begun to simmer. "Hope you like garlic."

"As long as we're both having it."

"You see, we know what we have to do to keep the prison running. This isn't a kindergarten. This is a max unit. We gotta come down hard on these motherfuckers or they'll set your ass up in an instant. You see what went down today? I know this girl, Terry. She's not a bad girl. She just got taken in."

"Does that happen very often?"

"It happens. We're all human. But it hurts. It hurts all of us."

She stirred the sauce, tested a strand of pasta; looked directly at me. "It's also being divorced," she said. "That makes it tough to warm up to someone new."

"I know."

She drained her glass and poured herself more wine. "Just don't feel comfortable," she said with a small shrug.

"I feel the same way."

"I mean sex, you know, with someone not my husband—"

I nodded and poured myself more wine. I was beginning to relax. "I know," I said. "What do you do? The AIDS thing and all—"

"Not very much," she said, laughing. "I get tested regularly."

God, it was an ugly subject. How do you become romantic with something like the Black Death hovering over you? "Well," I said. I didn't want to get into the whole AIDS thing, whether or not I had been sleeping with someone else. Since my wife had left, I had gone to bed with two women, pick-ups I had met with Phil Kleinmutz at a Bakersfield country and western nightclub.

It had been clumsy, the whole condom thing. It just seemed to be barbaric—a man in his forties playing around with rubbers, "safeties" as we called them when I was a kid. And yet what could you do?

I quickly downed my wine and poured myself another glass and another one for her. "You get used to a certain person," I said.

"Yes," she said.

"Get out of practice," I said.

"Yes," she said. "Do you—?"

"What?"

"—feel like practicing?"

I leaned back against the kitchen counter and laughed and she laughed, too. "Like football or basketball," I said.

"Should be like riding a bike," she said. I continued to laugh. "I don't know—".

"What do you mean?"

"I don't know how to behave. I guess we should—" She stopped and shook her head and poured herself more wine and drank it right down and I poured myself another glass, also.

"What?"

"We should start slow."

"Okay," She was leaning up against me now and her breasts were warm against my chest. Her perfume had suddenly whisked my youth back to me. "'White Shoulders,'" I said. I hadn't smelled it in years.

"How did you know?"

"When I was a kid, all the girls wore it." I was back in Pittsburgh and high school, making out in the backseat of my dad's Dodge. All my teen years sex on my fingers smelled like "White Shoulders."

I turned her face toward me and kissed her. She pressed against me and we kissed for a long time, then she pulled back. She studied me. "Not bad," she said.

I held her tightly, smiling. "What?" she said.

"Practice makes perfect." We kissed again and she was thrusting herself against me. She made a small effort to pull back, to stop, then she gave in and pressed hard against me and pushed her sex in against me and pumped hard against me. "The spaghetti," she breathed. She could hardly speak. She was churning against me.

"What about it?" I said.

"Going to be limp," she said.

"I don't think so."

I turned the fire off under the spaghetti and the sauce and led her upstairs.

She slipped out of her dress as we entered the bedroom and her panties and bra were off by the time she reached the bed. She stretched out on it and she was gorgeous, her body small, supple, breasts exquisitely formed.

I had never had a woman other than my wife on this bed. My wife had been spectacularly put together I had always thought, but Macklin was a miracle, one of those creatures created to be naked: with clothes on, she was attractive; nude she was astonishing, wondrously, delicately shaped, skin like cream, not an ounce of fat.

She pulled me down on her and I entered her and I fought not to come and she worked with me in an astonishing fashion. All my unease and tenseness disappeared. Our bodies moved together as though we had been doing this for years.

"Yes, yes, yes," she said over and over, gyrating against me. "This is so good." She came and I came and we both fell back on the bed and I felt wonderful and astonished that it had all gone so well and easily.

After a while she reached over and took a pack of cigarettes from her dress pocket and lit up. "We didn't even need to practice," she said.

"No," I said. "I have to tell you something. This is embarrassing."

She picked at a fleck of tobacco on her tongue. "Okay."

"Well, this is kind of a first for me."

"What?"

"First time I've been to bed with a woman that—"

She appeared suddenly annoyed and in that moment she reminded me of my ex-wife. "What?" she said, snapping her fingers to hurry me up.

"—I didn't know her first name."

She gazed at me in mock surprise, then she began to laugh. "You're something," she said.

"What do I call you? Officer Macklin?"

"That's really funny."

"Never got around to it."

"You had other things on your mind."

"Yes."

"My name is Rita."

"Good. You don't look like a Rita."

"What does a Rita look like?"

"I don't know. Dark. Sultry."

"What do I look like?"

"A Wendy. Or Debbie."

"Yuch," she said. She sat up in the bed. There were some copies of my books on a shelf across from the bed. She got up and crossed to the shelf and took down several of the books and looked at them. She looked at the pictures of me on the backs of the books and compared them to the way I looked now. I had no wrinkles then.

"I think you're more handsome now," she said. "I don't like people without any lines. You need lines. It shows you've done some living."

"I've done that," I said.

"You know what you look like?" She was studying me in the mirror behind the bed.

"What's that?"

"Cowboy gone to seed. I like that look. Marlboro Man." She studied one of the books. "'Funhouse Mirrors?' What does that mean?"

I didn't know what to say. I never knew what to say when people asked about funhouse mirrors. How could I explain the funhouse mirror my life had become when I had ventured onto the Plain of Reeds?

Entering Moc Hoa hamlet in the fog, discovering the butchery there, it was as though I had walked into another dimension, a warp in reality: Dogolov through the looking glass, forever after in the funhouse. Nothing was quite real after that. Blisters on the heart.

"I don't know."

She returned to the bed with the book. She leafed through it, read a couple of sentences. "Well, you wrote it," she said. "Don't you know what it means?"

"No," I said. I knew nothing. Most of all, I knew nothing about that morning on the Plain of Reeds. My men had been accused of the most horrific acts—I know they didn't do what they had been accused of, they couldn't—and yet.

And yet, I knew I hadn't been told everything. I would never know everything. No one ever knows everything. "Sometimes you write things and you don't know what they mean."

"Look, I'm just a dumb redneck broad who's read maybe three books in her life and two of them were comic books, so I don't want to come on too strong here, but shouldn't the writer know what his book is about?"

"I know it," I said. "But not up here." I pointed to my head.

"Here?" she said, indicating her heart.

I shook my head and took my finger and pressed it against her belly. "Here," I said. "It's in your gut."

I remained quiet for a while. She was watching me. "You were in the war?" she said.

"Yes."

"Which one?" I suddenly realized she might not know anything about Vietnam. She must be twenty-seven, twenty-eight. She would have been a baby when the war ended. What did they teach kids in school about that war?

Would they have talked about the Plain of Reeds?

"Not the Second World War or Korea," I said.

"I know that," she said. "You're not old."

"That means one other war."

"I know. Vietnam. I was just a little kid, then," she said.

"I wrote about something that happened there."

"Happened to you?"

I stared at myself in the mirror behind the bed and suddenly I seemed very old, blasted. A child was on the bed next to me. What are we doing, I found myself asking myself?

"What was it?" she said.

I just shook my head.

"You killed people?" Macklin said.

Yes, yes, I had killed people, enemy soldiers, people who were trying to kill me, people who were killing my comrades, my men. Yes, I had killed. "I'm not proud if it," I said. "But I never killed innocent women and children. I was very young when I went over there."

She had pulled her legs up to her chest and she had her arms around them and she shook her head and smiled in disbelief. "I would have never thought," she said.

"I'm not what I seem."

"No," she said.

"And neither are you. Nothing is what it seems."

She sat there on the bed, holding her legs, staring pensively at her twined fingers. "Horrible way to live your life," she said.

"Funhouse Mirror," I said. "You see, that's what it means."

We didn't speak for a while. She lit another cigarette and stretched back on the bed and stared at the ceiling. "This kid, Wells," I said.

"Wells?"

"The one they call 'Poet.' What was he convicted of? He killed his grandfather and—"

She turned on her side and looked at me and took her hand and smoothed it over my face. "I told you before," she said. "You don't want to know…"

"He did something more?"

She didn't answer.

"How did you become a guard?"

"Not much work in this town. There's the supermarket, the cement factory, and the prison." She got up and walked to the window and stared out at the prison lights. "Amazing," she said quietly. "The prison down there. They all look up here. 'Star Wars', they call it."

"One of the men told me."

"Don't ever let them know you live up here. Don't let them know anything."

She sat at the window for a long time and I felt myself drifting off to sleep. I started to fight it, and then I gave in.

I was in the middle of Travis Wells' story. I was sitting in a chair in a mobile home. A man came toward me, trying to speak. Nothing would come out. I didn't recognize the man. He might have been Asian, I'm not sure. Then I saw that he was holding a baseball bat. He raised the bat over me and swung at me and hit me. I could feel my blood flying from me and now there was blood everywhere.

I awoke. I looked around for Rita Macklin and she was gone. I called out to her. There was no answer. She had left.

I moved to the window. Her wineglass was on the floor next to the chair she had been sitting in. The glass was filled with cigarette butts.

The sky was gray with early dawn. The lights of the prison were still on. I stared at the lights. A hawk glided in the sky, hovered, dove.

I tried to shake off the dream's residue. I felt a sense of disconnection. It was something I felt often. The first years back from the war, I was convinced that I was insane. I feared that one day I would be locked away in a veteran's hospital.

And then I read a Japanese philosopher who said that if you imitated the wise man, even insincerely, you would become wise: the person who acts insane is in fact insane; the person who says he is imitating a murderer and then kills someone *is* a murderer.

And so I became well by imitating sanity. Because of this, there was a certain tentative quality to everything I did. I felt my reality was fraudulent. Who knew when the mask would no longer fit?

I told him he had done good work, to put it in prose form. "You going to steal it from me?" he said.

"Steal it?

"We," he stammered, "we in here…and we don't know what you doing with… our writing. You… could be making… big money off them."

"No, *I don't think a market* for your work is there yet."

"Well, I do. I know there's big money there."

"Okay. But I won't be stealing it from you."

Sergeant started to recount a story about Vietnam. He had come upon a wounded buddy. His midsection had been blown open; his guts were hanging over his knees. He begged Sergeant to kill him and Sergeant could not do it and it haunted him to this day. "He told me I'd kill an animal that was suffering. Why not him? He begged me to kill him. I couldn't do it. Later, though, I could kill. Yessir, I got over that hang-up."

"Are you writing this?" I asked.

"Thinking about it," he said. "Can't think too long, though. Gives me bad dreams."

"That happens," I said.

"You know that?"

"Yes."

Culpepper had begun a story of his childhood, how innocence had been betrayed; he had been thrown into the prison system when he was eleven years old; he had been brutalized at that young age; he had learned to be a real criminal. He had become a murderer.

It had a touching, child-like quality to it, an innocence, then the nightmare, real and frightening. "What were you sent to the Youth Authority for?" I asked him.

"I had run away from home. I wasn't getting along with my step-mother and she had me sent away. She wanted my Dad all to herself."

His gravel-voice had become soft, pained. Sitting there, across from me, was a middle-aged, hardened con; his wiry, prison-tough body was covered with tattoos needled-on in a half dozen prisons in American, elaborate graffiti of the body and soul. He had killed more than once. And yet the pain of the memory of how he had been abandoned as a young child was an open sore on his heart. "I cried so many tears then," he said, "that I thought they were blood. I thought I would bleed to death, so I stopped crying." An eleven-year-old in the body of an old man was staring at me and his expression was sorrowful in the extreme. Wasted life, wasted, wasted life.

"You have to write this," I said and he answered yes, but I wasn't convinced. I thought the pain might be too great.

Shea was working on a story of his days on death row. Robinson was writing about the family of the man he had killed. McMullin, too, was working on something about his childhood.

Poet read from his story. He seemed to have gained confidence from our last session. His voice was stronger now. "'They questioned me for fourteen hours. I had scratches on my face. My grandfather had traces of blood under his fingernails. They said it matched my type. But there was something else involved. When I found my grandfather's body, he was clutching something in his hand. A turquoise amulet I had given my girl friend. And he had splinters under his forefinger. I tried to pry his hand open and I got a piece of this wood in my hand. They tried to say I had beaten him to death with a baseball bat. He had tried to fend off the bat and that's how he got the splinters—'"

He stopped. He looked up at me, gazed directly at me. He seemed relieved, as though in reading the story a weight had been taken from him. "That's as far as I've gone," he said.

"How do you explain the scratches?" Culpepper said.

"My girlfriend and I were making love and she scratched me."

"Did you testify to this?" Culpepper said.

"She denied it."

"Why?"

He didn't speak for a moment. "I don't know."

"Why did they say you wanted to kill him?" Culpepper said.

"Some people thought he had money hidden in his trailer. Which was ridiculous. He had nothing."

"And the amulet," McMullin said. "I didn't get that—"

"It had been a gift from my grandfather to me and I had given it to her. My girlfriend testified that she had given it back to me and that I was wearing it that evening."

"Were you?" I said, feeling uneasy talking about the real case. We were supposed to be dealing with his story as a story, not re-trying his case. But I had been sucked in. I wanted to know if, in fact, Poet had killed his grandfather. Not as a story, but as reality.

"No," he said.

"How'd it get there?" Culpepper asked.

Travis Wells did not answer.

"I don't know, man," El Negro said. "Blood under your grandfather's nails—"

"It was type O, most common type."

"What was your girlfriend's type?"

"I don't know."

"You know, man, don't you?" El Negro said. "Hey, check it out—I got cracked on a murder rap just like you, but I admit I did it. This doesn't sound good for you. How'd the blood get on the bat?"

"My grandfather and I had been horsing around a couple of weeks before he was killed. We were hitting stones with the bat. He probably had a cut. I'm not sure. I think his blood got on the bat then."

"You're talking now strictly on a level of the writing," McMullin said. "Literature. Nothing to do with the actual case."

A few of the men laughed. "I loved my grandfather," Poet said. "Why would I kill him?"

No one spoke for a while. Then Crow said, "If we all knew the answer to 'why' we done what we done, I don't think too many of us would be here."

Poet now seemed intent on persuading me—perhaps all of us—of his innocence and that surprised me because up till now there had been a reticence in talking about the actual case. He poured out a whole litany of injustice, how everyone involved, including his own attorney, had set him up; how evidence had been altered, testimony perjured.

Even his girlfriend had betrayed him, lying to the police and to the court and how that was the most painful and disillusioning thing at all.

It was as if all the anguish over the case had welled up in him and overflowed as he had begun to write about it.

The men in the class challenged him on aspects of his story and I could see he was becoming upset; the whole thing threatened to get out of control. I stopped it and again made the point that we were challenging his *story*, his work of literature, not the actual case.

Was his fictional story believable? Did it work?

It worked for some of the men, but I was surprised at how tough other of the men were on him. Joker said, "I don't get it, man. It don't hang together for me. This is your grandfather. I just don't get it."

Poet looked pained and uncomfortable and at last said, "That's the way it happened! What can I say? That's the way it happened! I swear to Almighty God."

And I found inside me something that believed him. Yes, it was messy as life, as messy as the truth. Truth is not neat.

El Negro wanted to discuss a problem he had, his "story": "I tried writing this," he said, "but I don't have the English—"

"Write it in Spanish and we'll get someone to translate," I said.

"Yes, I know. But I want to be able to write this in English—"

"How much do you have?"

He held up a sheet of paper, embarrassed. "Some notes. That's all."

"Tell us about it."

He, thought for a while, then nodded his head. He began to speak almost apologetically: "In the town I'm from in Ecuador there is a family, Molinas. They are very wealthy and since I was small I worked for them. I shined their shoes, I cleaned their stables. The favorite in the family for me was the oldest son, Jacinto Molinas. I came to the States and I did many bad things. And one day I am in Los Angeles and I get a call from Jacinto Molinas." He paused as though trying to figure out if he wanted to go on.

"Yes?" I said. "You got this call—?"

"He is living in Los Angeles. He is wealthy. He has a house in Bel-Aire. He imports various things from Latin America. I visit him in his great mansion and he treats me as though I were his son and he tells me, 'El Negro, I have a problem. A Cuban is making my life a hell. He waited at my house and he shot me in the head and I survived, but the police can do nothing for me. Will you kill him for me?' This is an old man, a man who I have great love and respect for and yet I tell him I cannot do this. I was about to go on trial and I could not do this. I said, Jacinto, I would do anything but this for you. And since I did not do it, he did it himself and they arrested him and one day I am on the yard and I see an old, bent man walking the circle in the far yard and it is Jacinto Molinas. He is on this very yard now. He speaks to no one but me. I am his only friend. You know this old man you see me walking with on the yard? This is Jacinto Molinas. He lost everything, his house, his wife, his family."

"Can you write about this?" I said.

He smiled. He was missing an upper tooth in the front. He seemed embarrassed. "If this was Spanish, yes."

"Write it in Spanish," I said. "Then we'll translate it."

"Okay," he said, "because, you know, it hurts me to see what became of Jacinto Molinas. If I would have known I was going to lose my case I would have killed the Cuban for him." He was lost in thought. He smiled gently. "You know, Señor Paul, no one owns life. *Pero* anyone who can pick up a knife owns death." He said this gently, sadly.

When the class was over, Poet hurried away across the yard before I had a chance to talk further with him. He appeared troubled at how his story had been received by the other inmates.

It roiled inside me, the story. It was untidy and a lot of it didn't make a whole lot of sense, but that was the way life was. I had an instinct, a gut feeling, that he was telling the truth and that disturbed me.

I shivered as I crossed the yard. The men had all gone back to their cells, "inline", they call it, and the yard was deserted. The yellow yard lights, the razor-edged concertina wire, the bleak concrete of the walls, created in me a feeling of terrible desolation. Inside, I was as bleak as my surroundings. How did these men endure it? They were lost, lost.

Macklin showed up at my house just after dark. An immense bank of cloud had moved into the valley and it loomed below us, obscuring the prison lights. There were flashes of lightening on the mountains beyond the prison, followed by thunder, low rumbles at first, then tremendous cracks and Macklin looked alarmed and I held her close to me. Sheets of freezing rain lashed the house. The whole building shook with waves of wind. The large windows overlooking the valley bowed with the force of the storm.

We made love while the storm roared all around us. We had skipped even the pretense of having dinner and had gone right at it and it was fine and as lovely as the first evening. We just seemed to click together and our lovemaking was free and uninhibited and it was as though we had known each other for years.

She encouraged me to go at her with fury, calling out, "Harder! Harder! Harder!" And I thrust myself into her and our bodies clashed and we were pouring sweat and she screamed out in what would be pain, what would be murder if we were not lost in passion, and it was primitive and beautiful.

The storm raged and the house shook with the wind and great sheets of rain lashed the windows and then the storm quieted and the rain fell softly and we relaxed. The air was cold and fresh and damp with rain.

"I like you," she said after we had both climaxed and she had rested back on the bed and taken her cigarettes out of her skirt pocket and lit up.

"I like you, too," I said.

We lay there for a while and she smoked and seemed to be lost in thought and I was lost in thought, too, thinking of Poet and his story and I felt stupid, his crime clattering around in my brain while an exquisitely sexy young lady lay next to me. "Can't get that thing out of my mind," I said.

"What?"

"The inmate, Wells. He claims the D.A., judge, even his own attorney, railroaded him. Grandfather was beaten to death with a baseball bat. Splinters of wood under the grandfather's nails from the bat. Grandfather's blood on the bat."

"You're funny," she said, shaking her head.

"It's just on my mind."

"*Funny.*"

"He says he was horsing around with his grandfather a few weeks before the murder and that's when the blood got on the bat. I don't know."

"You should never think about these guys." She raised herself up on her elbows and stubbed out her cigarette. Her gaze was turned inward, her thoughts somewhere else.

"You said you thought he might be innocent."

Now she looked directly at me. Her expression was somber. "Of the guys I've seen there, yeah, I think he could be innocent. This guy is not a murderer."

"You look so serious," I said, and laughed.

"That's the difference between you and me. I look serious, but I'm not. You look pleasant and you're not."

She got up and walked to the window and stared out at the night. You could not see the prison lights. Dark clouds, immense and swollen, the remnants of the storm, closed out the valley, even the tops of the mountains opposite. She began to dress. "Got to go," she said.

"Why?"

She shrugged a tiny, little girl gesture. "Can't sleep with a man. Even with my husband. We had separate rooms. Goofy, huh?"

"You'll end up sleeping with me," I said.

She smiled, then kissed me and it was an intimate kiss, not passionate, but a kiss from someone who cared for me, someone who knew me well and this surprised me and made me feel good. I longed for that kind of intimacy, the intimacy I had once had with my wife. I longed to be friends with a woman again.

"I'll call you," she said. "I promise."

"There's no strings on this."

She stared at me and the dark, opaque quality to her gaze was there for an instant and I didn't like that. I wanted that wall to be gone forever, but sensed that it might not be and that troubled me. "That's good," she said. "That's how I like it."

That look—the men in the group had it. Pure emptiness, deadness. Maybe prison did that to you. Maybe I, too, had it. I prayed not, for the sake of my children.

There was something more. She hesitated, thought about it, then spoke. "Your wife hurt you a lot."

I shrugged, embarrassed. "Your husband and you?"

"I did the hurting." She was gazing at me and smiling and there was a sadness there. She kissed me and moved from the bedroom and I heard her footsteps down the stairs and out the front door. I heard her car start up and drive off.

I fell asleep and I dreamed of a man being beaten by another man with a baseball bat. Both men were strangers and yet in the dream I knew them and I kept asking this question: Why are you doing this?

In the dream I was happy. I was thankful that I was not dreaming of the war.

Chapter Eight

The mountains had been cool and drizzly and I had driven down into the San Joaquin valley's heat to meet Phil Kleinmutz.

Bakersfield, even in the spring, is murderously hot. It was the kind of heat that forces the breath out of you. You could see it, a heavy mist thick like syrup steaming from the irrigated cotton and onion fields surrounding the town.

It was late afternoon and we drove out to the batting cages near Sam Lynn Field and hit baseballs for about an hour and I was slamming them out and Phil would get a hit now and again and we had a fine time despite the heat. It felt good to smash something clean: that marvelous sense of connecting with *something*, if only a baseball.

After, we dropped into a saloon nearby, Bakersfield's idea of an upscale place. Founded by cowboys, Bakersfield for years was a ranch town. Then someone discovered oil in the surrounding hills and it was an oil and ranch town. Then someone else figured out you could irrigate the fields and agriculture boomed and the dust bowl destroyed Oklahoma and the Okies poured into the town and the surrounding farm areas.

This is John Steinbeck "Grapes of Wrath" territory and the faces you see in the city are mostly the sons and daughters of Okies, with some old cattle and ranching folk also there, leathery skin, the lean slouch of people comfortable on a horse or in a field.

It's a western redneck town and the saloon we were in, though upscale and aspiring to big city slickness, was filled with people in cowboy garb, the high-end stuff, Stetson hats, hand-stitched Bronco-label shirts, Stacy Adams boots. These were oil and ranching folk, with oil and ranching money.

The music in the background was Bakersfield country, which means Buck Owens, Merle Haggard, Bill Wood and Spade Cooly. They were all part of the rough, outlaw tradition of the town. Merle Haggard had spent time in prison and Cooly, who lived in the Mojave just south of Tehachapi, had axed his wife to death. Ol' Spade was visited by swift and celestial retribution. Playing at a Sheriff's benefit dance while on leave from prison, he ruptured an aorta. He was dead before he hit the floor.

Phil insisted we play chess. From time to time we would go at it and though I'm only middling at the game, I always beat him. As a player, he was passionate, but inept.

They had a set behind the bar—the owner of the place also liked the game; he would often play his customers for their tab—and the bartender fetched the board and pieces and we agreed to play one game for the evening's drinks.

As we were setting it up, Kleinmutz lectured me on behavior and how to improve myself: "If you run through the streets, saying you imitate a lunatic, you are in fact a lunatic."

Kleinmutz loved to pull this one on me. I had made the mistake of telling him how I had saved my sanity after the war. "I know this," I said. "I told you this."

"If you kill a man, saying you imitate a murderer, you *are* a murderer. By the same token, a horse that imitates a championship thoroughbred may be classed as a thoroughbred—"

"Are you going to play?"

"The man who imitates the wise ruler, Shun—"

"Please."

"I'm only imitating the master," Kleinmutz said. "He who imitates Shun belongs to Shun's company. A man who studies wisdom, even insincerely, should be called wise."

"And a man who acts like an asshole *is* an asshole. You can sit here and act like a great chess player, and I'm still going to waste your ass."

He grinned at me, a wide smile that said he knew how much of a fraud he really was.

I gave him a knight spot and we went at it, looking ridiculous, I'm sure, hunched sweating over a chess board in the midst of all the boozing and shouting and music and dancing.

Phil had taken lessons from a Russian emigree grandmaster and he knew all the openings and tactics and strategy, but he had a way of playing that was listless. His game had no guts. He would always make sure you knew he didn't take it seriously, though at heart I was convinced he took it *very* seriously and was devastated when he lost; he would just never let you see it. It was much the way he lived his life.

If I attacked hard or made a surprise move, he would cave in. He had no stomach to fight. It was as though he were an out-of-shape prize fighter who you could feint and push around and who would get tangled up in his own feet.

There was a guy I used to spar with in the service whom Kleinmutz reminded me of. He knew just about everything there was to know about prize-fighting. He had read all the books, viewed the films, even had worked with a private coach for a while. As you sparred with him, he would give you a running account of how you were doing, how he was doing, how the bout was going. And all the while you were cleaning his clock.

It was the same with Kleinmutz and chess. He envied strength and yet there was none in his game, no grit, and that made me wonder about him as a lawyer. How many cases might he have lost because of this lack of any fundamental toughness?

I felt badly for him. I felt that he *did* care about winning, but cared so much he could not show it and so pretended to be a good sport, losing all the while, dying inside.

I made quick work of Kleinmutz, checkmating him in less than twenty minutes. He took it gracefully, as he always did.

We had put away near a quart between us of Irish whiskey, slugged down neat and chased with Coors. Kleinmutz, expansive now that he had lost at chess, desperate even, turned his attention to the women in the place.

While he whooped it up, calling out to the ladies, philosophizing, arguing, flirting, I sat there bored, trying to muster the strength to leave.

He was going on about a new weight-loss program he had discovered: it dealt with your whole package. "You start with the large bowel," he said. "*Colonics*! Ukrainian woman over on Union, she cleans you out, you can't believe. Can you imagine the caca that's backed up in your bowel? Suppose five years ago something rotten happened to you—it's in your shit."

"Please."

"All there in your shit. Ah, you don't know anything." He waved his hand in disgust. He took a deep swig of Bushmill's, gazed morosely at the wall. "Your break-up with your wife—it's all there. It's all up your ass."

"Yeah, yeah."

"It's still in your shit. If you look at my old photographs—before colonics and after—well, there's just no comparison. I rid myself of all that old *shit*."

He tone grew quiet now, mournful. Despite all the booze he had downed, there was no flush to his face; it was pale with fatigue. He seemed to me now suddenly very gray—his hair, his complexion—and old.

He talked about the end of his marriage, about how his life had come to nothing, that nothing mattered, that he had lost it all. I knew he meant what he said, I knew he was in pain, and yet it seemed comical to me, theatrical, foolish, a not really good performance. Is it possible, I was thinking, that there are people who have faked life so long that even when truly painful things happen to them, they can only continue to fake it?

And yet he was exhausted—no denying it. And he *was* in pain. And still it somehow *seemed* faked.

He grabbed me by the forearm and stared into my eyes. I realized his gaze was not focused. "This is very important."

"Okay."

"You have to take a high colonic."

I nodded, shrugged.

"I care. You son-of -a-bitch, I care for you. And you're in denial. I'll pay for it—it's $40 or $70—whatever it is. You have too much caca up in you." He continued the deathgrip on my arm while staring at me full in the eyes, his look watery and unfocused as though he were peering back into his own head.

"Listen, in the normal colon, 15 pounds; a distended colon, like Marlon Brando's—as much as 50 pounds of hard shit. The new shit goes right through the old, it clings to the walls and this woman, Jana—"

"The Ukrainian?"

"—sits there and watches television with the sound off, while the old shit is *purged*. Paul, you can't imagine what this will do for your life."

He sat for a while, staring at the whiskey bottle. When he spoke it was as much to himself as to me: "You know, Mao Tse-tung had severe constipation, as did most of the world's dictators. They were *full of shit*, as the phrase goes. If we could clean everybody out, there'd be no more wars."

I remained quiet. Mercifully he went on to other things. He now wanted to talk about women, how there definitely was a woman for him in this room. He had worked out some mathematical formula and come to the conclusion—well, I wasn't sure what it was he had come to. He was beginning to get boisterous again.

He desperately craved a woman and I suppose he figured that if he made enough noise someone would notice him. I wanted no part of it.

As far as I could tell the women here had spent too much time with their horses: outsized jaws and teeth of a size to fill them were rampant in the room. "What are you thinking?" he demanded of me.

"When I was young, I did things for the joy of doing them," I said. "Now, I do them to fend off boredom or despair."

"Yes," Kleinmutz said. "Has to do with caca. Paul, you're in pain. What is this pain? Your fucking wife, right?"

"I get very little out of what I do. I do things as an obligation, to fend off emptiness. That's the difference between youth and middle-age."

"I know it. Damn, they make hooters now, you just wouldn't believe." This was said as much to himself as to me.

I shifted to Travis Wells' situation and how I felt about it: "He claims the judge, the prosecuting attorney, attorney, and the cops all conspired to send him away."

"This is Joshua Crest you're talking about. Desert crazies," Phil said, not at all interested. He had his eye on a dark-haired woman, solid as a NFL linebacker and just as big. "Look at the hooters on that one!"

"The trial judge—?"

"I know all about it," he said, his attention on the woman unwavering. "Frog Phelan. His brother was a big crank and weed dealer."

"All right," I said.

"What do you want? Why don't you just forget it? We got us a place here abundant with *tits*. Hey, little sweetheart," he called out to the linebacker. She was wearing a fringed buckskin jacket, jeans, and mud-caked boots. Dancing by herself in front of the juke box, she had her eyes closed in ecstatic appreciation of the music thudding from the machine. The song was "Tie a Yellow Ribbon on an Old Oak Tree." "I love the way those peaches shake on your tree!" Phil Kleinmutz yelled out.

She blinked open her eyes, looked over at him and laughed. Save for her bulk, the hairy mole on her chin, and the abundant growth of black hair on her upper lip, she was not unattractive.

She had a girl friend with her who was dancing in small circles and made her look like a beauty queen. Kleinmutz's desperation depressed me deeply.

Drunk as I was, my mind kept churning over Travis Wells' predicament. "Don't you understand," I said. "Look at it this way—"

"I like this one. And yours is not bad either."

"If you like to fuck moose," I said.

Phil put his arm around me and hugged me to him. "Another drink and she'll look like Madonna."

"This guy, this Wells guy—"

"Forget it. He's guilty…"

"He told me—"

"He told you. Of course he told you. Paul, I've been defending these guys for twenty years and in all that time I think I found one guy who I really thought was innocent."

"If you just heard—."

"I'm sure he tells a great story. He's in prison for a long time. He has nothing to do but work on his story. This is a kid who killed his grandfather, for chrissake. This is a psychopath."

"He said his grandfather's ex-wife, 'Fat something-or-other—'"

"Belle Reiss. 'Fat Belle.'"

"Okay."

"She owns a poker club out there on the Barstow Highway. One tough lady. I know all about her. *Stay away from this thing!*"

"He says she was involved. I think this guy's innocent."

"They're all innocent," Kleinmutz said. "All I hear, all my clients. 'I'm innocent, I'm innocent.' " He called over to the bartender for more Bushmills and beer.

"First thing in the morning, I'm going to drive down there," I said.

Kleinmutz straightened, stared me straight in the eye. Behind the drunken veil I could see concern in his gaze. "You're being stupid here, you know that?"

"Okay."

"You don't want to do that. You go out in that desert there, they got bodies planted—why do you think the cactus does so well? Human body makes great fertilizer."

"I have to find out."

"They kill outsiders like nothing out there. It's like its own country and Frog Phelan is the king. You know what they say? He has no enemies, but, boy, is he ever hated by his friends. He's driven by an intense need to control everything. If he attends a wedding, he wants to be the bride. If he goes to a funeral, he wants to be the corpse."

"Phil, now look at this—listen to me. If this kid *is* innocent—it's a terrible injustice there—" I realized I was drunk. I was shouting.

"Who cares?" Phil said.

"It's a crime! If he's innocent—"

"*Who the fuck cares?*"

The girl who had been dancing came over to us. Her girlfriend followed. "What's going down?" she said.

"Me," Kleinmutz said, grabbing her about the waist and pulling her to him.

"Promises, promises."

"I'm Phil. This is Paul. And you're—? You look like a Virginia. Virginia Virgin, right?"

"You're right," she said. Her girlfriend, lumpy, acne-pitted face, goiterish eyes, was trying to look like she gave a care.

"Really? Your name's Virginia?"

"Hell, no. I'm a *virgin!*"

"In your left ear," the girlfriend said.

That set them both to laughing and Phil, too. They laughed loud and long. Kleinmutz pulled the linebacker to him tighter. "Move with a hero, not a zero," he said.

"Can't tell if the gas tank is full by the honk of the horn," she said.

"The gas tank is *full*," he said, nuzzling her belly.

"Hey, I like this boy," she said, giggling.

"I'm very spiritual. I commune with my higher power."

"Right," she said.

"Connect spiritually with my inner self. Only then do I go out and try to fuck people." Phil laughed loudly.

"He's a lawyer," I said.

"Shmoozer, shmingler, bingler!" he bellowed.

"If you say so," the linebacker said.

"Shmingle and bingle with the best of them," Kleinmutz said. "Listen, this'll be the greatest lesson you'll ever learn—"

"Hey," the linebacker said.

"When a man of money meets up with a man of experience, the man with experience usually ends up with the money and the man with the money ends up with the experience."

"Hey, I like that." the linebacker said.

Kleinmutz grew solemn. "You have to listen to time."

"What does that mean?" she said.

"All that's good in us comes out of stillness and solitude. Listen to time. It's telling us what it hears."

"*Deep* booger," the linebacker said, turning to me. "He's a deep booger, ain't he?"

"I'm a bullshit artist," Kleinmutz said.

I knew it was going to be one of those evenings. Kleinmutz, bogus to the core, had a slew of aphorisms he loved to trot out for the ladies; they were an indispensable aid, he felt, to getting laid. He thought women thought he was deep. Undoubtedly some did, but only the dimmest would fuck him because of his profundity.

A terrible fatigue came over me; it happened often these days. In a crowd, I'd become exhausted and filled with a sense of isolation so profound that I'd begin to wonder if I even belonged to the human race. "I have to be up early," I said, rising from the barstool.

"You don't like virgins?" the first girl said.

"*Virgin?* What's that," I said.

"A ten year old, very ugly," said Kleinmutz.

"I don't think that's funny," the second girl said. She spoke this tentatively, as though unsure it was an opinion shared by the rest of the table.

"I'm sorry," Kleinmutz said, looking contrite. I started away from the bar.

"Don't get yourself killed," Kleinmutz called after me and he and the girls all laughed and it sounded ugly to me and I was glad to be out of there.

I was up before dawn the next morning, roused by a dream which I now could not remember. Only the feeling remained, a sense of tremendous dread; something deeply terrible had happened.

My head felt as though someone had chopped into it with an ax. I downed four aspirins, boiled up a pot of coffee, and drank the whole thing black. I still felt rotten.

After a cold shower, I still didn't feel much better. I dressed, got into the truck and drove down the mountain, then out to highway 58 going east to the town of Mojave, a drab desert railroad junction between Tehachapi and Joshua Crest.

The morning was cool. The sun came up above the Eastern Sierras and the mills in the windfarms outside of Tehachapi were looping away, the blades catching glints of morning sun, filling the air with a soft whooshing sound.

The day was fresh and clean and I began to feel better.

At Mojave I stopped in a diner and had ham and eggs and several more cups of coffee. I continued east on route 58, the highway to Barstow.

Joshua Crest was about seventy miles from Tehachapi, out in the Mojave Desert. At Kramer's Corners on the Barstow highway, I turned north. I had never been in this part of the desert and I felt a certain uneasiness.

Some people find beauty in the desert. The Mojave has always disturbed me: unbearably desolate and harsh, a reflection of all that is parched and empty in us. I don't like the feel or the smell of it, the furnace-like heat in summer, ferocious cold in winter, incessant wind, sickening, overpowering, sweet-sour odor of sage and juniper.

There were scattered Joshua Trees, the scraggly ones, not the plump, full grown ones; mesquite; miles of sage and palo verde. The countryside was dusty, gray-brown, sere. The air tasted of dust and sage. A dry wind sent clumps of tumbleweed skipping across the roadway.

I had the radio on and pretty soon each station I turned to faded out; the Bakersfield stations first, then Mojave and Lancaster.

The road was a two-lane blacktop and there was almost no traffic. Occasionally I'd pass a battered pickup truck going the other way. I checked my gauge to be sure I had enough gasoline.

This was not a place where you'd want to run out.

I found myself questioning what I was doing here, why I was getting involved. A young man is doing life without parole for killing his grandfather and he writes a story for my class about how he didn't kill him and now I'm on an empty, wind-swept, bone dry, weed-infested road, heading for god-knows-where to find god-knows-what. Why?

It was life, I thought, and it moves on its own laws: the way people always say, "That's life." Life wouldn't be life if you could control it. Life is mystery.

I realized I just couldn't ignore the gut sense that this kid was innocent. If it were true that he had been railroaded as he claimed, I knew I would have to do something.

It was really eating away at me, this possibility that Travis Wells had been set up. I was looking at a life that had been thrown away and no one had even gone through the motions of trying to do something about it.

In combat I had seen how we turned away from injustice and misery, how men built systems of delusion to avoid the unfairness of what was going on around them. The suffering was too great and so people refashioned reality.

Weren't we all guilty of this? Hadn't mankind invented God because life's injustices were just too great?

In war I had lost any belief I had had in God. There had been a kid from Fort Smith, Arkansas in my unit. He had been shot up badly and was delirious. I held him in my arms as the medics fought to save him and he kept saying over and over: "He isn't. He isn't."

"Who?" I said, trying to sooth him.

He looked up at me and his eyes were wide and innocent, a child's eyes, really; his voice was wonder-filled, a whisper: "*God*. God isn't anything we think He is." He hung on the rest of the day, delirious, raving about an absent God. Then he died.

And I spoke about him with one of the medics, a religious kid from Tennessee, and he told me how he felt about it: "We're all spirit. We're dressed up in a suit of skin. And one day we're going to leave it behind."

And I would think about him. I would think about him and what he had said. Was God, as we think we know Him, a delusion? Was religion a part of this grand delusion?

And if this were true, how could people who *believed*—those *most* deluded—how could we expect them to comprehend the true nature of what we call reality?

Does anyone who shares a delusion ever recognizes it as such?

And then I would have another thought: what is the beginning and end of the universe? How many universes lie beyond our universe? And finding an end to that, what came *before*? If our *universe* is like one grain of sand in a world of sand and that sand is dust in a larger system, then how vast is—what? Is *this* God?

There must always be a beginning and a beginning before that. On and on like reflections reflecting in on themselves.

If that is *so*, and it *must* be so, then anything is possible. Even God.

What was I thinking about, I would ask myself? And why? Experience, I had read somewhere, is a dim lamp which only lights the one who bears it. Dim and uncommunicable.

Do not seek for God outside your own soul.

I checked the mileage on the truck's odometer and realized I should be getting close to Joshua Crest. I saw nothing that would indicate a town.

A dark cloud lingered on the horizon before me some distance away. I thought at first it was a thunder cloud and that made me uneasy: storms in the desert can be occasions for disaster; a dry arroyo, a dip in the road, might, within minutes, become a raging river.

I continued to fiddle with the radio, hoping to get a news channel and the weather, but all I could bring in, and only faintly, was a Mexican station out of Tijuana.

As I neared the cloud I realized it wasn't a thunderhead at all, but an enormous tower of black smoke rising from the desert floor. It reminded me of the news footage I had seen of the burning oilfields in Kuwait just after the war there, black smoke just raging across the landscape.

I drove closer. The smoke was coming from a factory complex set off a distance from the highway. Beyond the blackened factory buildings, I could see the outline of the town of Joshua Crest.

It was astounding, this isolated factory complex spewing out waste in the middle of nowhere. Industry here! Joshua Crest is an industrial town!

I had lived on the edge of the Mojave for more than thirteen years and had no idea that there was heavy industry out there.

I sped by a huge behemoth of dark, tangled iron, spirals of steel, girder helixes, huge metallic storage tanks, immense pear-shaped Bessemer converters spitting fire and smoke into the desert sky.

Though it was still mid-morning, the area was dark from the pall of smoke above the highway and the town.

There was a sign on the highway's edge which announced "Joshua Crest, pop. 23,000, 'Jewel of the Desert.'"

The two-lane became Main Street which was grim in the way Eastern factory towns are: a lot of neon, saloons, a pawn shop, tattoo parlor, diner, several strip joints.

A closed-down movie theater, advertised its last show, Arnold Schwartzenegger in "Terminator," which seemed fitting.

The place *was* terminal: you were sure of it; you could smell the finality, the death in the air, taste it, gag on it, end of the road, end of the world.

I turned off the main drag, down a street called River Vista. The only river I could see was a garbage littered ditch at the edge of the roadway. The factories dominated the landscape, great fire-and-smoke-belching dragons, hurling soot and ash over everything.

I drove by tumbledown stucco homes, grassless yards, rusting autos up on blocks, a mobile home park.

I turned back onto the far end of the honky-tonk district and then I came to the civic center, a post office, city hall, police station, library.

The library was a gray concrete structure of no particular distinction. A sign in front said funds for it had been raised by Moose Lodge 78. I parked in front and entered.

It was cramped and ill lit, stocked, as far as I could tell, with Readers Digest Condensed Books, paperback best-sellers, magazines, and news-papers. There were several desert-rat types huddled at the tables, older men, unshaven, with long matted hair. They wore stained, dust-caked overalls and undershirts.

They looked up as I came in and watched me for a short while, then went back to their reading. I checked out the fiction section, which was several metal book cases. They didn't have any of my books. I discovered a reference room at the back.

There was a skinny older man with a purplish, acne-pitted nose, at a desk, cutting articles out of a newspaper. I asked about a newspaper file.

"We have the Joshua Crest News. What you looking for?"

"Crime that occurred out here, I don't know, five, six years ago."

"Which crime's that?" His voice was as dry as the desert outside.

"Kid by the name of Wells killed his grandfather."

He moved to a section of metal file cabinets at the far end of the room. "Travis Wells," he said.

"Yes."

"We remember that one."

He removed a carton containing microfilm. "This should have it." He moved to a machine and threaded up the film.

"You knew him?" I said.

He was running through the microfilm strip now. "Since he was just a little snot. Spent a lot of time in the library here. Ray—his grandfather—would bring him. Ol' Ray was known in this town."

"How was that?"

He stared at me. "Who are you?"

"I'm just a writer. Just interested—"

"He was *connected*," the man said.

"Connected?"

"What are you, slow? *Politically.*" He stopped the machine. "That ought to do you."

He moved off and I sat myself in front of the screen. There was a headline: "**LOCAL FIGURE AND GRANDCHILDREN BEATEN TO DEATH. OTHER GRANDSON CHARGED.**"

I stared at the headline, uncomprehending, shaken. I tried to read the account of the crime, but I couldn't get through it. There were photographs of two young children, a boy and a girl, dazzlingly beautiful; I covered my eyes; I couldn't look at them. They were so young.

My hands were trembling as I manipulated the knob for the microfilm scanner.

Travis Wells hadn't only been charged in the murder of his grandfather. There had been kids killed, too.

I got up. The library man returned to get the microfilm. "There were—"

"What's that?"

"—children murdered, too?" My voice was constricted. The words barely came out.

"Oh, yeah. Travis Well's half brother and sister. Cute little things. Knew them all. That's what's so terrible about the whole thing."

He offered to Xerox the articles on the murder and the trial for me; I took them and hurried from the building.

In the truck again I looked over them and again I could not finish them.

The smoke cloud had cleared from above the town, blown clean by a stiff wind whipping in from the desert. The sun was out now, searing hot. The reflection off the hood of my truck was a blinding white and you could feel the heat rising from the pavement and the hood. Everything radiated heat.

The town seemed ugly as the crime for which Travis Wells' had been convicted, and I was sick inside and I questioned why I had even come here. Children murdered, too. Kids the age of my own children. I was trembling. It came from deep inside me.

I sped from the town, across the bleak desert, past the fires roaring in the furnaces of the factories along the roadway and the landscape was thick with black smoke; the fire exploded against the black and the world seemed a place of evil. It reminded me of the burning villages in war, where children had been killed, also, and I felt sick inside and pulled over to the side of the road and vomited.

And even then I did not feel better.

Chapter Nine

Roderick Cook, Sergeant, read his story in a soft, hesitant voice. He had written about war, the ugly things that had happened in battle, and the matter-of-fact style of the writing intensified the horror of what he described. Civilians had been slaughtered. Old people, women, children. "I wake up at night and I'm crying," he read. His voice was hoarse and you had to strain to hear him. His tone was apologetic, as though he were saying, this was war, these things happened: I'm sorry.

Travis Wells sat motionless, staring at the tabletop. His face had paled. His expression reflected concern and—purity: the face of an angel. He appeared shaken and I watched him, trying to figure out what really was going on inside.

The depth of his feeling troubled me. It seemed achingly real and yet—Perhaps it was a sham, a shell game, with Poet palming his true feelings while offering us, the marks, a polished lie. I felt, with no justification, really, that no matter what he had done, his exterior would not betray him. His being radiated goodness; every gesture, every look, seemed unforced, true. And I realized, you could tell nothing by his appearance. You gazed on him and you felt with absolute certitude that he could never deceive you. And yet—and yet—it was too good, too pure. And so I was confused and uneasy.

His half brother and sister murdered and he had not mentioned this to me, had not written about it. And I wondered now: could he possibly have done it, killed two small children, also? Why hadn't he said anything about it? Why hadn't he written about it?

He noticed I was staring at him and he became uncomfortable and looked away. A moment later he glanced back at me, then quickly looked away again.

I was determined to somehow penetrate to the heart of him; to get past the mask, the sensitive poet's face, the gentleness, the shyness about him, the intelligence.

They called him *Poet*. Mask of the poet. I was determined to find *murder*, if it were there, behind this mask.

I could not penetrate it. He must be innocent. Look at him. This must be him; this must be real, the concern, innocence, purity.

And there was the savagery of what he had been convicted of: he had killed not only his grandfather, but two small children, his half brother and sister as well. Impossible, I kept telling myself.

The feeling I had had when I read the account of his crime had stayed with me, a chilling, empty feeling in the depth of me. I had slept badly these past few nights.

Sergeant's voice was soft and apologetic: "The town was Tay Ninh and we came into it in the evening. We had taken some gunfire and I was really nervous moving in and then I saw a VC crouching under a bamboo porch-like structure and I just blasted away at him and then I heard this woman crying and when I got over there, it weren't no VC at all, but a little kid, maybe ten years old. I had killed a ten year old kid." Tears welled up in his eyes. He couldn't continue.

I watched Poet. He was staring at the tabletop. His face, somber, as though made of glass. Not a solid chunk, but paper-thin. If I touch it, his face will crumble, I thought.

No one spoke for a long time.

El Negro shredded the butt of his hand-rolled cigarette; swept the leavings into a small pouch; cleared his throat. "Heavy thing to go through," he said. He looked over at me, moved. "I don't know what to say."

"Tough thing to live with," Joker said, staring at the table top. "All of us here have killed people, but not no innocent kid."

Even Blast seemed shaken. He was staring at me and there was pain in the depths of his gaze.

There was silence for a long time. "I never told anybody this," Sergeant said. "I've lived with this all these years. I can still see his face. I see it every night."

"What do you think, boss?" Culpepper said, turning to me.

I, too, had no words. I didn't think of it as writing. It had cut too close to me; it was too real. In my mind's eye I saw a line of children's bodies shrouded by fog.

And I saw the bodies of Poet's half brother and sister. "It's very strong," I said at last. "These things happen. Mistakes happen."

"Dude knows what I'm talking about," Sergeant said.

No one spoke for a while. "We'll break early," I said. The men did not move from the table. "Travis, I want to talk to you for a minute."

Baker, who was sitting next to me, said: "You can't just break class like that, boss. You got to get us back to our units."

"Can Macklin take care of it?"

"She can," he said.

"Would you—?"

"You want me to—?"

"Yes."

He stood and walked to the glass door to the guard's area. Macklin was on the phone. He signaled to her. She looked over at me and I pointed to my watch and let her know that it was all right to send the men back to their units. She looked at me without interest. We might have been strangers.

We hadn't spoken since the night she had spent at my place. She hadn't called. I didn't have her number. And when I had arrived earlier she hadn't been at her desk.

Several times I had asked her for her number, but she hadn't gotten around to giving it to me. It was something that nagged at me. Why hadn't she ever given it to me? Was it possible she had a boyfriend or a husband? That could help explain her guardedness toward me.

After placing a call to the tower, she went back to work without looking at me. The men started out. Sergeant came to me. "You *knew* about these things," he said.

"It's war," I said.

"They was a lot of people killed kids and woman and things. I just never been able to get it out of my head."

A question nagged at me. The killing of the child in war had been a terrible thing for him. But he had killed again. How did he feel about that? How had he done that? "What about the person you killed to get in here?" I said.

"Never think about him." He stood there for a moment, head nodding slowly as he considered what I had asked. He looked directly at me and his black eyes were the eyes of a child, and I kept telling myself, this man is a murderer and yet I like him and am moved by him. Why?

It had to do with the killing of the child in battle, his reaction to it. But what of the other one he had killed—a man in a botched robbery?

"Yeah. Never," he said. "Funny." He smiled and it was an engaging smile and I felt uncomfortable liking a murderer.

He shook my hand and his hand was soft like putty, void of energy. He moved off and out onto the yard.

Poet and I were alone in the library. Through the glass I could see Macklin watching us. "I've been thinking a lot about your case," I said. "It's given me a few sleepless nights."

"I never looked for sympathy."

"If you're innocent, then a terrible thing has been done to you. In the story you're writing, I believe it. I believe the writing. But there are certain things—now the splinters under your grandfather's nails—"

He smoothed his hair back and looked directly at me; I was thinking how open and honest his face was, how delicate, Christ-like, a face out of a Renaissance painting. "Cops tried to make something out of this—that my grandfather was beaten to death with a bat. He wasn't beaten to death with that bat—"

"How do you know this?"

"We had an expert testify that the wood under my grandfather's nail was some kind of composition board, mostly pine. The bat was white ash. And there were no gouges on the bat that would have been consistent with the splinters under my grandfather's nail."

He stared at me with gentle eyes. I felt uneasy. "Look, it's not important if anyone believes me or not," he said.

"In your story, is this everything that happened?"

He didn't talk for a while. He did not look at me. I said nothing. At last he said, "No. I left out certain things."

"What?" He didn't answer. "For any reason?"

He was upset. His face was tight, the muscles of his jaw working in spasms. He took a deep breath. A long while went by. "Some of it was just too—" I could see he was on the verge of breaking down. "This is difficult." There were tears in his eyes. "Whoever killed my grandfather also—beat to death—my brother and sister…"

And suddenly, his sorrow burst out; tears gushed from his eyes. He sobbed for a long time. "They convicted me of killing two little kids…" He cried and cried, fiercely, convulsively, his whole body racked with sobs. He turned away from me and wept, facing the mountains.

Through the glass Macklin continuing to watch us. Poet pulled himself together. "I'm sorry," he said, wiping his tears, smoothing his hair back. "I shouldn't have started this…"

"I think it's important," I said. "I think you have to follow this thing through. Write everything that happened. As honestly and as detailed as you can."

The door to the library opened. Macklin stood there, her face taut with anger. It had to do with Travis Wells breaking down, I was sure, crying: too human a moment between outside staff and an inmate. A prison guard could not permit it. "Shirt in!" she yelled. Poet immediately tucked in his shirt and assumed the inmates attitude of contrition. "Next time I see it, asshole, I'll write you up." She turned to me. "He has to get back to his unit," she said, then returned to her desk.

I walked Poet out into the yard. "What was that about?"

"Oh, she's all right," he said, "but she's a cop. She has to make her points from time to time. She's better than most, though."

He stood for a moment as though he wished to say something else to me, but he didn't. "If you're innocent," I said, "what you're going through is a terrible thing."

"I'm innocent," he said.

"Only you know that."

"Other people know that. Milly—my ex-girl friend—she knows it. And the ones who put me here. And my grandfather, my little brother and sister, know it."

We stood in silence for a while longer. I could see beyond Poet, Macklin at work at her desk. Men were moving back to their units from the weight pit and the handball courts. The day was turning cold. The sky looked ugly, threatening.

"On the bat," I said, "were there other blood traces?"

His expression was sorrowful. "Yes," he said. "They found traces of my brother and sister's blood." He shrugged and forced a smile. He shook my hand. "I want you to know," he said, "that the men appreciate your coming here like this. This is all we have."

He moved off. I entered the alcove. Macklin looked at me. There was annoyance in her expression and she reminded me of my ex-wife and it was not pleasant. "What were you hassling him about?" I said.

"It's my job. I could see he was snowing you and it pissed me off."

"But you said you thought he could be innocent."

"I can't be thinking about those things."

I didn't speak for a while. She didn't seem to much care "What's going on here?" I said at last. "I mean, what is it?" She looked and me blankly. "What's going on between us?"

"I like you," she said, without sounding as though she meant it.

"Why don't you give me your phone number?" I said. She didn't answer. She just stared at me. "I feel like I don't know you at all." I started out of the alcove, angry at myself for even having gotten involved with her. Too tough, I found myself thinking. She's just too tough.

"Hey," she called out. I turned. "I'll call you."

That night she came to the house and there was something guarded and tense in our lovemaking and when I asked her about it after, she said, "I don't know what I'm doing with you. We're just different kind of folk."

"I know that," I said. "But we have something together, don't we?"

"I don't know," she said and she looked very serious and then her expression softened and she smiled and she kissed me. "You're a good guy," she said. "Yes, we have something together, but I don't know what it is." And she laughed.

We made love again and things seemed fine.

Before she left she gave me her phone number. "Call me anytime," she said and she sounded as though she meant it. "Does that make you feel better?"

"Yes."

That weekend I picked up the kids. We had pizza and then went to the batting cages and Kurtie was hitting the ball well and Annie, also, and I continued to belt out the ball in the eighty mile-an-hour cage. I found myself thinking, I'm in my forties and I can still hit a baseball at eighty miles an hour. And I became depressed as I realized that it was the only thing I was now accomplished at.

We drove up to the mountain and I told the kids a Doctor Miracle, Noddy-noddy Land story. When they were asleep I poured myself a water-glass full of Bushmills, took out the Xeroxed newspaper accounts of Poet's case—I still had not read them through—and went over them to the very end and everything was more or less the way Poet had told it, though the slant the paper took was that he was guilty; he had murdered his grandfather for money the old man reportedly had hidden in the mobile home. He hadn't counted on his stepbrother and sister being there that night and he killed them to cover his crime.

It mentioned that the grandfather was from an old Joshua Crest family and was well known in the area.

I downed two more glasses of Bushmills, stretched out on my bed, fell asleep and dreamed. An old man was playing with two young children, a boy and girl. A figure moved into the scene, swinging a baseball bat. I couldn't make out who it was. With a start, I realized the boy and girl were my kids. The old man lifted his hand to stop the swing of the bat. He dug his nails into the bat, hard, and I could see long gouges form on the bat. I heard Kurtie's voice, "Daddy... Daddy..." I thought it was the dream but the voice continued; I awoke to see Kurtie standing next to my bed. He was tugging at my arm, fighting back tears. "I made pee-pee in my bed, Daddy," he said.

"Oh, Kurtie."

"On accident."

I held him close to me. "That's okay, little one," I said. "Accidents happen."

I led him from my bedroom back into the kids' room. The center of his bed was soaked; I began to strip the sheets from it. Suddenly I was seized by an enormous welling up of feeling for my kids; how fragile and precious they were, how they relied on me, how hard I tried to make things right and yet how far short I seemed to be falling in my efforts.

I remembered an incident that had occurred before Kurt was born, when Anne was just a little thing. It was evening. A field mouse had run onto the porch outside the dining room sliding glass door, a cute little thing with big Mickey Mouse ears. In those days we used to have a family of raccoons that would visit us on the porch from time to time and my wife had set out a bowl of water for them. The mouse dashed to the bowl, took a quick sip, then ran off. An instant later, he re-appeared, sipped again, again hurried away.

He continued rushing to and fro, sipping at the water. Muffin, our cat at the time, got wildly excited, as did Annie. I called the mouse "Mickey Mouse" and Annie jumped up and down, squealing, "Mickey *Mouse,* Mickey *Mouse!*"

Later, she kept walking to the sliding door, saying, "Mickey *Mouse.* Water."

In the middle of the night she awoke crying and I went to her and got her to lie down. I rubbed her back and she fell off to sleep. She was asleep for perhaps ten minutes and I was just about to steal from the room when she said, "Mickey *Mouse.* Water."

I was terrifically moved. I didn't know why. It had something to do with how we become humans, how dreams and reality flow past us, through us, and merge with each other within us, and how it continues as we grow older, reality touching us, moving into our dreams until dream and reality become one fabric. Was Mickey Mouse and water dream or reality to Annie then? Is God or Jesus or Buddha dream or reality to any of us? What is this life? Where have we come from? Where are we going? Mickey *Mouse.* Water.

And I remembered looking at her and seeing my mother in her. At that time my mother had been dead for years. And yet I saw her in my daughter: the same seed, the same soul. I was looking at the future and the past simultaneously.

There had been family and a closeness with my kids in those early days. Now, there was a gulf between us, the gulf of my divorce, the gulf of lack of family, of time with them, of really being involved in their lives. I was an outsider. A stranger had taken my place.

There was no father and mother together for them and I felt wretched and desolate and I grabbed Kurt and hugged him to me and sat with him on Annie's bed and hugged her, too. She stirred, but did not waken and I kissed her and my son and I ached inside for family, for a life with some sort of meaning.

"I love you, Daddy," Kurt said.

"I love you, too." I sat holding him for a long time. He fell asleep in my arms.

Chapter Ten

The day after taking the kids back to Bakersfield, I started out for Joshua Crest. I had no understanding of why I was making the trip. A powerful need pulled me there, into the dust and grimness of that town. I hated the feeling, and still there I was in my truck speeding into the desert.

What was it that was at work on me? The horror of the crimes? My growing disbelief in how they had happened?

More and more, I had come to feel that Travis Wells was innocent. A jury had heard the facts in the case and had rendered their judgement. I knew this, but—I was arguing with myself—innocent people certainly had been convicted. And how would we know? How would we ever know?

I would go over and over it in my mind: what he had written about the murder, the tentativeness of his reading in front of the class, the sloppiness of what he insisted had happened, how emotional he had been.

If he had faked it, wouldn't he have done a better job? Wouldn't he have tied up all the loose ends? It was just too messy, *messy*, to be a lie. And if he *had* faked it, why? To what purpose? What could he get from me?

And there was the feel to him, his shyness, the pain in his eyes, a sense of essential goodness, a quality of *purity* that you felt when you were in his presence.

Suppose I discovered *beyond a doubt* that he was innocent? Could I just ignore it, permit this bright, attractive kid to be stripped of his youth, his future, his *life* and not try to do *something*?

The day was overcast. Dark clouds raced above the immense and desolate expanse of desert. I sped along a blacktop straight as a line drawn with ruler, through undulations of sand and scrub, heading for Joshua Crest. The factories came into view. Balls of fire exploded against a bleak horizon.

There was something gloomy and unsettling about the town. Main Street was empty. No people, no cars. It reminded you of a corpse, rotting under its shroud of smoke. It reeked of sulphur, of eggs souring in the sun, of death.

I drove down the strip: the darkened movie theater, the tattoo parlor, the 7-11. A poster in front of one of the strip joints caught my eye: "The Sexscintillating Millie Coty!"

Millie Coty, I had learned from the newspapers, had been Travis Wells' girlfriend.

I pulled to the curb. I sat and watched the club for a while. The place seemed frozen in time. The air was heavy, the street unnaturally dark, the sun in eclipse. The smoke had blotted it out. Where was everybody?

At last I got out of the truck and walked to the front door of the club.

It had not yet opened for business. I tried to peer through the glass door, but it was dark inside; I could see nothing. I started away, then heard the door open.

A man in a wash-and-wear suit was standing there. He was large and fleshy with thinning, kinky hair. He stared at me. "I wanted to see if you were open," I said. He didn't say anything. "I'll be back some other time."

I returned to my truck. The man was still standing framed in the doorway of the club as I drove away.

I steered the truck to the far end of town and found the mobile home park where Poet's grandfather had been murdered. There was a sign in front: "Desert Lake Mobile Home Park–Recreational Oasis." The "recreational oasis," an expanse of rocky desert on which had been deposited, willy-nilly, collections of mobile homes. In various stages of disrepair, they sprawled there discolored and peeling.

Just beyond the gate leading to the place, an old man in coveralls worked at a cast-iron bench. With a hand-sledge, he was banging away at a large metal contraption that I realized had once been an air-conditioner.

He glanced at me, uninterested. He wore a kerchief around his neck that was soaked with perspiration. His skin was mottled from the sun. "Where's the lake?" I said.

"What lake?"

"Well, it says, 'Desert Lake Mobile Home Park.'"

He pointed with his sledge to the far edge of the mobile home area where a great pit had been dug into the rocky ground. It sloped away from the last mobile home, forming a crater of about five or six acres. The crater was littered with old cans, bottles, bags of garbage. "What's that?"

"The lake."

"Where's the water?"

"That's the fuck-all of it. There ain't no water. Twenty-five dollar a year assessment for water. Deadbeats here wouldn't pay it. Nice little pond there once. Used to stock her with crappie and bluegill. Recreation area."

"Look, maybe you can help me. I'm a writer."

"What you write, bad checks?"

"Books."

"If there ain't a lot o' sex, you ain't gonna get my money. I like my books filled with tits. Like 'God's Little Acre?' That's what I call literature." He continued banging away at the air conditioner with his sledge.

"There was a man murdered here a while back," I said.

"You got that right. They claimed the grandson, Travis, bashed in his head. Killed the two little ones, too. What about it?"

"Where was that?"

He pointed in the direction of the "lake," to the farthest mobile home.

"Is there anyone there?"

"No one living there now. Used for storage. Blood and bone and shit was all over the place. Who wants to live in a place like that?"

"You said they *claimed* the grandson killed the people."

"That's right."

"Didn't they convict him?"

"Travis never done it," the old man said. He banged away at the air-conditioner until a whole panel of sheet metal went flying. He kicked it to one side. "He loved the old man, his grandpa. Ray. I don't know why, but that's the fuck of it, that's this life. I never had no liking for Ray, he was more miserable than a rat with a cat's dick up his ass, but the kid loved him. And the kid loved the little ones, too. Didn't have it in him to bash 'em like that."

"Who did it, then?"

"This here's what it is. People out here'll kill you for your shoes. Got some mean fucks up here."

"I see."

"'Bout twenty years ago I was in this here shoe store—this was down in Barstow—with my wife and her sister, before my wife died. They was shopping and I was just standing there, not really looking around or interested in anything. This salesman comes up to me and says: 'Can I do anything for you?' And I says, 'Well, if you have a pair of Florsheim's, size 10, double A, I could use those.' So he says, 'Well, we might just have that—'"

"Well. Who do you think killed the old man?"

"That's not for me to say. Anyways, he comes back with that exact shoe, the only one in the place and he sells it to me for $7.00 and I still have them and they're barely scuffed on the bottom."

"Good."

"I never wear them."

"But you would definitely think that—"

"Just on special occasions."

"It's back there, right? Where he was killed?"

"Right. You like a good joke?" Before I could answer, no, he went right on: "You'll like this here. Pisser. Woman comes into a bar, holding a dog. Drunk at the bar says, 'What're you doing with that pig? 'I beg your pardon, this is a *dog*.' Drunk says: '*I'm talking to the dog*!'" The old man laughed. "Pisser, huh?"

"Oh, yeah."

"Sure."

"It's good," I said. "About the murdered man—"

"Ray?"

"Yes."

"Just come afoul o' the wrong folk is how I see it. Grandson was the perfect patsy." He picked up the sheet-metal panel and began to bang away at it again.

"What're you doing with that thing?"

"Going to make me a birdhouse. Someone just threw this away. I can make some good use of this. Steel birdhouse? Shit, some people'd give their eye-teeth for something like that."

"Look," I said. "Mind if I look back there, you know, where the old man was killed?"

He waved me off. "Anything happens to you, don't come running to me. No good fuckers around here. People who'll do that to a lake, 'ell do just about anything. I got another one for you. Know how to catch a fish with a can of peas and a hammer?"

"Not really. Look—"

"You row out to the middle of the lake, spread them peas on the water. When the fish come up to take a pee, you hit 'em on the head with the hammer." He returned to his furious banging on the air-conditioner. "Pisser, huh? Sure fire."

"Oh, yeah," I said.

I walked to the edge of the "lake." Set back from it, a distance from the other structures was a scarred and battered mobile home, its outer plywood shell rotted and peeling. I approached it and tried the door. The lock was broken and it swung open.

The inside was a mess, filled with gardening equipment, plastic drip line, broken tools, rusted wire screen; there were mouse droppings everywhere. I moved through this room to a rear room.

This room was empty.

There was a window in the back wall which looked out on the sere desert landscape, and a door; faded chalk marks on the floor, the residue, I surmised, of police work done years before: you could still see the faint outlines of the crime. Two small dark stains were encompassed by the chalk marks and I wondered if they marked the bodies of the murdered kids. The room smelled sour.

I knelt to study the stains. There was a soft sound of something moving quickly through the other room and I turned.

Poised in the archway between the rooms was a Doberman, sleek, black, spring-tense. He growled. His narrow ears were erect, pointed slightly back, his mouth partially open, revealing a yapful of yellowed, very long, very sharp teeth.

His body quivered lightly. He continued to growl, all coiled tendon, dreary agate eyes, ready to tear into me.

I stood very slowly. "Easy now..." Slowly, slowly I began to edge toward the rear door. The Doberman stiffened, growled louder. "Easy..."

I moved a step more and the dog leaped at me, snarling wildly. I put up my arm to shield my throat. He sunk his teeth into my jacket and flung me backward. I hit the wall, then the floor, the great dog whining eerily, digging at me, ripping at my clothes. I found myself gasping for breath, thinking, I'm going to die here, shredded, ripped apart by a dog. I flailed about. The dog hung on.

"Off, Jukie! Off!" A woman's voice overrode the terrifying sound. The dog immediately fell back. It hunkered low, continuing to growl.

The woman moved forward and with one hand snapped a lead onto the dog's collar. The dog sat next to her.

In her other hand, she held a large Western-style revolver. "What are you doing here?"

"Just looking around."

"Who are you?"

"I'm looking for—"

"I said, *who are you*?"

"I'm a writer."

She stared at me, the gun leveled on me. I had a strong feeling she knew how to use it. "What're you writin' *here*?" She was in her mid-forties and handsome; blonde hair streaked by the sun; skin reddish and lined, weathered. She had large, cold blue eyes and a body that was still attractive, but threatening to go to flab.

I could smell that she had been drinking and that didn't make me feel too happy since I was staring down the barrel of her revolver. "I'm not really—at this moment—"

"Are you a poet? You goin' to write 'Ode to a Shit-hole?' "

"I'm looking to get some information."

"Newspaper man? Is that what you are?"

"I'm not really a newspaper writer. From time to time I've done some work like that."

With the gun, she motioned toward the front of the mobile home. I moved past the dog and out into the front room.

"Maybe you can help me," I said. We were out the door now, crossing the mobile home park drive, moving alongside the "lake."

She laughed. It was mirthless and not particularly appealing. "Help you do what?"

"There was a murder here a while back and I'm doing some research on it. Is there a place we can go to talk?"

She slid the revolver under her waistband and let her suede, fringed jacket fall over it. "Sure, we can talk," she said. "What's your name?"

"Paul."
"Paul? What do you write?"
"Books."
"What are they about?"
"Different stuff—"
"Fuck books?"
"No. No."
"I like a good fuck book."
"Good."
"This Jackie Collins—"
"Yeah."
"She's good. Good fuck stuff."
"I write different kind of stuff. What's your name?"
"Why do you want to know?"
"You asked for my name."
"Kelly."
"Okay. First name?"
"Who gives fuck-all? We'll take my truck," she said. She took the lead off the Doberman and shooed him away.

Her truck was one of those outsized, off-road jobs, maroon with immense balloon tires and shocks that could have cushioned a railroad car. She spoke briefly to the old guy banging away at the air conditioner, then we sped off along the dusty road leading back to town.

"Guy told me there was a killing out here in the desert where some guy was convicted and they thought he probably didn't do it."
"Got that right."
"You don't think he did it either?"
"I know he didn't."

We came to a roadhouse called "The Way Out Inn" and she pulled into the parking lot. It was dusk. The sun was a huge red ball diving below the horizon. The air was thick with evening coming on. Swarms of little bugs filled the air. "Listen," she said.

"What?"

"The sage."

"What about it?"

"The sage knows things."

"Sage? You mean—like a wise man?"

"No, no, no. The fucking *weed*. It knows things." I nodded, not having a clue as to what she was talking about. "Not much. Keeps repeating itself. Over and over. But it knows a thing or two. Knows where the bodies are buried." She stumbled and I caught her. She didn't thank me. We entered the place.

There were a few cowhand types lounging around and a sprinkling of grizzled desert rats. No one paid us much attention, though two of the cowboys nodded at Kelly, tipping their sweat-stained Stetson's in a kind of mock gallantry.

We took a table at the rear of the place. "You look like a drinking man," she said.

"I've done my share."

She winked. "I know some things."

"Like the sage?"

"Like the sage."

"Where is everybody?" I said. "This is a factory town. Where're the people who work in the factories?"

She shook her head. "It's all automated. It's the Japanese, the English, the Danes. Automation."

She ordered a bottle of Seagrams with a pitcher of beer. When the booze arrived she lifted the whiskey bottle and stared at it. "This is a tough motherfucker," she said. "Can't shake this motherfucker. This here—" She turned the bottle beneath the overhead light. It gleamed gold. "This here *motherfucker*. This and dope. Don't get me wrong. I'm not a doper. *This* is my dope."

She placed the bottle before her and gazed at it sadly. "Most products you have to sell to the customer. This here, you sell the customer to the product," she said without animation. "Other goods, they try to make better. This, they just say, fuck it, just make the *customer worse*." She laughed her empty laugh and poured us out a couple of shots and we downed them and followed that with a long swallow of beer and then she poured out two more shots. I could see she was immediately drunk.

"Why do you say the kid's innocent?"

"I just know some things," she said.

"Okay."

"This is the thing here," she said. "You have the old man. And he has his two little grandkids out there with him. And then you have this girl, this slut that was going with this simple-assed kid. And she's carrying on with everyone—"

"Hooker?"

"Whoor," she said and she downed another shot and beer chaser. She poured one for me, but I didn't knock it right back this time, but sipped on it, realizing that I was getting woozy. I wanted to remain sharp for any information I might get from her. "Calls herself an *exotic dancer*. My sorry ass! She's still around, working the strip clubs on Main. So she was carrying on with all the big shots in town. And the big shots, they want the old man dead. And they want the kid out of the way. And they get her to testify. And that's it. They won it all. Sons-o'-bitches."

She stared down at her empty glass and I could see she was drunk and suddenly I was thinking that this was not such a good idea, that she was about to get maudlin and tell me her life story and I was going to have a weepy drunk on my hand. "You know what my life is?"

"What?"

"Butterfly dust." She blew on the back of her hand. "Poof!" She looked directly at me. "You're a good-looking guy," she said. "Married?"

"No more."

"Know that game," she said. "What do you look for in a woman? This is a game I like to play—ask men and women what they look for in the opposite sex."

"I look for different things." I said.

"Okay."

"There are sexual things you look for and then there are things apart from sex—human things."

"You don't think sex is human?"

"I'll take the fifth on that."

"A Fifth of Scotch," she said.

We both laughed and clinked shot glasses and belted another one back. "What I look for in human beings, men, sure, but particularly women—intelligence, wit, charm, and a certain quality—"

"Okay. Certain. Okay."

"—I call humanness."

"*Humanness?*"

"The quality that recognizes that we're all in this game of life together and we need each other." I was babbling to a drunk and I couldn't stop and she was tuning me out, gazing at her reflection in a mirror on the rear wall. "We're all going to die and on that road to death we should treat each other with respect and kindness. It's as though you and I were adrift on a piece of wood in a great ocean."

"Possible."

"We would help each other, we would respect each other. We would not prey on each other. The person who is a predator, who preys on others, is less than human." I was perspiring now, slurring my words.

"People are trying to survive," she said.

"The person who sacrifices his or her humanity in order to survive will never again be fully human."

"I follow you. I don't know where you're going, but I follow you."

"They'll go through life haunted by their being less than human. I would rather die than sacrifice my humanity in that way."

"Oh, please," she said.

"Suppose in order to survive you had to sell something that would insure the death of children? Could you do that? And I mean a *perception* of survival—to survive in a business, let's say—because you can survive, just not at the level you'd like."

She leaned forward as though imparting a great secret to life. "If you don't know where you're going, any road'll get you there," she said.

"Okay."

She stood. "Hey."

"What?"

"Let's get out here. I'm about to go kerplunk. You know what the good ol' boy said?"

"What's that?"

She laughed. "'I thought I was dancing till someone stepped on my fingers.' C'mon."

"Where?"

"My place."

"Why?"

"I'm going to fuck your balls off." And she shook her hips and her tits and they were very nice and there was something harsh and sad and appealing about her and who knows why, but I followed her out of the place, knowing that this could only be trouble.

Chapter Eleven

It was not quite night yet. The western sky over the desert was a slash of salmon color, orange and black. There was a chill in the air.

I tried to get the keys to the truck. Kelly danced away, mocking me. She opened her jacket and bared her breast. It was lovely. "What do you think," she said.

"Nice."

"Want to do it right here?"

"I don't think so."

I moved next to her, trying to coax the keys from her. She continued to toy with me. "I'd fuck a hunchback Chinaman on the steps of City Hall if I was so inclined."

"Would you now? Well, that's terrific. Give me the keys."

"Know what Calamity Jane said?"

"Haven't the foggiest."

"I don't care where you fuck—so long as it's not in the stable where you might frighten the horses." She laughed at that, a brittle, raucous laugh.

I tried to grab at her hand and she pulled away and jumped in the cab and started the truck up and I tried to turn the ignition off and she fought me off and put the thing in gear and we jerked out of the parking lot.

We sped along back-desert roads, veering from side to side, and I knew it was a mistake of immense proportion, my coming with her. We lurched over a rise and there were headlights coming right at us and she swerved at the last minute and we narrowly missed buying the farm head-on into an eighteen-wheeler. "Give me the key!" She just laughed.

I tried to shut the damn thing off, but she fought with me and I knew it was even more dangerous so I stopped and cursed myself for having come along with her.

We continued on through the desert. The evening had turned to night. The roadway was a snake of moonlight. A faint mist had formed and above it a starry grain. An army of Joshua trees stood at attention in the mist.

We came to an enormous adobe home that sat upon a rise at the end of a long drive. The home, lit by a array of floodlights, was surrounded by palms and shrubbery and a high cement wall.

She pushed a gadget in the truck and an electronic gate opened. There was a curved redbrick drive leading up to the house and she steered up it and parked in a area filled with other vehicles. There were a Mercedes and Jaguar, as well as an older Ford and a pick-up truck.

We got out of her truck. "Some place," I said. She shrugged, stumbling up the walk. "Belonged to my family. Pack of greedy fucks. Fuck a snake if they could get a buck out of it. Fuck 'em and the horse they rode up with."

The living room was immense. It reminded me of a set from an old Hollywood movie, one of those costume things full of camels and sheiks and a studio sky of cerulean blue. It had a high ceiling, great beams of dark wood. It was done in the style of a Moorish castle and, while there wasn't much taste here, it sure must have cost serious dollars.

She moved to a bar at the end of the room and poured us two whiskeys. She motioned for me to sit next to her on a wide overstuffed couch.

I took my drink from her but did not sit. "How do you fit with the mobile home park?" I said.

"It's mine," she said.

"Then you knew the old man who was killed?"

"Yes," she said.

"The kid who killed him?"

"Yes."

We didn't speak for a while. She was staring at me, measuring me—for what? Her bed, obviously. I was trying to figure how to get out of it. Burning building.

"You're going to make love to me," she said. "And I suggest you use a condom because, while you may know who you've done it with, I sure as hell don't know who I've done it with." She laughed and the laugh was throaty, harsh, predatory. "That's the way we rich 'uns are."

"Where's your money from?"

"Those factories when you came into the town? Belonged to my family once. Place is uglier than shit, but it sure has riches, tungsten, borax, gold. Grandpappy owned everything. My father did his best to piss it away. I managed to hold onto a few baubles."

She stood unsteadily and took me by the hand. "Come on."

"Where?"

"Don't play coy with me."

"I don't know if I can—"

"Perform? Don't worry about it. You'll perform all right. Leave it to me."

Her hand was warm and sweaty and she was leaning close to me, pressing her breasts into me and now, against reason and common sense, interest, shall we say, rose. A wise man once said, when your prick goes up your brains go to your ass, and there was nothing in my experience that ran counter to that.

The bedroom was done up in harem style, huge, an enormous oval bed, thick pillows. Everything was silken, soft, elegant. My feet sank into the carpeting to my ankles. There were mirrors everywhere. The walls, the ceiling. The walls were splinters of mirror.

She entered the bathroom and I could see that it was larger than my bedroom.

Behind the bed was a mirrored headboard and there were a number of family pictures set into niches, Kelly with a husky, dark-haired man who I assumed was an ex-husband, some kids, an older man, a teen-age boy.

She returned to the bedroom wearing a transparent, silk thing and her body was fine and lovely and whatever resolve I had had earlier to resist her had deserted me. I gazed around the room and there she was, dancing about me in silvered multiplicity. It was dazzling.

Still, I went through the motions, thinking of Rita Macklin. "I don't want to seem rude—"

"No," she said moving very close to me. "Don't be *rude…*"

She pulled me down on the bed, kissing me desperately, clawing at me.

I kissed her and her breath was sour with alcohol and she shoved her tongue hard into my mouth and we pushed against each other and then I held her away from me.

Her breathing was in spasms now and there was something crazed in her eyes and I was nervous and I laughed uncomfortably and picked up one of the photographs behind the bed.

It felt as though someone had cracked me across the skull. I gazed at it in stunned disbelief. It was a photograph of Travis Wells.

"My son," Kelly said. "The murder case?"

"Travis—"

"Wells. I'm Kelly Wells. He's my son. They said he killed my father and my other kids."

She didn't speak for a long while. She stared directly at me. "Now fuck me."

I lifted her gown off. She began to cry. She leaned against me and wept and wept.

She shook her head, weeping. Tears streamed down her face. "I keep seeing my babies." She wept bitterly. "They killed my babies. And they took my son away, the only one left for me."

She stood and moved away from me. She grabbed some tissue from a container on a bureau and buried her face in it. "Go," she said. She did not look at me. "Get out of here. Go. Go."

She continued to weep quietly and I tried to put my arm around her but she pulled away and I stood there for a long time and she finally stopped crying and then she looked up at me and her face was puffy and tear-streaked and she said very softly, "You play the hand you're dealt in this life." In the depths of her eyes were a profound sadness and pain. "You can't throw it back in and say, 'Give me three more.' You don't get to draw in real life. Now please. Take one of the cars…"

"I'm sorry."

She shook her head. I moved my hand to smooth her hair. "No," she said.

I could think of nothing more to do or say and so I left.

Chapter Twelve

Kelly's truck still had the keys in the ignition and I drove back to the mobile home park. It was dark. Behind a chain link fence, Jukie prowled. The old man was gone.

I picked up my truck and headed back toward Tehachapi. Speeding through the desert, I fiddled with the radio, trying, without much success, to get a clear signal. I did manage to bring in some mariachi and a preacher broadcasting out of New Mexico who faded then roared, then faded again; but mostly the radio crackled and shrilled. Chaos. It was almost dawn when I got home and I tried to sleep, but couldn't.

I waited until the late morning and called Kleinmutz. I could feel his hangover through the phone. He spoke as though he had a mouthful of cotton. "Who is it?"

"Who else calls you?"

"Yeah," he said. He sounded dispirited.

"I drove back out to Joshua Crest."

"Nitwit. That's what you are."

"Met the kid's mother. Travis Wells' mother."

"Oh, sure. Know her."

"Piece of goods," I said.

"Spoiled bitch drunk." He went off on a furious fit of coughing. Then, I could hear him pour something into a glass.

"Little early, isn't it?"

"Hair of the dog. Paint thinner and tabasco sauce." He smacked his lips. "Damn that's good! You can substitute Worcestshire, if you don't like the tabasco."

"Good."

"All right. What do you want?"

"What can I do here with this thing? This kid—he's innocent."

"Don't get involved here."

"I can't escape it."

"This is a mistake you're making."

"The kid is innocent."

"You don't know this."

"I'm leaning more and more to this conclusion."

"They wanted me to take the thing on appeal. I told you this. The mother wanted me to take it. I wouldn't touch it with your dick. This is dangerous business. All of them are involved in—something. Who knows who's doing what to whom? Fucking cesspool. I'm telling you, Paul. Please. Don't get involved."

"I *am* involved."

"It's crazy. Don't you see this?"

"I do," I said. "I just can't—I just—can't—"

"What?"

"—not try to do something for this kid."

"What do you think you can do?"

"Find out what really went on out there."

"You don't understand what you're messing with. One of the first clients I had out here, crank dealer, someone owed him money, one of the Phelan family. He goes to collect and he disappears. Mr. Keen Tracer of Lost Persons couldn't find him. Five years later, almost to the day, I get a call from a Sheriff out in the Mojave. They got a parcel for me. It's my client."

"How'd he look?"

"Not too bad. Had that nice leathery look, kind of a smile on his face. Could have been a grimace. Looked real tanned. It's that dry desert air. Mummifies you. I'd seen him look better, but I also had seen him look worse. If you're going to die—"

"I'll have to remember that."

"Desert rat fished him out of an abandoned mine shaft. Thought it was a sack of gold. He was in a burlap sack."

"They ever find who put him there?"

"Oh, no one put him there. Judge Frog Phelan ruled his death an accident."

"The burlap sack?"

"That gave them pause for about ten seconds, but they eventually figured it out. He was practicing—"

"Practicing?"

"Sack racing."

"In the Mojave?"

"You bet. Out there by himself practicing his sack racing, accidentally falls down the mine shaft."

"Works for me."

"Sure. Look, Paul, you'll excuse me. I have to throw up. Please don't go back out there."

After he hung up I tried again, without success, to get some sleep. I lay in bed and thought about Joshua Crest and Kelly and Travis Wells and even Rita Macklin and I felt as though I were tied in some kind of thin wire binding, as though it were being pulled tight around me.

Later, I came to the prison. I hadn't slept. I was bone-tired. I was uneasy about seeing Travis Wells. What was I doing?

McMullin and Blast were alone in the library. Big Mick displayed a copy of "Funhouse Mirrors" his wife had picked up for him in a used bookstore. He wanted me to sign it. Blast studied the photograph on the back cover. "You… look like a fag," he said. Mick reached to take the book back and Blast pulled away. "Don't he… look… like a fag?"

"Give it here," McMullin said.

Blast turned the book so that the picture faced McMullin and me. I was younger, of course. Deadly serious. The expression on my face reflected a pain so profound you wondered that anyone could endure it. How did I make it from there to here?

"Don't he look like a fag?" Blast said. "You ever… on…pipe?"

"Give Mick the book," I said. Blast dropped the book to the floor. "Pick it up."

"What…you… going to do?"

"I said, pick it up."

"You… gonna call the…guard? Have them write me up?"

"Don't you worry about what I'm going to do," I said. "Just pick it up." He didn't move. "You're going to pick it up. Believe me."

Blast looked over at McMullin. Then he began to laugh quietly. He picked up the book and handed it to McMullin.

The rest of the men arrived, Travis last. He took his seat without saying anything and I felt his gaze on me and I was uncomfortable. He knows I've been with his mother, I was thinking.

It was foolish, of course. How could he? Kelly would have had to have had information that I worked in the prison system, at the institution that held her son. How could she know that?

The feeling, though, persisted.

Through the glass to the library, I noticed Macklin also watching me. She, too, seemed to know something. What was it? Was my life so transparent that the whole world knew what I was doing and where I had been?

McMullin showed "Funhouse Mirrors" to the others and Culpepper asked what it was about and I shrugged it off. Sergeant asked McMullin if he could look at it and Big Mick gave him the book. He leafed through, making soft clicking sounds with his tongue. He asked if he could borrow it and McMullin said, yes.

Blast had brought in another of his quasi-literate rants against Jews and women guards. I was tired and fed up and cut him off. I could see he was angry, but I didn't care. He moved to a chair away from the main table and brooded.

Poet had done some more work on his story. It was a description of his relationship to Millie Coty, his stripper girl friend. "This is a girl you were in love with?" Mick said.

"Yes," Travis said softly.

"This is a young man and his feelings for a woman," Culpepper said.

"I know this," Sergeant said and the others nodded in agreement. Travis didn't want to read the new material. He wouldn't tell me why. "He's embarrassed," McMullin said.

Crow laughed and Big Mick looked at him in a very serious way. "This is not easy," he said and Crow nodded uncomfortably, apologetically.

"You write some good horny stuff?" Crow said to Travis.

"It's love stuff," El Negro said. "This is the toughest thing to write about."

"We have to get over this," I said. "If we're going to be true writers we're going to have to go deeply into ourselves, reveal ourselves. You have to bring out your life as though it were a corpse. You have to be ready to cut your heart and soul open."

No one spoke for a while. Poet fingered the pages he had worked on, trying to decide whether or not to read them aloud." Hey, you... gonna... read this dogshit or not?" Blast said.

"Hey," McMullin said.

"What?"

"C'mon, Youngster," Sergeant said to Blast. Blast smiled a tight smile and looked away.

Poet read quietly: "'You can't figure out why you care for a person. Why this person and not some other? I always felt in a very deep way that there was one person in the universe who fit perfectly with you. Your souls fit together. You were not complete without each other. You could look up at the stars and where two stars kissed, that was you and your girl. Millie was this girl. I was not a complete human being until I met her." He stared at the paper for a long while before he went on. He read so soflty and rapidly that the words ran together, a blur of sound: "And this had terrible consequences for me. The reason I'm here is because of the girl I loved. And I still love her. I don't know why she did what she did to me. She loved me, I'm certain of this. And yet she lied, she perjured herself, and destroyed my life and I don't know why. Why did I love her? Why? There was something about her that was so gentle and good and pure. She would look at me and it was as if we were the only two people on earth. I felt so *close* to her. It was as though our two souls had become one."

He finished reading and stared down at the paper. His face was flushed, his shame palpable.

"I don't understand," said Culpepper. "This is the girl that turned on you, right? Why would she have done that?"

He did not look up. "They put pressure on her."

"They?" I said. "Who?" He didn't answer and I found myself wondering why someone would want to set him up. To what purpose?

"Something doesn't add up here," said McMullin. "You say she loved you. Why, if you're innocent, would she turn on you?"

"You're fooling youself, man," El Negro said. "She don't love you. She never loved you. She was using you. And believe me, when it all comes out, it gonna be that *she* put you here for whatever reason. She's the one who done this whole thing."

When the class was over, Travis delayed leaving the library. I could tell he had something to say, but he couldn't bring himself to come out with it.

"Big Mick asked a good question," I said. "If she loved you and you're innocent, why would she set you up?" I couldn't hear his answer. "What?"

"Someone had a hold on her."

"Who?" He just shook his head. "So she's the key to this whole thing. If you're really innocent, she knows it."

Barely audible: "Yes."

"And her testimony put you here?" He remained quiet. "And you say you still love her?"

"I do."

"Does she still love you."

"I don't know. I think she does. Yes."

"Does she ever write you, visit you?"

"No."

Neither of us spoke for a while. He stared right into me. "I swear to you," he said, "she knows I'm innocent."

"What do you want me to do?"

"There's nothing you can do. No one can do anything."

"How about your family?"

"There isn't much of a family now. I never knew my father."

"Mother?"

"She has her problems." I remained quiet. "She's a drunk." He looked away. He stared at the mountains, as though he were imagining himself disappearing into them. "Not a polite, middle-class drunk. The falling down kind."

He grew quiet, now. Should I tell him I had been with his mother, had come very close to sleeping with her? If I continued my involvement with his case he was sure to find out. What would happen then? How to broach it with him?

I said nothing.

Macklin was watching us through the glass. She appeared angry. On the yard, Blast was pacing beyond the yellow "Out of Bounds" area. Poet continued to stare at the mountains. His voice was very quiet. "When my grandfather and brother and sister were killed, it just tore her apart. And then to accuse me of the killing, bring me to trial, *convict* me. She didn't deserve this. And she's stuck by me. Done all she can for me. And

I feel so bad over that. All that she's gone through. And she has to worry about me, too."

I didn't speak. I could think of nothing to say to him. It was the corrosive power of injustice. Something deep, deep was closing down inside me. If this kid was innocent, how ugly everything seemed.

Kleinmutz and Macklin were right: I never should have opened myself up to this. It was just too painful, too unfair. I was trapped by my caring.

"There's no one who can do anything for me," he said. "The truth of it is, I'm lost."

He didn't look at me. He turned and left the library. I watched him move off across the yard.

I could see Blast standing just beyond the OUT OF BOUNDS marker. He hadn't gone in-line, yet. He was waiting for me to come out onto the yard. I was aware that Macklin was watching me.

I exited the library. Blast gazed off, facing the far wall and gun tower. "You… treated me… like shit," he said.

"You're lucky I didn't do you some real damage," I said.

"Write… me up?"

"I don't operate that way. If things don't go right between us, we'll deal with it another way."

"What way's that?" I shrugged. "You mean a man to man way? You mean… we get down…" I didn't answer. "*What*? Because I said you look like a fag?"

"You'll treat me with respect," I said. "I've done nothing to you to cause you to treat me any other way, have I?"

"You… gonna write… me up?"

"You don't like the class, just withdraw." I started away, then came back to him. "You're doing what kind of a bit?"

"Little Bitch—Twenty-five… to life…"

"You're not getting out of here. You understand this?"

"If… I thought that…," he said, "I'd… kill myself…"

"You've heard this, I'm sure. You can do hard time, or you can work on things. Work on yourself." He didn't answer. "You hear me?"

"I… hear… you…" He stood standing there, not speaking, for a long time. He was staring beyond the administration building at the electrified fence that ran between the two main fences. A rabbit had made its way past the outer fence and was hopping about on the dirt path of the no man's land. "You ever have something you… never told… no one?" he said.

"Yes," I said.

"What?"

I didn't answer. I was thinking about what had happened after Moc Hoa. These were things that I hadn't told anyone.

"I…have… something," he said. He still did not look at me. He did not speak for a very long time.

"I have to go," I said.

"Yes," he said.

I started away from him. He called to me. "Teacher?" I turned back to him. "Remember what Sergeant wrote about? About how he killed a kid?"

"Yes."

He stared a long time at me. "I killed… this kid, too…"

"What kid?"

"This happened a long time ago," he said.

I walked back to him. "What are you talking about?" He didn't speak for a while. "When was this?" I said.

"I was eleven… years old… I killed this kid." He said it very simply, matter-of-factly.

"How did that happen?"

He remained silent for a while. He shook his head from side to side, staring inward. "I never told… anybody… about this."

"All right."

"We were… playing games… at lunch period…"

"This was at school?"

"Hoover Elementary in South Central." Again, he did not speak for a while. I could see he was trying to form the words, but his stammer had grown so strong he could not. I remained quiet. The rabbit in the no-man's land sniffed at the air. At last Blast continued: "There were these kids… from a another… school came by…"

"All right."

"And this… older boy… he dragged me down… into this hall that led to… a storage place… in the school…" I still did not speak; we both remained quiet for a while. "And he… he… took out… took out his… dick."

I said nothing.

"He tried… to get me… to suck it. And I hit him on the side… of the head… with a piece of iron—"

"Where'd you get something like that?"

"Scrap just lying there. It was like part of what you might use to jack up a car…" He spoke in a matter of fact voice, without once looking over at me.

"Then what happened?"

"I ran and…" He grew quiet again. He was looking back at the past. "I never told nobody… and the next day the janitor staff, they found… his body and… he was dead… and the police… they came and… questioned… us. But no one… saw him with… me."

"You never told anybody?"

"You the first one."

"Why're you telling me?"

He didn't speak for a long time. "I thought… you were…maybe… you could be… my friend." It was astonishing. The child in him was now standing in front of me. This fierce, tattooed convict seemed more like an eleven-year-old kid.

"You have other friends?"

"Outside?" He shook his head. "Just you."

He walked away without looking back at me. I stood stunned. The brutishness of lives, the horror, the sadness. An eleven year old boy had murdered another boy and never told anybody about it until he confessed to a stranger on a maximum security prison yard. A stranger whom he thought of as his only friend.

What world was I living in? What was this life?

Is it possible that an eleven year-old child murders and never says a word to anyone for twenty years or more?

The rabbit moved slowly along the path, not far from the electrified fence; hopped, sniffed, nibbled at a scrawny clump of sage; nibbled another, this one closer to the fence. And yet another. And one more.

With this, a jagged electric sound ripped along the fence. The rabbit jerked into the air, impaled on a spit of electricity. As the yard alarm shrilled, the rabbit was yanked into the electrified strand and immediately consumed by flame.

Spotlights snapped on bright in the towers. Guards came running from the reaches of the yard.

"It's a rabbit," I said.

"Damn rabbit," the Sergeant called out and the guards gathered and moved to the fence and gazed on the still-smoking carcass.

"Good eats," one said.

"Hey," another of the guards called out in the direction of the inmate housing units. "Dinner!"

They laughed and started back to their stations.

I left the yard feeling uneasy. I was uncomfortable over what Blast had told me. And I was thinking of Poet and his girlfriend, "like two stars kissing," he had said.

Later that evening I rendezvoused with Rita Macklin at the small bar behind the bowling alley next to the Mountain Inn. We both drank beer. We didn't speak much. "What is it?" she said.

"It's Travis Wells," I said and I was thinking of Joshua Crest and Kelly, his mother.

"Why should you care?"

I shrugged and could not answer. "He wrote this thing about this girl he's in love with…"

"What are you talking about?" she said.

"Travis Wells—"

"Yes?"

"Had this girlfriend who he says is responsible for sending him to prison—"

She was angry now. "This is just foolishness," she said. "How? How can you get involved in the life of a *stone* killer? And he killed kids, too, didn't he? Everybody knows this. This is not just some guy who got pissed off in a bar room."

"You said he could be innocent—"

"Let's just drop it. You're making me physically ill."

We didn't talk much after that. We finished our drinks. "I'm going to go home," she said.

"Fine."

"This thing with this inmate is not healthy. It's not right," she said.

"What do you mean? I think this kid is innocent—"

"All right. I don't want to argue. I'm tired."

She left and I had another drink and then I drove east, out of town, heading back toward Joshua Crest. I hadn't slept in two days, but it didn't matter.

Chapter Thirteen

I'm not sure what time it was when I arrived in Joshua Crest. The furnaces of the mills outside of town were banked down. They glowed a dull red. On the far side of the last mill, where the desert spread to the horizon, a huge slag dune, larger than two football fields, burned with orange and blue flame, like a great wall heater laid flat.

I went along Main Street, past the saloons and strip joints and tattoo parlors. I pulled up in front of the Kaktus Klub.

I parked the truck cattycorner to the curb and entered. The night was, as they say in the trade, slow: the ever-present desert rats, two at the bar, grizzled old guys in tank-tops, overalls, and work boots, with long greasy hair and beards, several more at tables. The club reeked of booze, stale smoke, and sweat.

Milly was at work on a small stage behind the bar. She had stripped down to a g-string. Lost in the texture of her skin, it was so scanty as to be non-existent.

I suddenly understood what Travis Wells had been writing about. She was beautiful beyond what I could have imagined; I was astonished at it.

It was the kind of spectacular beauty where your heart begins to race and you feel giddy and you think about becoming a poet. I hadn't expected it—not in this brutal, ugly, town, this rotting club.

She had raven-black hair, very white, almost translucent skin and eyes a kind of washed out blue that was extraordinary.

She was tattooed on one buttock, the inside of her thigh, her right shoulder, and just above one breast, small, delicate etchings too fragile to be clearly made out from the distance of the stage. She also wore a small diamond—or was it rhinestone?—in one nostril.

She danced in front of a full-length mirror to the lugubrious accompaniment of a scraggly drummer who seemed to be asleep, his broom-handle thin arms displaying skeins of knotty vein. He worked the sticks and skins as though he were only vaguely acquainted with them. A hunched piano player in an orangish toupee and unnaturally thick spectacles was equally uninterested. He was singing, but it was barely comprehensible, a kind of sloppy slur of sound. Neither men looked at Millie who stared at herself, entranced by her reflection.

The piano player continued slurring his song. The lyrics went: "Nobody loves me but my mother/ And she could be jivin', too," an old B.B. King blues.

Seated in a dark corner of the place was the large middle-aged man in wash-and-wear suit who had come to the door when I was here earlier. I sat at the bar. The bartender, hefty, with a badly pocked face, and a manner that hinted at scant doit of humanity, came to me. He didn't say anything. He stared at me with dull, chilling eyes. I ordered a draft beer and he poured one out for me and asked for seven dollars. I told him that must be some beer and he said it was, but he did not smile. I paid him and sipped at the beer and watched Millie Coty as she plodded through her dance.

At the finale, she snapped her g-string several times, removed it, and flung it to one of the desert rats, who put it up to his nose and inhaled without much animation.

She exited the stage through a curtain at the rear of the bar and I got up and started around the bar after her. The bartender put his heavy body between me and the curtain Millie had gone through. "I'm a friend of a friend," I said.

He just stared at me.

"Travis Wells," I said.

He continued to stare at me. He watched me for a long moment, then he looked back at the man in the corner. The man in the corner rose. "Where was that?" the bartender said.

"Tehachapi Prison."

I could see that the man in the corner was just standing there, watching us. "Okay," the bartender said, moving to one side. I started through the curtained entrance to the back.

I could see the man in the corner moving toward the bar.

There was a narrow corridor with a kitchen off to one side and another curtain masking an archway to the other side. I parted the curtain and looked in.

Milly, in a ratty flannel bathrobe, was seated before a mirror. She was reading—Dostoyevsky's "Notes From Underground." She glanced at the book, then herself in the mirror. She saw me in the mirror, but didn't acknowledge me. She went back to her book.

I came into the dressing area and sat in a wicker chair against the wall. She gazed at herself in the mirror. "How do you like the book?" I said.

"It's all right," she said.

"I'm a writer."

"What do you write?" Her voice was very soft and there was a deadness in it that canceled out her beauty.

"Novels. I also do some teaching." She was staring at me in the mirror, but she did not say anything more. "At Tehachapi Prison. Max Yard." She now turned to me. Her eyes were washed out, pale and dead. "Travis Wells is one of my students. He's been working on a story about his crime—and, he says he's innocent—"

"He's not," she said.

"In the story he, ah—"

"Read the transcript of the trial?"

"No."

"Read it."

"I will."

"Anyone who was close to him at that time knows he did it." Her voice was so quiet I had to strain to make out what she was saying; she spoke without emotion and she just went on as though reading the newspaper. "He told me he did it."

"Really?"

"Old man had all sorts of jewelry and cash hidden in that dump, is what he said." She continued on without animation, staring at me with eyes so dead I regretted having come to her: the kind of look that makes you question your own humanity, question the existence even of a species called human. "Was going there to get some of it. Hour later came back all bloody, shaking, told me when he got there he'd argued with the old man. Picked up a bat, smashed him. Didn't know the kids were sleeping in the front room. They come running in crying. He killed them. Killed them all."

"He told you this?"

She took a cigarette out of a beaded case and lit up. "That's right. I testified to it."

"What do you make of these splinters that the grandfather had under his finger?"

"I don't make anything of them. He hit him with a baseball bat."

"Why did he do it? just for the money?"

"That's what he said."

She continued to stare at me with those dead eyes. She took a deep, long drag on her cigarette and just stared at me.

"It just doesn't seem that he did it," I said. "The way he writes about it."

"He's very convincing. He's a psychopath."

"He loves you," I said. For a instant I thought I saw a glimmer of caring in her eyes, but it was immediately shut down. "He writes about that, too." She just stared at me.

The man in the wash-and-wear suit appeared through the curtain. "He bothering you?" he said.

"He knows Travis. From the prison."

The man came into the dressing room. He moved right up to me. I was staring at his belly which overflowed his belt. On the silver buckle the name RICH was embossed. "I want you to give Travis a message for me," he said quietly. "Okay, guy?"

"Who are you?"

"Just tell him Richie."

"Richie?"

"He'll know."

"Fine," I said. "Richie." He was staring down at me. I could see his ample belly moving up and down. I could hear his breathing, labored, snorting through his nose. Suddenly he reached down and grabbed me by the collar and yanked me to my feet.

Before I could do anything, he hit me. He hit me hard and my head went numb and I realized I was falling backward, but I could not go down because he was holding me and hitting me over and over. "Tell Travis from me that I live for the day when I can get my hands on him."

I could see in the mirror blood spouting from my nose and mouth. Millie had gone back to touching up her make-up. She was watching me with what I thought was a glint of concern; that surprised me.

"Fuck with me anymore," he said, "I'm going to kick me some three-pointers with your gonads."

I indicating his belt buckle. I spit some blood. "Do you wear that so when you take your head out of your ass, you can look up and know who you are?" He hit me again and I tried to punch back, but everything was closing down around me. He hit me over and over and I went to the floor. I could see Millie Coty watching me.

The last thing I remember is thinking, I have to stop being such a wise-ass, as the point of his shoe kicked at my head.

.

Chapter Fourteen

I awoke to stars, an ocean of them, moving slowly around, rotating above me. There was a velvet black sky and a great sweep of stars and I was gazing up at it. It was all turning slowly, gracefully. Abruptly, it stopped.

My stomach kept moving. I rose on my elbows and tried to throw up. I only gagged. "*What am I doing here?*" I was thinking. Beyond a lacy palo verde bush, I saw yellow, feral eyes staring at me. It was a coyote.

It stood on a small rise ten yards away, shock still, trembling slightly. The coyote lowered its head, eyes eerie and malevolent.

I picked up a rock and pitched it at him and he moved off in a curious, sideways trot.

The terrain was scraggly brush and grit and rock and sage and manzanita, with a few Joshua trees here and there. I was out in the desert, but where? How far out?

The sage knows a thing or two. Yeah. Maybe where and how I died.

My head felt swollen, enormous. It did not hurt; it was numb. My ribs were numb too and I could feel there was blood caked over my face and I knew I had taken a real beating.

I should have been frightened, but I wasn't. I was angry, as angry as I had ever been.

I stood and my legs were weak and I almost fell. In the distance I could see wavering headlights. I began to hike in the direction of the lights.

In the desert it's difficult to estimate distances. Too much space, the air too clear. You think something's a mile away and you're way off: it's twenty miles or more.

It took me better than an hour to reach the lights. I walked and walked and stumbled and walked. I could see, fifteen or so yards away, trailing me, hunched silhouettes of coyotes, black against a gray sky. They trotted along, a huddled escort. I would throw a rock at them and they would move off and then a while later they would be back.

I reached the highway. I could see the fires from the factories outside of Joshua Crest still father off. I continued down the road toward them. There was not much traffic, just an occasional car or truck.

I was desperately tired, but I kept walking; the town never seemed to get any closer.

I walked for hours: how long exactly I'm not sure—my wrist-watch was no longer working; neither was my wrist for that matter. The hefty man known as Richie had done a job stomping me all over.

My body was coming alive and it was not fun. The numbness was gone from my ribs and every time I took in air it felt as though a knife were slicing into me. I ached all over. I had a ferocious headache; I had difficulty breathing.

Occasionally a car would come speeding down the road and I'd wave. The driver would take one look at me and see how beat up I was and figure this was trouble and keep on going.

I thought I'd never get to Joshua Crest. I just kept walking; the factories seemed never to get nearer. To the west ahead of me, the sky began to lighten. I continued on.

The sun was well up, a fiery, blinding disc, when an old pick-up sped past me. It suddenly careened to the shoulder, then, in a cloud of dust, backed up. I limped to it. I couldn't see the driver: the sun blinded my view. I got in and we started off.

There was an overwhelming odor of perfume. I expected to see a lady driving. I immediately realized I had made a mistake.

It was a muscular man, large, bald and black with a hard, chiseled face. He was wearing tight, red shorts and a silk fuchsia shirt with cut-off sleeves. He had a tattoo on his forearm, a hammer and anvil and the words: "Man of Steel." His face was thick with make-up. "My, my, some-one's got himself all *tacky*!" Man of Steel said with a delicate lilt. He gazed over at me with large dark eyes. "What happened, doll?"

"I had some trouble."

"I can see that!"

"A *sissy* picked me up."

"Really?"

"Tried to get fresh."

"This world," he said, tsking.

"Think I look bad?"

"You don't look good."

"You ought to see how *he* looks. You're not like that, are you?"

"Like what?"

"Double-gaited, as they say in Texas."

"Honey, is the Pope a polack?"

"But you don't want to—?"

"No, no, no. Not after what you done to that other hussy trim. I'd say she had it coming to her. Cunt."

On his way to Barstow from San Bernardino, Man of Steel had decided to take a side jaunt to look at the desert; I don't think he was looking for the endangered Mojave Desert Tortoise.

He explained he was in the Air Force, stationed at Edwards. "I'm not usually attired like this," he said.

"I would guess not."

He dropped the lilt. "I can be as macho as the next butch stud-muf-fin. Believe it." His voice had suddenly dropped an octave and devel-oped a rasp. I liked that; I laughed. We began to chat.

He was a baseball fanatic—he had even played minor league ball. We talked about the finer points of the game, mechanics, strategy. He knew his stuff.

Before entering the service, he had had a stint with the Bakersfield Dodgers, before they became the Blaze. I probably had seen him play, though I couldn't be sure: he wouldn't have been in red shorts and fuchsia. He laughed.

"Got to be *tres* careful, honey," he said. "Not many of those *ball* players live up to their name, if you know what I mean. And not many are *switch* hitters."

We got into a discussion of batting technique. He was impressed that I could still hit the fastball in the mechanical cage. He spoke about pulling the ball with no strikes and one strike; cutting down the swing with two strikes. "I could drive that ball with the best of them," he said, "Or, if need be, stroke it to all fields." He demonstrated, snapping his wrists to the left, center, and right.

We talked about hitting the fast ball and he assured me he had no problem with that. He could even read placement of the ball, where the pitcher spotted it. "That wasn't my problem. My problem was with Charlie."

"Curve ball?"

"Mister C. Never could solve it, never could lay off it." Once the opposing pitchers realized he couldn't hit the curveball, his career was over. "I could have got on by in the low minors. But I would never have even made it in Triple A. And also there was the strain of my sexual orientation."

"Can't be much better in the Air Force," I said.

"Don't ask, don't tell."

We came to Joshua Crest. He brought me right to the police station. "Hope you get your face and everything put in order," he said. He leaned forward, his grotesquely whited-out face serious. "You sure you don't want a blow job?"

"I'm sure," I said.

He looked sad, but shrugged it off. From a leather case, he offered me a cigar which I declined. He lit up, a massive heater; looked to be Cuban, the real thing. I began to laugh.

"What?" he said.

"You have a certain, I don't know—" I said.

"Gender confusion? You might say so. But isn't that what makes life interesting?" He blew me a kiss and drove off. I entered the station house.

There was a uniformed cop at an elevated desk. With a plastic fork, he was attacking a bowl of some kind of Chinese food, noodles, chunks of chicken. Behind him, the clock read a little after eleven. He was studying Guns and Ammo Magazine. He looked over at me without concern. "Someone beat the living shit out of you," he said.

"That's right."

"Better get you a cop."

"That's why I'm here."

"I'm on my dinner break." He broke into a wide grin, revealing scrambled, yellow front teeth. He pressed a button on the phone, then went back to his eating and reading.

A plain-clothes detective, a young, crew-cut guy, came out of an office. "Where'd this happen?" he said. He didn't look as though he much cared.

"Kaktus Klub—"

The detective looked me over, nodding his head. There was a shadow of a smile on his face. He moved back into his office.

He returned with another man. The man stared at me without compassion. It was Richie. "Hey, Baby-cakes," he said.

"Know him?" the detective said.

"Oh, yeah." Richie put his lumpy face right up to mine. His breath smelled like horse-shit. "Hey, guy, next time you try to sexually harass one of my dancers, I'll hang a rape charge on you," he said.

"Oh, please—"

"Please *what*?" He was pushing his whole body at me.

"I never touched her."

He swung out and hit me again. I went down and the marble floor was hard and cold and I was spitting blood. I got up slowly. I felt god-awful. My mouth was bleeding again and it tasted of old blood and new blood and I felt about to throw up but I didn't.

I went after Richie, kicking and flailing about and he laughed and the uniformed cop and the detective grabbed me. "Naw, naw. You don't want to do nothing," the detective said.

"This police work is a young man's game," Richie said, gulping air as he brushed himself off. "It's a contact sport." The detective laughed.

I was breathing hard, also, not so much from exertion, but rage. I wanted so bad to get a kick in, just one. "I came to her because—"

"I know why you came to her, guy," Richie said. "But you don't know what you're getting into here. Now get out before I book your ass."

Book me? Oh, this was news. Serious. "He's a cop?" I said to the detective.

"Oh, yeah," he said. "You listen to him, now. Get."

Richie stared at me. He jutted his jaw out at me, Mussolini-style. Oily, ridged with acne scars, his face was like a fist, something to batter you with, one of those beauties that could make a freight train take a dirt road. The fury I felt was immense. "Hey, Baby-cakes, mess up in this town," he said quietly, "and you're going to find yourself at room temperature."

I could see he was waiting for me to come at him. He was eager. It would give him an excuse to really do me again. Oh, I wanted him bad and I knew I'd get to him—sometime. Another day, another place.

I left the station and walked down Main Street. My truck was still parked in front of the Kaktus Klub. I drove off down Main, heading out to the mobile home park.

It was nearly noon, and the old man who had been there the day before was back in the same place, out in front in the grassless yard. He had yet another heap of metal on his iron table and he was banging away at it.

The day was ugly and hot, the air dry and thick with the gunk from the factories outside of town. You could hardly breath from the heat and the stench of factory fumes. I had no reason to stay here, but I knew I wouldn't be leaving. Not right now.

I got out of my truck and approached the old man. "How's it going?" I said.

"Any day above ground is a good day," he said. "You know, I'm not an *old* man. I'm a young man that something happened to." He laughed a dry laugh.

"That's good," I said.

He glanced over at me. "See you're getting to know our town."

"Oh, yeah," I said. "Nice place."

"If you like dried out *shit*. You look like something a fucking mongrel dog done throwed up."

There was a sound of gunshots from behind the mobile homes, a rapid volley. I flinched and the old man laughed. He kept right on banging away at the metal. "Mrs. Wells," he said, "Keeping sharp for the assholes round here. Hey, what are the three words, you don't want to hear when you're making love?"

"I don't know."

" 'Honey, I'm home.' "

He laughed and laughed at that one and I walked behind the trailers and mobile houses. Kelly Wells was standing at the edge of the dry lake bed. At the bottom was a line of empty liquor bottles. .45 revolver in hand, she was blasting away at them; she hit them every time.

She paused to reload. She noticed my battered face. "Did I do that," she said.

"I went looking for Travis' girl."

"Okay. When I'm drinking, you know, I do things and—" She finished loading the gun.

"I found her. Also found a guy by the name of Richie—"

"That fuck worked you over?"

"That he did."

"He's a cop," she said.

"Tell me about it."

She rested the revolver at her side. She looked off in the distance, but her gaze was turned inward. She ran her tongue over her upper lip. "Why are you getting involved in this?" she said.

I shrugged.

She said: "You see it's Richie and the D.A., Corcoran. And Froggie—"

"Froggie?"

"The Honorable Judge, Wilson Xavier Phelan. Frog. And I'd even throw in my son's attorney, Whittaker. Between them they have gall enough to gag a maggot."

"Where do I find them?"

"You don't want to get into this," she said.

"Yes, I do. I don't like the way I've been treated here."

"You want to run with the dogs you got to get down off the porch," she said.

"I mean to. Where are they?"

"Tungsten Club, at the far end of Main. Sit around counting their money, figuring who they can fuck over next…"

The Doberman, Jukie, appeared, sleek, black, evil-looking as hell. He stared at me, bared his teeth, growled. "Speaking of dogs," I said.

"It's okay, Jukie," Kelly said. "It's okay. Come here." She pulled the dog over to me and he sniffed me and she kept saying that I was okay and I petted him and he grew friendly. He stretched out at my feet.

Kelly turned from me and went back to shooting the bottles.

"You got your truck?" I said.

"Yes, I did."

"Thanks."

"No problem," she said, without looking at me. "Do yourself a favor."

"Okay."

"Get far away from here."

She gazed at me now. Her expression was tired. "Stick around," she said, "and they're going to kill you. And you can take that to the bank."

Chapter Fifteen

At the far end of Main Street, the look of the town changed. The buildings were older, adobe or brick, stately, with heavy oak doors and shutters. One had been a church in the old Spanish Mission style. You could still see the concrete cross atop it. A brass sign on the stucco wall surrounding the building said: "Joshua Crest Tungsten Club—Members Only."

I left the truck, went through a high wooden door in the outside wall, climbed a set of concrete steps, and entered the club.

It was anything but small-town; a lot of decorative oak, elements of the original church still in place; pews, stained glass windows. Down a few steps, in what would have been the apse of the church, were tables, filled with lunch-time diners, prosperous-looking folk in Western chic, designer boots, styled jackets, elaborate Stetson's.

A red-jacketed maitre d' hurried to me. "I'm looking for Judge Phelan,"

"Is he expecting you?"

"Tell him I'm a friend of Travis Wells."

Like a matador, he moved back into the room, dancing between the tables.

At a far table four men sat. Richie was one of them. Another man, large, beefy-faced, stood nearby. The maitre d' leaned down to one of the men. The others turned to look at me.

The maitre d' returned with the beefy-faced man. He was immense, six and a half feet, near 300 pounds, edging toward flab, but with plenty of muscle still there. He had a strabismic left eye which roved the room while his good eye fixed me with an ugly stare. I could see a bulge under his jacket and I assumed it wasn't his wallet.

"I'm here to see the judge."

"He can't be disturbed."

"He'll talk to me."

"Don't be a hard-on." He spoke so softly I had to strain to hear him. His voice was light and he had a vague lisp and you got the feeling that he was very tough and dangerous. "You don't want to look any worse than you already do." He winked his bad eye at me without humor.

"I don't want any trouble."

"Of course you don't."

"But Judge Phelan—"

"—is busy."

He winked again. I nodded and winked back, then moved quickly past him. He grabbed at me, but I yanked away and hurried toward Phelan's table. Roving-Eye came after me. I could see Phelan hold up his hand in a signal to let me go.

It was not hard to tell why Phelan was called Frog. He was a short, reptilian man with a broad, reddish face, full lips, and enormously thick glasses, Coke-bottle bottoms. The two other men were sleek, in their early forties, clean-cut business-types. They wore Western suits, string ties. Their Stetson's were on wooden pegs behind the table.

Richie sat with clenched fists, looking as though he were about to leap the table to get to me. "Hi, guy," I said to him.

"What's your problem?" Phelan said. His voice was deep, stentorian as befits a judge used to bossing around a courtroom.

"Who said I have a problem?"

"Appearances," Phelan said. He smiled. It was not an attractive smile: too many teeth for his mouth. They were crammed in at ugly angles.

"This fucker here," I said, indicating Richie.

"Richie? Really?"

"He did this, then dumped me out in the desert. Didn't you, guy?"

"Watch your language in front of the judge," Roving-Eye said.

"Fuck you."

"Fuck me? Fuck *you*!"

"No, fuck you!"

Roving Eye's errant orb, like a pinball racking up major points, flicked angrily from side to side. "Your *crocodile* mouth's going to get your *hummingbird* ass in trouble," he said, starting for me. Phelan again motioned with his hand and he stopped. "Won't you sit down, Mr.—?"

"Dogolov."

I sat. Phelan motioned for a waiter. "Have you had lunch?"

"Not exactly hungry just now."

He glanced sidelong at me. "What happened? Looks like you took a good licking."

"Yeah," I said. "Ol' Richie Rich here. The *guy* here. Baby-cakes."

Phelan laughed; it was a dry, mirthless laugh. "Knowing Richie, you must have done something to provoke him."

"He was just trying to be a hard-on—"

"Richie?" said Phelan. "I can't believe this."

" '—I'm the big tough cop and I'm going to go Third Degree on your ass,' " I said.

"Not in this town," Phelan said, smiling. "We would never mess with *Third Degree* here. Drink? How about a brandy? Corvassier?"

"As my old dad used to say, 'If they give, take; they take, holler.' "

"Wise man," Phelan said. The waiter had been standing a few feet off and Phelan nodded at him and he moved away. "We haven't introduced ourselves. I'm Frances Xavier Phelan. *Judge* Phelan. And this is Ron Corcoran, who prosecuted Travis Wells."

Corcoran had blondish hair, close cropped, and a light moustache. He nodded. The other man, dark and balding, said, "Alton Whittaker."

"The Wells kid's defense attorney," Phelan said. He indicated Richie. "Of course, you know—?"

"Oh, yes," I said. "Hi, *Baby-cakes*."

"Richie has told us that you're interested in Travis Wells' case. You had dealings with him in Tehachapi Prison?"

"Something like that."

"I don't know what Travis told you," Corcoran said, "but he was guiltier than hell. Everyone knew it. We were lucky to keep him out of the gas chamber."

"I'm not so sure he was guilty," I said, waiting for a reaction. No one spoke. They just stared at me. "And since coming here I'm getting more of a sense of the way things are."

"Really? What sense is that?" Phelan said.

"People get fucked over in this town."

"Really?"

"Oh, yeah. Get fucked over big time."

The waiter arrived with my brandy. I rolled it around in the snifter, then tossed it back. "Travis said there was a fat lady—"

"Fat Belle," Whittaker said. "Witness or anything, she was worth squat. Her alibis had alibis."

"Travis insists he's innocent."

"Isn't that what they all say in Tehachapi?" Judge Phelan spoke quietly, but with authority, as though addressing a class or lawyers in chambers. "There are people, and not all of them are in prison, who like to criticize our society and its leaders. Happens everywhere, not just in Joshua Crest. Universal thing. Not long ago I was thinking of all the jobs I've had and the various businesses I've had some knowledge of and the awareness came over me that not one of them was wholly honest. Every business, in my experience—and, since my experience has been widespread, you could extrapolate that this applies to *all* business—every business has an element of dishonesty to it. Perhaps business cannot function without a touch of the dishonest. Perhaps the world cannot go on without someone cheating someone. But here, then, is a major problem in our society: we are raised with values, ethics, what's right and what's wrong. And yet when you become an adult, you see that things don't work like that. Then, you either become very disillusioned or neurotic or hypocritical or self-delusional or Quixotic, in order to survive."

I stood there listening to him, wondering what the hell he was going on about? The others watched the judge with feigned great interest.

"That's why *justice* is so important. Regarding this, I recently had a memory of my childhood. This was during the Second World War in San Bernardino. The wealthiest and most envied family in our area was the Rooneys"

Corcoran smiled and nodded in agreement. "Ranchers. Made their money in black market meat during the war, didn't they Judge?"

"Yes they did. I realized, then, even as a kid that justice was not an either/or proposition. Black or white. There were shades of gray. There was one justice for this person, a different one for that. And I swore then that I would help find true justice in this world. I would stand for a purer justice."

"How have you fared?" I said.

"I've done my best." His eyes, grotesque behind the lenses of his glasses, remained on me. "As to Travis Wells—Travis Wells was guilty as a suck egg dog." He had taken a small ivory toothpick out of a case and was digging at his teeth. "You want to tell us what brought you here?"

"Driving the Mojave for the hell of it. Figured check this corner out. Get some clean desert air."

"You often drive the Mojave?"

"Almost never."

"Well, I trust you've had your air," Phelan said "Time to move on."

"The air was—I don't want you to take this personally. The air was disappointing."

"In what way?"

"It's—well, how can I put it?—*rotten*. You can't really *breathe* it. And this place—"

"Joshua Crest?"

"—is a slime bucket."

Phelan gazed at me with huge eyes from behind the thick lenses of his glasses. "Industrial development, Mr. Dogolov. Reversing what's gone on in the Rust Belt." He wiped a hunk of gristle reclaimed from his mouth by his ivory pick onto a napkin; he then replaced the pick in its case. "A few fumes, hardly anything to get a spastic sphincter about. People out here have work."

"Maybe Travis is guilty. I don't think he is. But there's something ugly here. I'm thinking about writing an article: 'The desert sky is a sickly yellow, but that's nothing to compare to the pus at the heart of Joshua Crest, a sheikdom halfway between Los Angeles and Death Valley...' L.A. Times. Start it with something like that."

"*Sheikdom*?" Corcoran said. "There are no *Arabs* in Joshua Crest."

"You're a writer?" Richie said, his voice thick with contempt. "Is that what you are? Know-it-all, arrogant cocksucker going to tell us how to run our town? Slicker than dog snot on a door knob. We don't like no one out here likes to look down at folks. If I was you, guy, I wouldn't be messing around out in the desert here."

"I wouldn't be messing around," I said.

"You don't know what happened with Travis," Richie said. "We all know him. Knew ol' Ray. Knew the kids..."

"I'm just looking to find out what happened," I said. I didn't take my eyes off him, sneaky bastard.

"He was convicted by a jury of his peers," Phelan said.

"Must have been a real neat trial. Judge, prosecutor, defense attorney, all playing kissy-face with each other. I'll bet my guy, Richie, here was the investigating cop."

Phelan gazed at me, pale with anger. The forced affability was gone. "Mr. Dogolov, you're talking out of ignorance. Complex situation here.

Whole thing house of mirrors. Trickier than braiding a mule's tail. Leave it be. You came out here for our desert air. I trust you've inhaled. Now leave it be."

"I wouldn't waste any time," Richie said. "Somebody might do you."

"Now, now," the judge said.

"Do you proper."

"Is that right?" I said.

"I might not read too many books, but I sure know sic' 'im from go fetch."

"Fascinating thing about stupidity," I said to the judge. "Intelligence always has limits. Stupidity is bottomless."

"That an insult?" Richie said, eyes narrow and suspicious."Trying to insult me?"

"You know what you need?" I said.

"I don't need you to tell me." He glowered at me, tilting his chin up in a challenging gesture.

"An *octorectomy*."

"What's that? Supposed to be some big word? What is that?"

"That's where they cut the cord between your asshole and your eyes because you have a shitty outlook on life."

"Trying to be a big brain with big words like that? Is that it? Call me an asshole? *You're* an asshole!"

"Richie, Richie," Phelan said very quietly. I turned from him and started around the table. I could feel Phelan's frog-gaze still on me."

"You hear me, asshole? *Asshole!*"

Richie had a plate of food in front of him, a pile of Mexican stuff, tostados, rice, beans, guacamole. As I went by, I knocked the mess in his lap. He rose to go for me and I hit him. He went right down. Roving-Eye dived at me and I hit him, too, hard enough to hear his nose break. He fell to one knee, dripping blood.

Richie had drawn his service revolver; Phelan pushed it to one side. "That's enough!" he said as though he were a school teacher calling a class to order.

"Don't fuck with me cause as long as I can suck some wind I'm going to be coming at you, Baby-cakes," Richie said, trying still to appear tough. His voice, however, came out as a whine. "There's going to be some serious butt-kicking. It might be my butt that's kicked, I don't know, but I'm going to keep coming at you as long as there's air to be sucked." He looked as though he were about to cry. He tried to thrust his revolver toward me again and Phelan grabbed it from him.

"I said, enough. Hear me, Richie?" He had positioned himself in front of Richie. He glared at him. "It's all even now, Mr. Dogolov." Several busboys had rushed to the table and were applying ice to Roving-Eye's face.

I leaned close to Richie. I stared right into him and I did not blink and I meant what I was saying as much as anything I've ever said in this life. "You don't know anything about me, about what I've done in my life. Don't fuck with me, either. Baby-cakes."

And I turned and walked from the club, hoping I wouldn't trip or appear stupid in some other way. I felt good. I felt I had made a point.

Chapter Sixteen

I killed a few hours driving around the town. I came upon a roadhouse just outside of town and had something to eat. In the men's room mirror, I saw myself for the first time since Richie had worked me over and there was this terrible sense of disorientation: another man stood in my place. It took me an instant to realize it was my reflection.

I was a mess, face blood-caked, swollen, clothes torn, dried blood everywhere. It wasn't me. It was this bloated, pummeled, lump.

I looked at myself for a long time, feeling not so much anger as disgust. It was as though all the other beatings I had taken in this life, were now worn on my face, those things you swallow and never talk about.

I washed up and rearranged my clothes and though I still looked like a dimes worth of dog meat, I figured in this town no one would look at me twice.

The roadhouse had satellite television and I drank beer and stared at baseball. It was the Dodgers and the Expos, but my mind was on other things and the game ran its course and I never even caught the score.

I was thinking about Travis Wells and his mother and Frog Phelan and all the rest. It was nasty business and I hadn't an idea how to handle it. I also thought about Kleinmutz and his warning to me about ending up as fertilizer for cactus. All of that didn't seem so outlandish now.

It was near midnight when I left the place. The night was cold with a wind that stung my face and hands and cut right through my jacket. The windows on the truck were white with frost.

I drove back down Main Street to the sleazy side of town. The area was deserted. Not even the desert rats were out prowling the streets. A thick, yellowish fog hung over everything; there was a pungent odor that stung your lungs and I realized it wasn't fog but a noxious, syrupy haze of factory effluvia.

I parked the truck and walked past a closed-down tattoo parlor, a store-front advertising tea-leaf readings, several bar and strip joints whose facades sported great slashes of neon: cocktail glasses, gyrating hula dancers, tropical birds. Music from the strip spots thudded dully through brass-studded, Leatherette-padded doors. I entered the Kaktus Klub.

The desert rats were there at the bar and tables, matted hair, scruffy beards, leathery faces and hands. There were also some cowboy types in dusty boots and oily denim jackets and trousers.

Millie was up on the stage behind the bar, dancing a plodding strip to her reflection in the mirror.

I sat at the bar near where she was dancing. She saw me in the mirror and spoke to my reflection: "Richie's message didn't get through to you?"

"I need some help from you."

"What do I look like, Mother Theresa?"

One of the cowboys at the bar spread his arms wide. "Hey, Mother," he said.

"What's your problem?"

"Well, now, hey there —" The cowboy raised his glass in a toast, smiling sweetly. "Why don't you just kiss my ass?"

"If it looks anything like your face," Millie said, "I wouldn't do it for a million bucks." The cowboy's friends laughed at that and he smiled foolishly.

"I need a place to stay," I said. "Figure you know the town."

"If you had a quarter more brain" she said, "you'd be almost a moron." She did a slow turn around, peeling off her g-string. She kicked it down the bar at the cowboy. He dunked it in his drink, then leaned his head back and squeezed the booze into his mouth. His friends laughed some more.

Millie said quietly to me: "I'll get off after this set. Wait out front."

I moved away down the bar. Millie was back facing the mirror again, massaging her breasts at her reflection.

I pulled the truck to a space in front of the club and waited. I waited a long, long time, nearly an hour. I was about to return to the club when Millie came out.

She was wearing a long, ratty something that was meant to be fur but whose involvement with anything animal, other than alley-cat, was tenuous. She also had on a pair of gold, spike-heeled shoes. The diamond in her nostril had been replaced with a surgical-steel ring; and she had drenched herself with a perfume so cloying that I prayed for a skunk on the road that I could hit to mitigate the sweetness.

"Head toward Barstow," she said. She lit up a cigarette and leaned forward to turn on the radio. She had only her costume underneath the fur; her breasts were kind of flopping around in a flimsy black-net bra and, though I had seen them in the club, at this nearness they were exquisite.

There are small things in this life that are can-openers to the soul. They set free some good stuff, enthusiasms, deliriums, passions, but also a freight-car of foolishness. You feel as though your breath has been knocked out of you; you want to behave goofily, recite poetry, even propose marriage. Her breasts made me want to do something really stupid; fortunately I was old, wise and depressed and the impulse quickly vanished.

She searched for a station on the radio while I watched the road and her breasts. There was just static for a while. At last a mariachi band came on. "Only station we get at night," she said.

"So I've noticed."

"Mexican national anthem. They're through broadcasting for the day." She punched the radio off. We drove in silence for a while.

"The sage," I said. "The sage knows things."

"The sage?"

"The weed. Knows many things."

"I don't know what the fuck that means."

"It means I don't know fuck-all in this life."

"I believe that."

We neared a fork in the road and she told me to bear right. A sign read "Barstow 75 Miles."

The road was empty. There was nothing coming in either direction. Off to my left, I could see the fires leaping at the horizon beyond Joshua Crest.

After a while, we came to a motel, a drab place that looked as though it had hung on from the 1940's. Wooden cabins, once white but now badly in need of paint, lined a gravel parking lot; a faded wooden sign announced: "The Desert Flower Motel."

"What flower's that?" I said. "Stinkweed?"

"You're safer out here."

"If I'm not eaten alive by bedbugs."

I parked and got out of the truck. There were three other vehicles in the lot: business at "The Desert Flower" was not booming.

The motel office was empty. A sign behind the desk let you know that there was a 10% discount for Christians. There was a bell on the desk and I banged it and no one came.

I glanced out the window. I could see the glow from Millie's cigarette flare in the interior of the truck. The wind was blowing outside, raising grit; several large tumbleweeds went skipping across the parking lot. The whole place had a godforsaken, abandoned feel and I stood gazing at the night, thinking of my life, of how I had been tossed willy-nilly from the mills of Pittsburgh, to war, to the Max Yard at Tehachapi Prison. To here, the asshole of the world.

At times I would get into one of these ruts. You begin to question everything about your life. You look back at what you've gone through and marvel at it and wonder why you were still around.

I stood now at the motel window, staring out at the dancing tumbleweed, lost in loneliness and desolation. The world had dropped away from beneath me. I was lost, lost.

Once in war, just before battle, I had come to a black edge. It was deep night, no stars or moon. I could feel ground beneath me, a kind of shale, slick, flaked, but what was in front?

Precipice, river, lake? I was alone. There was no sound. I couldn't bring myself to shine a light for fear the enemy was there in the black. Stretching before me was endless darkness. And I grew damp with fright of the unknown.

I moved away from this black edge and we went on and I never found out where I had stood or what was beyond it. But the sense of desolation remained with me.

And I felt it now gazing out over the parking lot of the "Desert Flower Motel," the blowing wind, the tumbleweed, the glow of a cigarette end.

I banged the bell over and over. At last a woman in a terry-cloth robe shuffled out of a room behind the office. She was not young at all, with a face like a week-old Halloween pumpkin, all scrunched and caved-in and wrinkled with sleep. If she had false teeth, she had not thought to put them in. She carried a large .45 revolver. "You John Law?"

"No, ma'am."

Gimlet-eyed, she watched me while she shifted sign-in cards around. "Two things out here," she said. "Desperados and John Law and you don't look like no desperado."

I signed the card, gave her my Visa plastic, and she passed a key over to me. "What's the attraction for desperados?" I said.

Through the window I could see that Millie was out of the car now; she was making a call at a pay phone on the outside office wall.

"How the hell should I know? I was a good Christian once, went to the Assembly of God Church over there by Kramer's Corners, but eight years out here—let's put it this way: I was on my way to bein' an asshole an' this place pushed me over the edge. Out here—well there ain't no one out here. You can do what you want. You makin' meth, some other of your narcotics, dope in other words, you use ether in the process there, and that stuff will smell up a city block. Out here, shit, wind just blows it away."

"Speed…"

"Speed capitol of the goddamn world," she said. "Hell, I ain't tellin' you nothin' you don't already know." She flashed a wide grin, revealing two rows of gums without teeth. "John Law."

I started out of the office. "String 'em up by their balls," she called to me, "see if they'll sing 'America The Beautiful…'"

Millie was just hanging up the phone. We got into the truck together. I could see the old lady watching us behind the office curtains as I steered the truck to the farthest cabin on the lot.

"Lady runs this place said this is a hideout for dope dealers."

"What they say."

"Who'd you call?"

"What're you, my daddy?"

We entered the cabin. It was what you'd expect from the exterior, walls a faded green, gouged plaster, peeling paint. There were dark smudges on the wall above the bed where years of occupants had rested greasy heads. The coverlet on the bed had more stains than good hygiene would dictate. You felt that if you got out of there with just crabs you should thank your stars. There was a strong odor of bug spray which I took to be a positive.

Millie said, "Mind if I get comfortable?" Before I could answer she was out of her coat and peeling off her stripper's costume. "After a while, begins to chafe," she said.

She stood before me completely naked. I had seen her at the club with the requisite g-stringy geegaws, so it wasn't as though her beauty was news to me; I knew how exquisite her body was. Totally bare, though, it was breathtaking beyond imagining, an exponential gorgeousness, dizzying, extraordinary. There was the purity of her, the sweet curves, rich smoothness, that caused you to ache inside; marblesque skin so white you'd think she was carved, lines so delicate they cut right into you. You felt your heart would break. I ached for her, not only in a sexual way, but in the way you ache to come near to astounding art.

I could now make out the tattoos: snakes that twined about her thighs and buttocks, dazzlingly fine, precisely limned foliations which bloomed and twisted across her porcelain skin. I took my finger and traced one of the snakes and she did not stop me. "Don't get any ideas," she said, hard. "You're not fucking me."

"What is it, the town style?"

"What's that supposed to mean?"

"You're the second one."

She raised a warning finger. "Hey," she said.

"'No' means 'no,'" I said.

"People got to learn that." She stretched out on the bed and lit another cigarette. I sat in a chair opposite the bed. She didn't speak for a while. "'Did he really say that?" she said at last.

"What?"

"That he loved me? Did he write that in your class?"

"Yes, he did. He wrote movingly about you."

She shook her head slowly. "Truth is," she said, "Travis killed his grandfather and the kids. I know it. And the fact he says he loves me, well—" She let the thought hang in the air.

"How do you know he killed the grandfather and kids?"

"He came to me. He was covered with blood. And he told me. And he had the old man's money."

"How much?"

"Oh, there was enough. The old man was kind of like a go-between with the dopers, manufacturers, and the distributors."

She stared at the ceiling, drawing on her cigarette. I tried to read her thoughts, but couldn't get past the opacity of her exterior. She was weighing something, turning it over in her mind, but she gave no hint of what it could be. There was this coldness that you couldn't get beyond. She gave away nothing and that was scary.

"What's Richie to you?" I said.

"My boyfriend."

"That's great. What happens—?"

"—if he finds us? He'll blow your ass away."

"Blow—?"

"—your ass *away*. Desert justice."

"That's really terrific. If I'm going to get my ass blown away don't you think I ought to at least get laid first?"

That brought a smile to her face. "No," she said, almost shyly. The change was striking, from stone hard to a little girl in a flash and I wondered at how little in my years I had learned about our nature. The human heart was an abyss, unfathomable to anyone: even our own heart was impenetrable to ourselves.

"You called Richie, didn't you?"

"No." She sat up. She flicked her cigarette ash into the ashtray, toyed with the glowing tip. "Besides, you're not doing nothing."

"Tell Richie that."

She laughed. "Probably kill you before I got it out."

We didn't speak for a while. She lay still. She stared at the ceiling. What was she thinking? Her body was like a magnet to me, the coolness of it, whiteness, exquisite curves, luxuriant hair, nipples like two firm eraser heads. She ran one hand over her legs and across her belly and I knew she was teasing me, but what else could I expect? This was her profession.

"Travis' mother said he didn't do it."

"Kelly? What do you expect? She's his mother."

"Those were her kids that were—And her father."

"Yeah."

"And the Fat Lady?"

"What about her?" She shook her head. "Just a good ol' gal, eats like a hippopotamus and looks about like one. That don't make her a killer."

"Why'd you come here with me?" I said.

"You said you needed a room."

"Directions would have been fine."

"I don't want you to get hurt. You're into something here, you can't even imagine. Just go." She stared at me for a very long time. "Do you want me," she said.

"No," I lied, knowing that she would either continue to tease me or come across. And truth to tell with that fatal disease out there, I wasn't sure I wanted her, even with a condom as thick as leather.

"Good," she said. "Let's get some sleep."

I began to make myself comfortable on the chair. "Come here," she said. "If you don't try to fuck me, you can sleep here."

I went over to the bed and lay down. I kept my clothes on. "I don't want you to get me wrong," she said. "You're an attractive man. I just don't like to fuck."

"Don't you get me wrong either. You're an attractive woman—"

"You don't like to fuck, also?"

I smiled, but did not say anything. Oh, yes, my darling, I was thinking, I'd love to fuck you, but the world is going too fast, speeding right by me; moving through space at spectacular speeds: I can't keep up with it.

I missed my wife and I felt that loss now, the good times we had had together, the fun times, the small jokes between us, the intimacy. I would never have her again. The past was a chunk ripped out of my heart.

Her breathing had deepened. She was on the edge of sleep. "What's this world coming to?" she said. "I have this problem—"

"What's that?"

"Life's been dealing me cards from the bottom of the deck for so many years pretty soon even the aces and kings start to look marked."

I thought to myself how peculiar it was: first Kelly, now Millie, comparing life to a card game. "Yeah," I said.

She looked over at me and gave me a heavy-lidded, languid look. Her eyes were barely open. "Kind of hard to trust the dealer behind that," she breathed.

I turned off the lamp next to the bed, rolled over and kissed her lightly on the cheek. She was already asleep.

I lay back and stared at the dark and began to ruminate about war, my deep night ritual. I was thinking about promises. We had been on a recon mission northwest of Saigon in what they called the Duong Minh Chau bastion, War Zone C, moving through a banana grove, through stands of bamboo and water palm. There was no gunfire, no evidence of the enemy. All was peaceful. Suddenly there was the sharp crack, a rifle shot—one shot, that was it, nothing more—and the man next to me fell. He had taken a bullet through the back. It had bounced around inside him, destroying his organs. His life was oozing out of him. The medics worked on him, but he was beyond saving. I knelt next to him.

Before he died I promised that if I got out of there alive I would visit his family and tell them about what kind of soldier he was.

He had come from a small town outside of Memphis, a cotton mill town that was dying when I finally got there. His father was a middle-aged black, a man who had worked all his life in the mill. His mother had died not long after he was killed. His father lived alone in a clapboard house not far from the closed-down mill. He was in his Sunday best when I came to call. The small living room was filled with pictures of his son from the time he was very young in short pants, to his high school days in football and track gear, to his days in the service, soldier-straight with an all-business look on his face.

The father began to weep when I spoke of his son and how he had soldiered and how he had died. "He promised me he would come home," he said, sobbing. He said it over and over, embarrassed at his sorrow, yet unable to control it. Nothing I could say would divert him from his son's promise. He could not come to terms with the idea that his son had not fulfilled his promise to him. His son would never break his promise and therefore his son could not be dead. "He promised me he would come home…"

And then, lying in bed now, I recalled a Colonel who had counselled me after a particularly bloody battle. My nerves were shot. I was burned out, and he told me this parable: In ancient times a king called in all the wise men of the land and asked them to instruct him how to govern. After ten years they returned with thousands of volumes for him to read. He told them that he could not, he hadn't the time: they must give him advice in a manageable way. They went off and returned ten years later—this time with only a hundred volumes. Again, he told them he had no time to read all of this. They must return again with a more manageable course of study. Five years later the king was on his deathbed. The wise men returned with one slim volume. The king was so sick he could not even look at the book. One of the wise men interpreted for him: "Man is born. He suffers. He dies."

I thought about this and I thought about Vietnam as I did always in the deep of night and then I was asleep also.

I was in a room writing a letter. I was writing to a town in a far-off land, apologizing to its inhabitants for the killings that had taken place there so many years before. I was worried. If every one had been killed who would be there to receive the letter?

I could see the back of a man seated in a chair. Another man moved near, holding a baseball bat. He swung the bat, hitting the seated man. He hit him over and over again.

There was a loud banging at the cabin door and I was awake now, my heart racing, my body drenched with sweat.

I looked over at Millie. She was fast asleep. She looked young, a teenager striving to appear older, her expression, child-like, innocent.

The man with the bat had been a dream. The banging on the door was not.

Chapter Seventeen

I got up and started for the door, glancing back at the bed. Millie was lying nude on top of the coverlet and I folded it back over her. "Who is it?" I called out.

"Just open up."

Millie was now awake. "Open it. It's okay," she said.

"What do you mean, it's 'okay'?"

"Police," the voiced called from the other side of the door. Millie moved past me. Naked, she opened the door.

A man came into the room. He wore a denim jacket, cowboy hat and boots; his face was friendly-looking, if damaged, with a gnarled, prize-fighter's nose and skin severely weathered by desert wind and sun.

Millie stood in the center of the room for a moment, then shaking the sleep out of her head, made her way back to the bed.

Outside, a ferocious desert wind was blowing. "Close the damn door, Butt Hole," Millie called to the man and he shut the door.

"Don't worry none," he said to me in a voice high-pitched and with a twang. His face was a map of lines, leathery skin, sun-cracked lips, prominent cheek bones, sandy hair, sprinkled with gray; raw-boned frame. He looked like your typical cowboy.

"This is Wild Bill," Millie said by way of introduction.

"Who the hell's that?"

"Her husband," the man said.

"Divorced."

"Not in the eyes of God."

"Shove it, Bill," Millie said. "I just thought the two of you should meet."

Wild Bill sat on the edge of the bed. He took out a small sack of makings, rolled a cigarette, and lit up. "You two been doin' the nasty?" he said.

"Hell, no," Millie said. "what do you think I am?"

"I know what you are. Damn whore, that's what you are."

Millie turned to me, unmoved. "Talk like that undermined our marriage," she said.

"Your fucking everything that walked undermined our marriage," Wild Bill said.

"That's your opinion."

"Right." Wild Bill turned his attention to me. "Millie tells me you're a friend of Travis'?"

"I know him."

"Helleva good kid. But he done a bad thing. Whacked three people."

"You know this for a fact?"

"I was the detective ran the case."

"Detective?"

"You thought I was kidding when I said, 'police'?" He reached inside his jacket and brought out a leather holder with silver badge.

"Head of homicide," Millie said.

"You got a thing for cops," I said. "First Bill here, then Richie."

"The dickless wonder!" Wild Bill let out a high-pitched whoop.

"Don't you wish," Millie said.

"Man's a pawn. Bought man. Fuck him!" Wild Bill stood and began to pace the room, inhaling deep on his cigarette.

"Bill's problem," said Millie, "he's an honest man."

"Way I was raised. But, look, I don't know what Travis told you, but he was guilty as shit. Now just get out this place here."

"Why's everybody so hot to get rid of me?"

"Want to save your ass," Bill said. "Bad people here. You're sniffing around about Travis, but who really knows?"

"He's giving you the office," Millie said. "Know how we met? He arrested me. I was a teeny-bopper. Burned me with my mouth, then wiped me out with my brain."

"What little brain you had in them days," Bill said.

"That's true. I was tweaking bunches then." She raised one bare leg from under the coverlet and displayed a tattoo. "Hey, Billie, this here one's new. This is a rattler, Mojave Green! Like it?"

"Great." Bill was glum, hardly looking at the coiled reptile.

"Most poisonous snake in the Southwest," Millie said.

Bill's attention was on me. "Goes over to the old guy's place, wants to shake him down for his money. Gets into an argument. Hit him with a baseball bat. Kids come running in, takes them out, too. We had him cold. Had the bat, had his finger prints. Millie told us what he told her."

"What about splinters under the finger nails?" I said.

"Had that."

"He said it was a different kind of wood from the bat."

"Way I see it," Wild Bill said, "splinter of wood is a splinter of wood. His attorney come up with that one." He turned to Millie. "Get dressed, I'll drive you back to town." He lifted her outfit from the chair where she had flung it and waved it at me. "Joke, huh? Get dressed…"

He threw the costume to Millie and she got into it and went to the mirror and began to fuss with her make-up. He passed me a business card. "My number. Have any questions, call. My best advice, though: get your ass out of here."

Millie was into her coat now, heading for the door. "Nice sleeping with you," she said.

"Did she sleep with you?"

"She said, 'no,' and to me, 'no' means 'no.'"

"She was lying balls ass naked next to you?"

"'No' means 'no.'"

Wild Bill walked to Millie who was waiting at the door just watching us, looking tired and disgusted. "Can we get him on sexual harassment, sweetheart?" Wild Bill said.

"He was a perfect gentleman."

Wild Bill cocked his finger like it was a pistol firing at my heart. "Take care," he said and he and Millie left the cabin.

I went to the window and watched them. They were stopped beside his car, in deep discussion about something. Bill opened the door and shoved Millie inside. He hurried around to the other side, got in, and I could see his hand came back. He hit her and she pushed away from him and started to get out of the car and he pulled her back and began to slap her over and over again.

She had her hands over her head, trying to protect herself and he continued to hit her. She leaned her head back on the seat and Wild Bill put the car in gear and drove off.

I returned to the bed. On the nightstand was a piece of jewelry Millie had left, a turquoise bracelet. I turned it over in my hand. Engraved on the back, it read: "Love Grandpa."

I said, the hell with it, no more sleep tonight, and splashed some water on my face and got out of the cabin and drove back toward Joshua Crest, thinking that I had stumbled into a pit of vipers.

The tattoos on Millie's extraordinary body told the tale. The most poisonous snakes in the Southwest. Yes, this place was definitely ugly and poisonous and I found myself thinking of Travis Wells and how he *was* innocent, done in by these reptilian desert folk. What should I do now? I was in this deep. I couldn't back off. But I had to have a plan of action. What was I looking for?

Poet had said that Millie knew he was innocent. She was the key. I'd have to win her confidence. But how?

And how dangerous was she to get close to? Snake tattoos. Snake soul.

I drove to the diner where I had been the night before. It was an all-night place and I had an early breakfast and there was a San Bernardino paper someone had left and I read it and then I got into a discussion with a huge, jelly-like trucker, a quivering mountain of bluster and bullshit wolfing down burgers by the handful, about the relative merits of Ted Williams and Carl Yazstremski and how many men had hit .400 in the history of baseball and who was the greatest player of all time. I said Babe Ruth. He insisted on someone called Mose Solomon.

"Never heard of him."

"They called him the Rabbi of Swat."

I laughed and he became heated and I saw he was serious. "Read your record books. Mose fucking Solomon, Jewboy, batted .375 for the New York Giants in 1923—"

"The Rabbi—?"

"—of Swat. That's right. Before the Giants he led the Southwest League in doubles, homeruns, runs, hits. Batted .421! That's the greatest hitter of all time! The Rabbi of Swat! The sheeny Babe Ruth—"

"Never heard of him."

"You don't know shit about the old days." He turned to me, fat face bathed in sweat and exasperation, breath rank enough to fell a wart hog. "The Giants brought him up at the end of the '23 season. John Magraw wanted him to stay on the roster for the World Series, but he wouldn't pay him extra. The sheenie said fuck you, went on to Columbus, Ohio to play pro football. Magraw said if he left he'd make sure he never played another game of major league baseball. Mose said kiss my ass. Magraw said, I'll show you kiss my ass! That was all she wrote for the Rabbi of Swat. Ruined him. The greatest hitter the game ever knew died in obscurity in Miami Beach in 1966. He was a bell-hop when he died."

"This is fantasy," I said.

"Look it up! The Rabbi of Swat!" Suddenly, for no apparent reason, he shifted the subject. "You been in the army?"

I didn't say anything.

"Seen combat?"

"About the Rabbi of Swat—"

"Forget the Rabbi of Swat! Look it up in your record book! You know Nam?" I didn't speak. "What do you know about it?"

"We're talking baseball—"

"You know shit. You been there?"

"I don't want to talk about it."

"Well, I been there, too."

"All right. We've both been there."

"I seen things there nobody should see. I was with the Americal Division when we went into Pinkville! You don't know shit!"

"Pinkville was My Ly," I said.

He leaned in to me to make his point. I found myself wishing he hadn't had garlic and clam sauce for dinner. "That's what everyone thinks! But there was *three* Pinkvilles! And Calley was sent in with a platoon and it was supposed to be all V.C. They fucked up! It weren't Calley. It was Westmorland fucked up. Wanted to fight on the U.S. terms, but you can't do that with the V.C. They was fighting the French for 25 years."

"I don't care. I don't want to talk about it."

"You don't know nothing!" the trucker yelled, spraying me with sweat and saliva.

"I know something," I said.

"What? What? Come on ass-face, tell me something!"

"Tell you what?" I said. He didn't answer. He began to grumble to himself. We didn't speak for a while. I thought about death.

He grumbled, without looking at me: "Mose Solomon was the best, what you could call an idiot savior." He rambled on, mixing baseball with war, the Rabbi of Swat with My Li and General Westmorland.

I did not follow him. I was lost in fog and death. I was thinking now of Millie and her snake tattoos and Wild Bill and Richie and Frog Phelan and the ugliness of the crime that had been committed here in Joshua Crest and how ugly the group of characters were who had been responsible for Travis Wells' conviction.

I thought, too, how rotten it was for Travis Wells to be serving a life sentence for a crime he didn't commit—if, in fact, he didn't commit it. I thought of the war, of the heroism I had seen in it, what men went through in battle; how some were taken prisoner by the enemy and tortured and how, under the most brutal of circumstances, there were those who did not crack. I thought how rare it was even for the bravest not to be crushed and broken by the force of life—not only in extreme cases like torture, but in jobs, marriages, relationships with children and friends; dreams; ideals. Who is not ultimately ground down?

I saw the faces of so many people who had been killed, comrades, enemy, children. The children were blisters on my heart.

I thought of Millie and her ex-husband. I thought about him beating her. And I thought of Travis Wells' mother, how life had worked her over, slaughtered her father, her children; sent her son to prison for life.

How to break through all this? How to find out who had done what to whom and why?

I drained my cup of coffee. The trucker was still expounding on Pinkville and the Rabbi of Swat: "You check your record books, there. You find that sheeny kike."

"I will." I was suddenly very tired. I got up and paid my check and started for the door. It was daylight outside. The man, relentless, called after me: "Babe Ruth would uppercut the ball. That's not the way to hit. Anyone'll tell you that."

"You're right," I said, mumbling, on my way to my car. I was talking into the wind, fed up, berating myself. "I'm wrong. Wrong about everything. About baseball. About war. Wrong. Wrong."

The air tasted like death. Morning in Joshua Crest was enough to make you throw up.

Chapter Eighteen

I drove to an Arco station and filled up with gasoline, then parked in a far corner of the lot and fell asleep. I slept for a couple of hours and woke hot and sweaty with sunlight stabbing into the car.

I washed in the men's room and had a cup of coffee from the take-out island. It had been there all night and had simmered down to a thick gunk that caused your teeth to ache, and, although I drank it, I couldn't help but think I would have been better off pouring it into the crankcase of the truck.

I had to gain something more from Travis, I realized. Should I tell him what I knew so far? He must know why Millie had turned on him.

What were the motives of Richie and Phelan and the others? How did Wild Bill Coty fit into it? I had to learn more from Travis.

Just past noon, I motored out of the town. I raced thunderclouds across the desert; they burst as I climbed the highway grade from Mojave to Tehachapi. The rain came in torrents.

It was late afternoon when I reached my house. I shaved and showered and cleaned up my battered face; then I drove to the prison. The rain had subsided but the air was heavy with moisture.

The guards at the bubbles eyed my swollen eyes and lips uneasily. On the lower level, I stepped out onto the yard.

The place was eerily quiet. I gazed on a scene that was bizarre and disquieting. A thousand men were lying spread eagle on the ground.

From the library, past the handball courts and weight pits, to the far cellblocks, they lay in the mud and rain.

Arms and legs apart, their faces thrust into the muddy ground, they lay there motionless.

I entered the library area. The anteroom was empty of guards. Even Macklin was not there.

Sergeant, alone, was in the library room. Hunched over a large legal volume, he looked even more gnome-like than usual. "They on search mode," he said in his raspy voice.

"I need to talk to Poet."

He smiled. "Be my guest. He's having himself a mud sandwich with the rest."

"What happened?"

"It were that dumb youngster, Blast. Got himself stabbed. They brought the boys outside so they could do a search for the shank." He studied my battered face. "Who did you like that?"

I shrugged. "Nothing," I said. "Misunderstanding. And Blast?"

"It weren't shit, one of them, 'I'll kill you motherfucker, there, there.' And he stabs Youngster in the fleshy part of the ass. He be all right. I was lucky I was here else I'd sucking mud, too."

We didn't talk for a while. Sergeant had pulled out a large law book and was looking for something. He found what he was searching out and took a note on it. "You think that's going to do any good?" I said.

He shook his head. "My case been lost a long time ago. This is for a friend. Says he's innocent."

"Is he?"

He shrugged. "Hey—everyone in here is innocent."

"What do you think about Poet's case?"

"What should I think about it?"

"Think he did it?"

Sergeant grew thoughtful. He nodded his head, rubbed his chin. "So many dudes in here claim they're innocent. Nobody likes people thinking of them as a killer. Oh, maybe some crazy youngsters looking to make a name. But most people don't even want to admit to *themselves* that they snuffed out another person's flame."

He didn't speak for a while. It had begun to rain again. The rain gusted against the library glass. "Damn, look at that," Sergeant said. He stood at the window, staring out at the rain. "With Poet something else going on. I been down almost twenty-five years. I've served up at Quentin and at Old Folsom. I know a lot of dudes killed people. This kid's not a murderer. I've been with him on the yard here, six years, right after he was sentenced and shipped. This isn't a killer."

"You think he's innocent?"

"I do. And I'll tell you, most guys on the yard who get to know him, know that this kid's innocent."

"It's painful," I said. "If a man's innocent."

"It is painful. I seen what it's done to this kid. He's changed in so many ways. He's changed cause he knows he's never going to get out of here."

I walked to the window. The rain was falling in a soft drizzle now. The men still lay there on the yard floor. "You were lucky," I said.

"Got in just before the alarm sounded. C.O. told me it was Blast, I had to laugh. Mexican dude got tired of his shit. Didn't want to kill him none. Just give him a nick."

He sat on the table-top. He lit up a cigarette. "You were in Moc Hoa that time?" he said. "What happened there? " I didn't speak. "I was at Kien Tong, not far," he said.

"Small world."

"Oh, yeah," he said. He sat there smoking.

"We probably got laid side by side, To Do Street," I said.

"I don't know about that." We didn't talk for a while. "A lot of folks were killed down there," he said. "We came into Tan Thoi the day after that thing happened." My heart was pounding heavily in my chest. He stared directly at me. "A lot of killing done there."

I gazed out at the rain. The men still lay spread-eagle on the ground. Wasn't this cruel and unusual punishment? "That morning when we went into Moc Hoa the V.C. were waiting for us," I said after a long while. I hadn't talked about this in years.

"I know this," he said.

"Weapons they captured from us, M-1's, carbines, Thompson subs, standard .30 caliber belt-fed machine guns, Browning Automatic Rifles."

"Oh, sure." He inhaled deeply on his cigarette.

I saw Moc Hoa in my mind's eye. "Terrain, the weather—perfect for an ambush." I was talking to myself now as much as to him. "The village was a short distance from a large canal."

"I know that," he said. "Creek there with tree lines on both banks. Conceal any movement there. I know that. I know Moc Hoa. There's an irrigation ditch—"

"That's right."

"Sure. Large dike following the edge of that ditch. Trees on top of the dike. I know this area, this terrain."

"You know what I'm talking about, then."

"Oh, sure."

"V.C. had foxholes dug into the dike under the trees. The dike was built up above the paddies in front like a levee."

"That's how they do it."

"Couldn't see anything, from either the ground or the air."

"You're talking about your tree lines there, they're banana and coconut, you got stands of bamboo and water palm. Oh, sure. This is typical."

"Undergrowth—"

"Thick motherfucker, right?"

"They dug their foxholes here—"

"Sure. Don't tell me. I seen this many times. No foliage disturbed. Cut them fresh branches, put them over the top and sides of them foxholes."

"From a low-flying L-19 spotter or a helicopter, all looks normal. And there was ground fog that morning—"

"You can't see nothing even from one of them L-19's. Or a helicopter. I know this so well."

"We had a support group of South Vietnamese. At the first barrage, they fall back. I'm trying to keep them in place, yelling out orders in a mixture of Vietnamese and pidgin English. 'Di, di!' I'm shouting."

"Yeah, 'Go!', but they don't move. Sure. I know them little sneaky motherfuckers."

"They huddle against the bank of the levee. Then they begin to retreat. They're flailing through the water of the rice paddies. I yell myself hoarse, then I'm pinned down. My men are taking it all about me—"

"Sure they are."

"Dying."

"I know this."

"I look for the South Vietnamese. They're no where to be seen now, lost in the fog."

"I heard all about this."

Why was I telling this? Why was I talking about it? "We lost a lot of men, a lot of dead and wounded. I could hear firing from the village, pop, pop, pop and I knew people were being executed."

"That's what they was doing."

"Killed all the women and children—"

"Because the village was friendly."

"That's right. Punishing us."

"Ain't that a motherfucker."

"Then the V.C. moved south."

We didn't speak for a while. My heart was surging now in my chest. My fingers trembled. Sergeant finished his cigarette. "I have to go," I said. "I'll see if I can talk to Poet in the morning." I started for the door to the yard.

"I remember the inquiry," he said. I waited at the yard door. The men were stretched out in the mud. The rain poured down. "There had been a second village below the dikes," Sergeant said. "There was some men went there."

"Tan Thoi," I said.

Sergeant was watching me with deep, dark eyes and I saw now what I had tried so hard not to see. My men, too, knew well how to kill. And the bodies were piled high that afternoon, piled in a huge pyre, women, children, old people. And it was set on fire.

And you could see the cloud of smoke for miles around once the fog had cleared. And you could smell the burning flesh.

The inquiry never dealt with that. And I never dealt with it.

"Let it go," Sergeant said.

The yard lieutenant moved into the library. "Your class is canceled today," he said. He noticed my battered face. "How'd that happen?"

"Batting cage. Baseball came back up and—bounced the wrong way."

"Lot of damage," he said. He turned to Sergeant. "You're supposed to be out there."

Sergeant and I walked onto the yard together. It continued to drizzle. "See if you can do something for that kid," he said to me. "For myself, I done what I done and I deserve what I get. Not the kid, though. The kid is innocent."

The lieutenant moved Sergeant off the walk. Sergeant got down on his hands and knees in the mud. Then he stretched out spread eagle like the rest of the men.

Chapter Nineteen

I slept badly that night. In the morning I returned to the yard and attempted to get Poet called up to the library. The men were on lockdown. No one could get out of the cell units.

I drove back out to Joshua Crest. It was late morning when I got there. I drove up the long drive to Kelly Wells' mansion. A maid answered the door, a diminutive Mexican. I could hear loud voices, a man and a woman's, from a room off the foyer.

The maid asked who I was there for and I told her it was all right and moved past her into the living room.

Kelly was seated on one of those large, overstuffed chairs upholstered in bright colored, zig-zag Navajo pattern. She was writing something. Richie stood above her. She finished and tore a slip of paper out of the maroon leather-covered book and handed it to Richie. It was a check.

When they realized I was in the room, they looked startled. I said, "Excuse me, I didn't know—" and Kelly waved her hand at me and said, "That's all right. He was just leaving." Despite the early hour, I could see she already was half in the bag. Richie started for the foyer. "So you'll take care of the other thing, too?" he said to Kelly.

"Don't I always?"

"Thought you left town," Richie said to me.

He had a little ratty smirk on his face and I wanted badly to hit him again. But this time I knew he'd use the .38 Special I was sure he had

189

under his jacket. I had the feeling he was itching to do me for good. In this town he was the law and who would fight my posthumous battle for me? "No such luck," I said.

He paused at the entranceway; looked me up and down with contempt. "You two make a nice-looking couple," he said. Then he left.

I waited at the entranceway, not knowing whether to come in or go out. "I didn't know—"

"What?"

"—you two were—friends."

"Hardly," she said. "Hate his fucking guts. Want something to drink?"

"Little early," I said. I moved into the room, catching sight of myself in the large antique mirror that ran along one wall. My appearance hadn't improved since I had last looked in a mirror.

There was dried blood caked about my mouth; the area around my eyes was swollen; I hadn't shaved in several days.

Kelly moved to the bar and poured herself a water glass-full of Glen Livet. "Breakfast," she said, sitting on the couch. She leaned back, stared at me.

"Spent time with your son's ex-girl friend last night."

"Richie know?"

I shook my head, no. "Her ex-husband did, though."

"Wild Bill Coty," she said. There was a trace of bitterness in her voice. "Part of the whole thing."

"He claims he's not. And the girl supports him. He says Travis is guilty."

"He's in like Flynn with the whole thing. They set my son up."

"Said your father was involved in dope."

"My father was a drunk who was just trying to get by in this life! They're the ones up to their eyeballs in dope!"

"Wild Bill, too?"

"I don't know," Kelly said. She shook her head and I could see there were tears in her eyes. She continued to shake her head for a while. "All I know is, they did this to my father, my kids."

She downed her drink and stared into the bottom of the glass and she looked sad and lost and I wanted to get out of there but I didn't move. "What was Richie here for?"

"Money."

"How does that go?"

"You don't know? You don't get it?"

"No, I guess I don't."

She looked directly at me and she did not appear drunk now or sad; just matter-of-fact. "He's my husband," she said. "Father of the little ones."

And suddenly she was weeping, hard. She buried her face in her hands and sobbed and sobbed and I went to her and held her and she was trembling in my arms, weeping so hard I thought she'd never stop.

And then she pulled away and stared at me and her face was bloated and tear-streaked and her expression was a bit crazed, but, also, strangely, there was something beautiful in her look. I think it was the love and pain she felt for her son. "And you think Richie killed his own kids?" I said.

"I know he did it."

"How do you know?"

"I just know." She began to cry again. She wept and wept. I held her close.

She turned her face toward mine and we kissed. Then she led me upstairs. "You don't even have to love me," she said. "You don't even have to like me."

We made love and it was passionate and pained for her, while for me—I was outside the whole thing, just watching both of us; watching myself and my life, not really involved. Just outside everything.

After, she lay back and lit up a cigarette. She smoked in silence for a while and I stared up at the ceiling, feeling completely separate from everything in this life. Small flashes of war, of combat, passed through my head.

"For a mercy fuck, you did all right," she said. "Can't believe you're a writer. Seem more like a cop."

I didn't say anything. "Soldier?" she said and I didn't move or say anything, but my mind was racing. And then she said: "In country?" And I was wondering, how did she know? Was it indelible on my being, a snake tattoo of the soul?

I must have nodded, but I don't remember that. I only remember lying there, numb, cut away from everything except small flashes of dead children like lightening in my mind. Kelly shook her head as though trying to make sense of something beyond sense. "You killed—?"

And I said, very softly: "Many times," and I ached inside. "Came out all fucked up—" Why was I telling her this? There was no sense to it, no sense to my life. Snake tattoo of the soul. She had seen it.

Somewhere I had read that holograms are magical in many ways: not only do they re-create reality in full dimension, they hold onto the complete image even when you shatter it. Take a section of holographic film representing, say, a child; cut that in half and then light it by laser: each half will contain the entire child. Divide these halves again and again, and the image of the child will remain in each diminishing section of film. Unlike normal photography, every fragment of holographic film contains all the information recorded in the whole.

Some of those who study this phenomenon insist that memories are distributed in our brains in this way. Like a holographic image, every fragment of our brains contains all our memory. And so, like the child dividing and remaining whole in the holographic photo, so the shattered bodies of the children at Moc Hoa did not fracture beyond what war had done to them; they did not fade or dissolve in my mind. Instead, they permeated every molecule of my memory and haunted me to this day.

I said to Kelly: "So I wrote a book. Married. Divorced. Went to work in the prison system, teaching writing."

She was sitting now, staring at me in disbelief. The connection. I had never given her the connection. "The prison system," I repeated, "where I got to know your son."

There was a long pause and she looked at me and her eyes were deep pools of disillusionment and her expression was dark with suspicion. "You know Travis?"

"Yes."

She didn't speak for a long time. "How does that go?" she said at last.

"He wrote about what happened to him for my class."

"Then you know he's innocent," she said.

"I *don't* know. That's why I came here."

"He didn't do it. You know it!" I didn't answer and she grabbed my arm and dug her nails hard into it. "He didn't do it! I swear to you! They set him up! They ruined his life!"

"Tell me about the Fat Lady," I said.

She got up out of bed, walked to her make-up table, lit another cigarette. She had a glass half-filled with liquor there and she took a drink and then began to brush her hair. She brushed her hair furiously as though she were trying to brush away the skin on her head. "She and her husband were in on it. That poor kid is going to rot there for the rest of his life! They set the whole thing up!"

I could see her face in the make-up table mirror and it was rigid with fury. "Why?" I said.

"The way things are here. They have it all sewed up. My father wouldn't go along. Travis loved my father. The two of them were going to do something, I don't know what it was—and they found out— through that little whore! She was playing Travis. I caught them together and I told her if I ever found her in bed in my house again I'd kick her tiny-hiney to hell and back! So she set him up. And it worked!" She began to cry again and now it was a wail of pain. "It worked," she said and she smashed the liquor glass against her reflection and the mirror shattered and she had cut her hand, not a bad cut, just a little slice on the fleshy part and she wrapped a piece of Kleenex over it and I was thinking, I'm almost through with my last seven years bad luck, what's this going to do to me?

"Where can I find the Fat Lady?" I said.

"They run a poker parlor just outside town. 'The Oasis.'" She entered the bathroom and I followed after her and she washed the blood off her hand and turned to me. "Why're you doing this?" she said.

"The idea of a kid spending the rest of his life in prison for something he didn't do—it doesn't set right with me."

I moved back into the bedroom and began to dress; she came back into the room. "Your father had splinters under his nails from the bat," I said.

"Whittaker ran tests. It wasn't the same kind of wood."

"The jury bought it."

"They brought in an expert and—"

"Think I'll go see Whittaker."

"He's as much as part of it all as any of them."

I was dressed now. She said: "You don't have to kiss me. It had nothing to do with affection."

I found myself nodding and fighting to find something to say and all I could think of was, hope I don't have seven more years of bad luck, and knew that was not an appropriate goodbye, so I said nothing.

She walked downstairs with me. At the door she said, "In the visiting area of the prison, in the ladies room, someone wrote on the wall: 'No light—darkness. No life—death. No science—magic. No justice—revenge.' I copied it down. I memorized it. I think about it all the time."

She wanted revenge. Of course she wanted revenge. And I had nothing to say about it. I just left and felt rotten about it, felt rotten about the whole thing.

Chapter Twenty

On the drive back through town, the empty feeling stayed with me. I felt old and tired, disgusted. I was nearly fifty. People will tell you that's middle-age, but how many men do you know who have lived to be a hundred?

When I was eighteen my Dad was seriously injured in an accident. He was a steelworker for Jones & Laughlin just outside of Pittsburgh. Working the second level of the open hearth, shifting rods to the regenerative furnace below, he fell from a catwalk and broke his pelvis. He spent months at home recovering and I would help him get around and I remember watching him as he sat bent over in pain on the edge of his bed and thinking, "How old he's become!" He was thirty-nine.

At Kelly's house I had caught sight of myself in the mirror and I was my father; I looked that old, that beaten. No, more so. My father had only been thirty-nine. I was nearing *fifty!* My body ached and it reminded me of those times when I was in high school playing football and how it would feel the day after a game and how quickly I would snap back and I thought of a lot of things that were nice about being young and I yearned for those days, at least yearned for my body to perform the same way, and then I felt stupid. The saddest thing, I told myself, is to spend your years of maturity waving back at your youth.

Alton Whittaker's suite of offices was in the old section of town, not far from The Tungsten Club. I parked and moved up the flagstone walkway to the building, a folksy house, really. Granite-stoned, covered with ivy, it reminded you, in its quaintness, of something that might be found in a French or English village.

I entered into a foyer and reception area, filled with heavy European antiques. I glanced at myself in the mirror. The angle of the light somehow washed my figure out. It was blue-gray, hazy. The light about me was diffused as though shot with some exotic Hollywood lens. My edges were blurred. A stranger stared at me. Someone fading. For an instant it was as though I had disappeared and a ghost had taken over.

A middle-aged receptionist directed me to Whittaker's office. It was down a narrow, wood-lined hallway. The office had a great deal of oak—table, bookcases, paneling, beams. Whittaker sat behind the massive desk, his handcrafted, silver trimmed cowboy boots up on the desktop. His balding head reflected the Tiffany-style overhead light above the desk.

He pointed me to a chair and gazed at me, smiling. He toyed with a rubber band, stretching it and snapping it, waiting for me to speak. When I remained quiet, he said, "You look like all kinds of shit. I imagine you don't feel too good neither."

"Got that right."

"Well. What's rubbing your hemorrhoids wrong?" He grinned as though we were old friends. "This Travis Wells thing? Got you all keyed up? Just relax. Just simmer down. Travis Wells was as guilty as any man I've ever defended." His voice was low, folksy.

"The bat was white ash. The wood splinters as I understand it—"

"Smoke and mirrors. Got some professor over at Bakersfield College testify about cellulose composition, wood fibers all kind of mumbo-jumbo to just sow some *doubt*." He leaned forward and inserted a coin in an antique gumball machine behind the desk. "Gumball?"

He gazed at me and for the first time I realized there was something off-center in his look, something tense and unattractive. I couldn't figure out what it was, but it made you feel uncomfortable. I wondered how it went over with a jury.

I shook my head, no. Whittaker stuffed several gumballs in his mouth. "But we had his *girlfriend* come into that court and she testifies—"

"I know."

"And then the dog—that was very persuasive with the jury—"

"There were other people the dog would know…"

"Ray's ex-wife—"

"The Fat Lady—?"

"—was out at her club. Her husband, also. Travis's mother—she had an ironclad alibi. Who else?"

"The girl friend. The dog knew her."

"Tried to work that angle. Jury wasn't buying it."

I didn't speak for a long moment. Whittaker continued to snap the rubber band. "Did you want to get him off?" I said at last.

He wasn't smiling now. He stared out the window. "I'll tell you the truth, no. That doesn't mean I didn't give him the best defense his mother could buy. But *I knew* he had done this crazed, brutal act. And somewhere, I guess, I didn't want him out to do something like that again."

"Did you try, really, to get him off?"

"God's honest truth. And I don't take the Lord's name in vain. You got one big problem when you're defending someone who *you know* is guilty. There is no defense you can put up that makes any rational sense. And juries feel this."

I wasn't getting anywhere with Whittaker. He admitted he had had no real belief in his client, no true interest in saving him. Kelly had been right about that. With that, he had copped to about as much as he was going to. What were his motives? Was it as he insisted: He had done his best, and was unable to come up with a defense that worked? Or had he purposely set out to do Travis Wells in?

What was he thinking? Was he above-board or toying with me? Perhaps he was honest; perhaps it was just his damn lopsided gaze that made him look so guilty.

I got up to leave. "You making a mistake," he said.

"Really? About what?"

He didn't answer me. "What are you going to do? You're going to be writing an article?" I didn't say anything. "Write your article, whatever, but the kid was guilty. And you see there's another reason you're getting people *edgy*."

"What's that?"

"While back this area took some heat, big Federal dope bust, a lot of people got hurt bad. Not a bunch o' brain-fried desert-rat hippy-dippies. People of standing in the community."

"Phelan's brother?"

He looked somber, genuinely saddened. He stared at me and it was lopsided, disconcerting. Something with his face—it was out of kilter. "Great blow to the Phelans. This was the baby of the family, all right he was a little misguided, but a Federal Court gives him fifteen to life. This was quite a blow here."

"Phelan's brother goes to jail and there're still prominent people messing with that?"

"I didn't say that. This is a small town, but I don't know everything going on here. I'm just saying, this is a good place to live. Good All-American place to raise your children. I don't think we need another black eye."

I was at the door now, Whittaker right next to me. There was a thin line of sweat on his upper lip. "The Fat Lady's joint, where is it?" I said.

"Barstow road, beyond the motel." He looked at me with grave, lugubrious eyes. "Can't really appreciate how vast that desert is out there till you get into a car and drive those back roads. While back, couple of ladies on their way to Death Valley, took a wrong turn. Were a hundred yards over a rise from the town. Found their bones months later. Desert disorients people. Lot of bodies out there."

"Is this a threat?"

"Just want to caution you. Driving the back roads, get lost, who knows when you'll be found? Not enough even to identify you. Coyotes, buzzards, pick your bones clean."

He winked at me and it was a thick, clumsy gesture and suddenly I realized what was so disturbing in his gaze: his right eye was glass.

Chapter Twenty-One

I drove along through desert vastness. Great thunderheads loomed on the horizon. I could see a slash of neon on the horizon and I headed toward it.

The wind had started up and sand began to blow across the road and the neon on the horizon would appear, then fade in the blowing sand.

It was dusk now. I kept on and it seemed I would never reach that smudge of neon off in the distance.

At last I came above a rise and there it was, a neon sign proclaiming, "The Oasis Poker Parlor—High and Low Ball—Hold 'em". There were three cars in the dirt lot in front of a concrete block building. I parked my truck and got out.

The wind was blowing harder now. The cars in the parking lot rocked in the wind. The air was sweet with the smell of sage and manzanita. Everything felt gritty. The sun was just going down behind me and I shielded my eyes from the blowing dust. The stuff got into my mouth and my eyes and into everything.

The club was not elaborate, cement floor and walls, a long bar, a dozen tables, a few tacky wall hangings with a Western theme—a cowboy on a bucking bronco, men around a campfire, several horse-shoes and branding irons.

There was action only at one table where two cowboys sat hunched over their cards. A mountainous woman, The Fat Lady, I was sure, make-up thick as putty, perhaps sixty years old, was dealing. She had a ring on each of her thick fingers and I couldn't help but think that once on those rings would never come off. The flesh seemed to have grown around them.

There were several other people at the bar and a skinny twig of a man behind the bar: he was gray and wrinkled and he reminded me of wood that's been baked in the sun for years.

"Down and dirty," proclaimed The Fat Lady, "the game is Hold 'em, quarter a hand, table limit. What's you pleasure?"

I took out a twenty and passed it to her; she exchanged it for chips. The play went on. Despite her thick mitts, the Lady dealt with a professional's casual ease and dexterity.

"Bet to the Queen," she said. "Take another?" There were various grunts from the cowboys, clicks of chips, nods. We played several more hands. The cowboys busted out. It was just me and The Fat Lady now. "What's your pleasure?" she asked.

I was down to my last five chips. I put out one chip. "Cut the cards," I said. We played a desultory game of high card, low card. I won a few; she won a few. She was bored. The place was cool—an ancient swamp cooler groaned away behind the bar—but she was perspiring. "Where you from?" she said and I knew she couldn't care less.

"Near Bakersfield."

"What brings you here?"

"Writing an article."

She continued without looking at me. "You're that guy," she said.

"I guess I am. Murder happened here a couple of years ago," I said.

She paused to stare at me and her gaze was hard. "What of it?"

"I heard you were involved."

"Plain horse*shit*! I was involved with *shit*!" She shook her head hard and the wattles under her chin sprayed perspiration on the table. "Tried to pin it on me. Said I knew where the money was. Said the dog knew me, said this, said that. Only problem was, fifteen people told 'em I was right here, dealing cards. Kid done it. Don't have to be no genius to see that."

"Your grandson?"

She snorted in derision and looked around her as though pleading her case to a roomful of people. "No way. I was Ray's third wife. Buried the two before me, tried to bury me. Old bastard could be nasty. Always on you for this and that, I'm humping this guy, I'm humping that one, none of it true." She paused, trying to contain herself, then roared on, talking not really to me, just rambling: "One day, there's this guy worked construction out by Kramer's Corners where they're putting up these big power lines. We get to drinking and one thing leads to another and I do hump him. First one I ever done it with. So then I come home and tell Ray, 'I'll never go to bed with you again, ugly butt-hole. I did the ring-dang-doo this afternoon with someone who was so fantastic.' And he won't believe me. When I wasn't doing it he's always accusing me, but when I do it, he won't believe me. 'You bag of shit,' he says, 'that never happened.' Boy, did I get a laugh out of that."

She shuffled the cards over and over, cutting them, making precise stacks with them, then reshuffling them. "It was that snot-nosed kid who done Ray. Carrying on with this slut, she threatens to leave, he needs money. No, sir, don't have to be no genius."

"Some people think he's innocent."

"Some people. Some people believe a crew of Martians killed John Kennedy. I don't want to talk about it. Aggravates my gastritis. What're you, a cop?"

"Also heard there was a dope angle, that Ray was involved."

"You're tramping on some sensitive stuff here," she said. Her voice had gone high and shrill. "You're just behaving like an asshole. What're you, out of your fucking mind? You're going to stick your nose in that?"

"I heard that this dope thing was a major industry in these parts—"

She slammed the deck of cards down on the table and began furiously racking chips. "Get out of here!"

"I just heard—"

Get out of here!" she bellowed. "This table's closed!"

The old guy behind the bar moved over to us. "Problem here, toots?"

"This guy's a dilly. Hassling me—"

"You a dilly, mister?"

"Who the fuck knows," I said.

"Let's keep it decent," the old guy said.

"He is a dilly!" the Fat Lady crowed.

"I believe you are" the old guy said.

"Goin' on about Ray's death—"

He moved up very close to me. His eyes were wide and watery and he smelled of sour sweat and cigarettes. "What's your beef?"

"No beef. I just explained, I'm doing an article."

"Well, the lady has suffered enough over this tragic incident. Now take a walk." His frail chest was right up against me; he wheezed when he talked.

"Excuse me, old timer."

"Don't old timer me, get your ass in gear!"

"Look, I don't want any—"

The old timer thrust his chin up at me. "What? You want a piece of me?"

"Don't want to hurt you. Don't want to hurt anybody—"

He nodded his head in a knowing manner, as though he were privy to a secret no one else possessed. Jaw thrust forward, he barked: "Hurt me. Come on, hurt me. I love for you to hurt me."

I reached forward and grabbed his shirt front and flung him to one side. He went right down, skidded across the floor and landed with a loud thunk at the base of the bar. "That weren't no fair fight," he yelled. "Fight fair. I'll show you a thing or two." He was on his feet now, pleading with The Fat Lady: "Belle, I could've taken him. He didn't fight fair."

"Shut up, Geezer!" She pushed by him and waddled over to me.

"You just pissed me off, mister."

"Look, I had no beef with the geezer," I said. "I'm sorry."

"*Sorry*," she shouted. "Come in here, toss the Geezer across the floor like he's a sack o' shit, and you say you're *sorry!*" She was right up to me now, her face pale with anger, enormous breasts heaving with anger. She quivered as she spoke. "Come in here, accuse me of *killing* someone—"

"Lady, look here. I never—"

"Mistreat the elderly!" Her voice was a wail now, ear-splitting. She was as angry as anyone I had ever seen. "The Geezer here, treat him like he's a *sack o' shit!*"

Her face was in my face, the enormity of her right up against me. Suddenly she reared back and walloped me. Her punch was like a fistful of concrete, like the kick of a horse. There was a poker table behind me and I went into it, then clear over it.

I got up, embarrassed. The Fat Lady was rolling up her sleeves. Damn. Before I had a chance to do anything she was on me, belting me with lefts and rights, slamming them at me from every angle, heavy punches and hard which shuddered my whole body, jolting me even to the nerve-endings of my teeth.

She was getting off like a trained heavyweight. Everything was spinning lights, numbness, floor, ceiling and walls tilting and rotating around me, an intense shrill sound, a fire alarm ringing in my ears. I was aware, dimly, that I was in trouble, that the alarm was in my head. "Left hook, Belle, left hook," The Geezer was shouting.

"Shut up," she yelled back as she continued to clobber me. She had me around the neck now and was slamming my head into the wall. I felt everything begin to go hazy and I fought to get out of her grip and she tossed me around like a rag doll.

The Geezer had the door open now and The Fat Lady pushed me toward it and I tried to get in a punch and she slugged me again and I was stumbling backward. The Geezer was on me now, trying to stomp on my groin. I tossed him to one side and The Fat Lady drove into me with her shoulder and I hit the ground.

I was on my ass in the grit and gravel of the parking lot. The Fat Lady stood framed in the doorway to the club.

My mouth was thick with blood. Again. I spat and staggered to my feet. "What you got under that dress, a pair of balls?" I yelled.

"Come here again, jagoff," she yelled back, "you may get better, but you won't get well, no good, skinny-assed motherfucker. My face is your case." She waved a meaty fist at me. "Want to find out about my balls, come on. Yessiree. Is a frog's ass waterproof?"

I started back to my truck. I could hear The Fat Lady screaming curses at me—butt-hole this and butt-hole that, "Sometimes you eat the bear, jagoff, sometimes the bear eats you!"—on and on—then the door to the club slammed, and with effort I climbed into my truck.

Oh, I was whipped, beyond feeling old and disgusted, way beyond that now. My body no longer ached: I could feel nothing. I was numb. What was happening to me? What had this town done to me? Physically, I had always been able to handle myself. I had been a prize-fighter in my younger years in the service, and after. I had been good. There was a time that I had even considered making boxing a career. Lucky I had changed my mind, I was now thinking. Ass whipped by an elderly, fat woman. This town had taught me a *lesson*. I had just been whopped good by a sixty-year old woman. Damn, what was happening in the world?

I looked in my side mirror and tried to get some of the blood off with a handkerchief, but there was just too much, old blood, new blood.

What the hell was I doing here? Phil Kleinmutz had been right: these desert folk were meaner than scorpions. What the *hell* was I doing here?

My kids liked to jump rope and they had a little ditty they sang; and I found it now bumping around in my head: "Not last night, but the night before/ Twenty-four robbers came knocking at my door./ I ran out as they ran in/ And this is what they told me:/ 'Little Spanish Dancer do the splits./ Little Spanish Dancer do high kicks./ Little Spanish Dancer touch the ground./ Little Spanish Dancer get out of town.'"

I considered just giving up on the whole thing, leaving Travis Wells to his fate, going back to my life. Snake-bit and ass-whipped as I was, I considered it. But I knew that I couldn't, I wouldn't.

I opened the truck door and spat out a mouthful of clotted blood and told myself, no sir, when I departed this town it would be on my own terms, when I wanted to go.

I wouldn't be leaving soon, *fuckers*. No one was going to *run* me out.

Chapter Twenty-Two

I didn't have to wait long for my resolve to be challenged. As soon as I pulled out of the lot things began to go weird. I heard this great engine roar, then the sound of gears angrily meshing; headlights came bouncing toward me.

There was a dirt road running behind the club and a truck moved out of that road, an immense off-road machine with raised shocks and massive balloon tires.

I turned onto the highway, heading toward Joshua Crest. The truck hurtled after me. It drove up very close and then snapped on its rooftop fog lights and high beams. I adjusted my mirror to cut down the blinding glare and tried to race away, but the monster continued on right behind me, bearing down on me. I don't know what size motor it carried under the hood but the clamor in the night was like a tandem of eighteen-wheelers.

It pulled right alongside me and the roof fog beams were swiveled on me and I was momentarily blinded by them; then the truck went ahead of me half its length and angled in toward me and I moved to the edge of the road. It backed away and let me go ahead and then came roaring after me. I could see two men in the truck; the fog beams wouldn't let me make out who they were, but they seemed to be laughing. They were playing cat and mouse.

They got behind me and tapped my rear bumper and then let me pull away. They then sped up until they were alongside me, then cut into me. Then they went ahead of me, then dropped back, playing this taunting game at eighty plus miles an hour.

We went on about a mile or so like that. At last they just tired of the game and they cut hard in against me and I went off onto the shoulder of the road and spun out in sand.

I got the truck going and went a ways off road and then I was really mired deep in sand and couldn't go anywhere and the large truck, its fog beams directly on me, came roaring at me.

It stopped a few feet before my front bumper and two men got out and started for me.

Blinded by the beams, I couldn't make out who they were. As they came up to the door of my truck, I pushed hard on it, and jumped into the sand.

I was running into dark. I could hear footsteps slamming the ground after me. I could hear their desperate breathing and the pounding of their feet in the sand. Fear will ride herd on you and I ran as I hadn't since the rice paddies and buffalo grass of Vietnam and I widened the distance between us.

A gunshot cracked the night. I had a terrible sinking feeling; I heard myself say out loud, Oh, no and, though I felt no pain, wondered if I had been hit.

A voice, hoarse, breathless, called out to me: "Just hold it right there. Or you're fucking dead, guy."

I stopped, turned. The two men came right up to me. One had a flashlight which he shined directly into my eyes. I put my hand up to shield myself from the light.

I could make out who it was: Richie. Of course. *Guy.* With him was a very large man in cowboy duds. Both were heaving with exertion.

"What is this?" I said.

The cowboy grabbed me and pushed me toward their truck. I could see now it had police markings on it. "Get in," Richie gasped. A thick vein stood out on his forehead. The cords of his neck appeared about to explode.

"What's the problem?"

"You don't know, you cocksucker?" he shrilled at me. *"You don't know?"* Eyes wild, face flushed and swollen, he raged out of control. *"You don't fucking know!"*

"Know what?"

He grabbed me hard and shoved me inside the truck. He smashed my face into the dashboard. We drove off. They had me between them. The cowboy was driving.

My mouth was bleeding again; my nose also. I leaned my head back to try to stem the bleeding. "You look like rat puke," Richie said.

"What is it?" I said. "Can't seem to make friends around here. What is it? My deodorant?"

Richie snatched a snub-nosed .32 out from under his jacket and he shoved it against my forehead. "How would you like a second asshole right between your eyes?'" He pushed hard against my head. The barrel of the revolver dug into the bone.

He had a sap in his other hand and he punched me hard in the stomach and all the wind went out of me and I clutched my mid-section and tried to suck in some air and he hit me on the side of the head and now I was on the floor of the truck, curled into a fetal position, saying to myself, Jesus, not another one; not *another* beating.

He grabbed me by the hair and yanked my head up. "You're in some big trouble, guy," he said. "I mean big. Big, big trouble."

And he hit me again. His hand with the sap in it felt like a ton. And again. And again. It didn't hurt. Just this enormous numbness spread over my body. *"Cocksucker! Cocksucker! Cocksucker!"* he yelled over and over. A small voice in my head said, "Fuck it all." And everything went black. Mercifully.

Chapter Twenty-Three

"C'mon, get up. Hey, get up!" There was something bright and harsh stabbing at my eyes. My whole body ached terribly. I realized I was on my back on a cold concrete floor and an overhead light was shining on me.

Someone was kicking me and yelling in my ear. I turned my head and the pain increased, my neck, my jaw, the top of my head. I tried to move my hands and realized they were cuffed to something metal, a bed frame.

I was in a jail cell. Richie and the prosecutor, Corcoran, were standing above me. Corcoran was kicking at me, not hard, just nudges. "Let's go," he said. A beefy jail-cop leaned down and uncuffed me and dragged me to my feet. It was the man whose nose I had broken at the Tungsten Club. His eyes and nose were puffy and discolored, but he was smiling. He was gazing at me, strabismic eye and all, and enjoying the sight.

"What going on here?" I said through swollen lips. "What happened here?" I put my hand up to my face. My fingers felt my face, but my face could not feel my fingers. My face had no feeling and that was a little scary. It did not seem like a face; much too big, immense, in fact. It felt like a basketball.

They didn't say anything. The jail cop cuffed me again, then led me out of the cell and pushed me ahead of him down a cinder-block hallway, which smelled strongly of piss and, weaker, disinfectant. There were smears of what looked like blood on the walls. I staggered and almost fell and the jail cop grabbed me and continued to push me forward.

"You got the brains of a fucking flea," Corcoran said.

"What's going on here?" I said. I thought I might be dreaming all this and I demanded of myself to wake up, but the whole thing continued.

We came to a steel door; the cop unlocked my cuffs. "In there," Richie said.

It was a police squad room, greenish in color, reeking of stale smoke and perspiration. There were windows on one side, coated with dust so thick daylight barely could make it through. There was a bright overhead fluorescent light.

Three detectives got up and stood in a line and Richie shoved me in among them at the center. As I was the only one there with a face like chopped hamburger, I was sure no one would have any difficulty picking me out as a perpetrator of something. "Bring her in," Corcoran said.

A side door opened and a cop brought in the desk clerk from the Desert Flower Motel. She didn't look a fraction of a second at any of us before she said, "Him." She was pointing at me, of course. "What happened to him? He sure looks like one big hunk o' shit." One of the detectives lit up a cigarette and handed it to her. She gulped at it, coughing the smoke out.

"He was suicidal," Corcoran said. "He was beating his head against the jail cell bars."

"Yeah, well, some people should kill themselves. Criminal class, you know?"

"Yes." Corcoran said.

"Asshole fooled me," she said. "Never figured him for a desperado. Thought he was John Q. Law for sure."

She was taken out through the door she had entered and the detectives immediately began occupying themselves with other tasks. "What is this?" I said to Corcoran.

Richie lunged at me and hit me and knocked me to the floor and began to kick at me. The other detectives jumped on him and tried to pull him off. He was screaming: "First my kids. Then her!"

"What are you talking about?" I said. My mouth was filled with blood again; blood was pouring from my nose; and the basketball that was my head felt as though it was about to explode.

One of the detectives, tall, with a moustache, yanked me to my feet and shoved me out the door and down another hallway to a small, windowless room. Another shorter detective followed after.

In the room, they uncuffed me. The tall detective offered me a cigarette, which I refused; he gave me a Styrofoam cup of cold coffee.

The short detective read me my Miranda rights. "Look," I said. "I don't know what's going on here. Richie and another guy grabbed me, beat me, I wake up in jail. What is it?"

"You killed his girl friend," Shorty said. "The stripper—

"Millie Coty," the other detective said.

"*What*?" I wasn't sure I had heard right. I could feel my heart racing wildly. My whole body went weak. Millie Coty *dead*? And they were trying to get me for it!

For the first time since coming to this godforsaken place, I was truly frightened. This was deep, deep *shit*. Murder, deep. Dear, God. How do you claw your way out of this?

They had set Travis Wells up and he was one of their own. It would be a cinch to railroad me. What could I do?

The two detectives sat there just watching at me, waiting for me to offer something. My mind was chaos. Images of the night before whirred in my head, slide projector clicking through scenes: swirling dust, flare of a cigarette in my truck, greasy walls of the motel room. And Millie, naked on the bed, her body alabaster, precise snakes curled across its whiteness. And, then, she was being slapped. And then her ex-husband drove off with her. And then someone killed her.

"I want to see a lawyer," I said. Neither of the detectives reacted. It was as though I hadn't spoken at all. "Phil Kleinmutz. His office is in Bakersfield."

The tall detective sat on the edge of the table just above me. The short detective walked to one corner of the room. He didn't look at me for a long time. "You're in some real shit," the tall detective said quietly. "Don't take this lightly."

"I'm not."

"That's good. 'Cause this is some shit you're not going to get out of."

They started pounding me with questions. I barely was aware of what they were saying but this much was clear: some time that morning Millie Coty's battered body had been found just off the Barstow Highway. She had been beaten. She had been shot through the eyes. The back of her head had been blown away.

I was the last person known to have been with her. I knew differently but I wasn't going to say anything until I had an attorney.

The detectives were determined to open me up. They kept coming at me, first one, then the other, bombarding me with questions, shouting, cajoling, threatening . Maybe I had a right to an attorney, but I didn't see anybody making an effort to get me one.

They went at me for what seemed an eternity, though it probably wasn't more than an hour or so. They slapped me around, but not too much.

I guess they figured they couldn't do more than had already been done.

"Why the hell would you kill her?" the tall detective kept saying over and over. "Nice piece of trim like that. Why?"

"I didn't kill her," I tried to say; I choked on the blood in my mouth. "Get me Phil Kleinmutz."

The detective slapped me lightly across the face. He just went across my face, back and forth, very softly, almost caressingly. He seemed to care for me. "Don't be Mr. Peckerhead," he said. "Come on, let's play a little ball, you give me something, I give you something back. We build some trust, here."

"Fuck him," the short guy said, spitting in a corner. He turned on me. "Fuck you in the ass. Perverted bastard. Mess up a beautiful piece of trim like that? Fuck you in the ass."

"Call my lawyer."

"You tell us what happened," the tall, pleasant detective said, "we'll work you up a murder two. Seven and a half years with good time and you'll be out."

"It's my turn," I said.

"For what?" hard guy Shorty said.

"To say, 'Fuck *you* in *your* ass.'"

He would have hit me really hard if the other guy hadn't stopped him. Then, again, maybe he did. Things went black again.

Chapter Twenty-Four

I'm not sure if I passed out or just fell asleep, but I was lying on a steel cot in a jail cell when I heard voices down the hallway. I opened my eyes. My face was up against the concrete wall, my cheek grazing the word, "Lobo", where someone had scrawled "Desert Lobo." A lone cockroach lambada'd across the scrawl. From the next cell, the sound of snoring rip-sawed the air which was thick and dank and reeked of a body stench so stercoraceous it caused me to gag, fetid underwear, putrefying socks, god knows what else.

It's stunning how we're defined by our surroundings. In a jail cell I was a criminal. I felt an immense loneliness, abandonment. Family, esteem, accomplishments, *a sense of who I was*, had fled me. Concrete and steel proclaimed I was a loser and that was it, that was me.

I thought of the men in Tehachapi and realized that whatever humanity they ever had had, prison had canceled that mail. In the jail block now, the walls exuded despair, hopelessness. And danger.

There was a fury just below the surface. You could feel it in the stone and steel. I was a captive of it and my own imagination. It pressed down on me.

When you are trapped in the lower depths you become a soul of the lower depths. That is your identity. You cannot be otherwise. You attempt to tell yourself you don't really belong here. This is a mistake.

You're not a *criminal.* This is temporary—but—but—deep down you feel that all of this is right. You deserve this. This is where you belong.

People become their circumstances: a cop puts on the uniform, he's a cop to the core; the man who steals, a thief, murders, a murderer. You have done nothing and yet you are where the criminals are, and so, this is what you are.

If you've ever returned to the home of your childhood, you know this. No matter where you've been or what you've accomplished, you are what you were as a child. Every corner, every alleyway, every playground cries out how insignificant you once were. And when you meet old friends, the relationship at light's speed reverts to what it had once been. You can't hide from yourself. Money, fame, accomplishment—none of it will protect you.

We are always two things: what we had been in our early years and what we are at this very moment. We are nothing in between. Nothing in between can rescue us. Captive of memory and present circumstance, the man, who as a joke, decides to be a convict for a day, will discover how deep in his soul he truly is a convict. A man, lost and pathetic as a kid, returning home, will once more be lost and pathetic.

I thought of this and other things in that stinking jail cell. None of it caused me to feel any better about what was happening to me.

Footsteps approached and my cell door opened and the jail cop entered. He put on the handcuffs and led me out into the hallway to a room beyond the cells where Phil Kleinmutz was waiting for me.

The cop pushed me into a chair and removed my cuffs. "They did a job on you," Kleinmutz said.

"Yes," I said, but barely: my tongue was thick, the inside of my mouth caked with blood and swollen.

"He was depressed," the strabismic cop said, voice serious, funereal, bad eye shifting clumsily in its socket. "He tried to commit suicide." He sighed, weighted down by the obligations of justice. He left the room. I pictured him flicking me the finger as soon as the door swung shut.

"You should be in the hospital," Kleinmutz said.

"I'm all right." My voice was hoarse, raw. "I'm happy to see you."

"Look at this. Look. I lost two pounds." Kleinmutz showed me a notch on his belt. "Colonics."

"Two pounds?"

"Isn't that great?"

"One dump, that's all it is."

"This is two pounds of body fat. This is not caca."

I laughed. It hurt, but I couldn't help it. Someone had tried to play soccer with my face and Kleinmutz was singing the praises of therapeutic defecation. I laughed and laughed and Phil watched me, grinning sheepishly.

"Oh, it's so good to see you, Phil," I said at last. "I was really getting worried. I'm surprised. I just never—I figured they would just, they would never—"

"What do you mean?"

"I figured that they—they just wouldn't call."

"They didn't," he said. "No one called. I was driving to Mojave for a court date. Heard it on the radio. Stripper was raped and murdered. You had taken her—where? Motel?"

"We were at a motel, but nothing happened. I didn't kill anybody. They didn't call you?"

"They were determined no one was going to see you. Phelan's coming down now, middle of the night. Wants to steamroll the arraignment. They're intent on doing a number on you. They want to send you up in the worst way."

"I was with her at the motel. Nothing went on. She had called her ex-husband—"

"Why was she there?"

"She was the girlfriend of the kid—"

"What are you doing, Paul? Are you crazy?" Kleinmutz was serious now, upset. "I warned you about this place, not to fuck with these people."

"Said she was willing to talk with me, took me out to this motel—"

"A motel to *talk*?"

"I needed a place to stay. She knew this motel—"

Kleinmutz shook his head. He walked away from me and continued shaking his head and I was feeling stupid and vaguely sick. I had come into this whole thing like some naive kid playing cops and robbers and now I was in it, deep. I could tell by Kleinmutz's expression that he was genuinely worried. "This is a son-of-a bitch," Phil said. "A fucking son-of-bitch." He took a deep breath and continued to shake his head and pace the room. "Damn. Damn."

"Phil, this is what happened—she takes me out there, then she calls her ex-husband to pick her up—"

"Ex-husband?"

"Homicide detective, Coty—"

"Wild Bill?"

"You know him?"

"Wild Bill Coty. Crazier'n a shithouse rat."

"So he drives out to the motel and picks her up. They're in his car and I'm watching from the window. He begins to slap her around, then they drive off."

"You think he killed her?"

"How would I know? I'm telling you he was beating her—"

"They question him?"

I shrugged. I didn't know. "I didn't tell them about him. I wanted to wait until I saw you."

"This is great. You're accused of killing the ex-wife of a *homicide* cop. Great."

The door opened and Phelan and Corcoran came into the room. There were two uniformed cops with them.

Phelan didn't look at me. He took Kleinmutz to one side. Corcoran joined them. Phelan lit up a cigarette which he smoked through a short ivory holder. Though they were ignoring me, I could hear every word that was said. "Boy here got himself in a mess," Phelan said.

"I'd like to hear what the prosecution—" Kleinmutz began.

Corcoran cut him short. "We got a case, Phil, believe it."

"What about Bill Coty?"

"What does he have to do with anything?" Corcoran said.

"Paul told me he picked his wife up at the motel."

"Isn't he the one went on vacation?" Phelan said.

"Yeah, he went on vacation," Corcoran said. "Left last night."

"Convenient," Kleinmutz said.

"So you understand now," Corcoran said, "I'm asking for no bail here."

"No bail? You must be kidding."

"Murder One, special circumstances," Corcoran said.

"Phil, looks like your boy here took the wrong train," Phelan said.

"Explain that to me, Judge," Kleinmutz said, "I'm getting a little dense in my mid years."

"You take the wrong train," Phelan said, "and every station you come to is the wrong one."

"All right," Kleinmutz said.

"We'll work this out at the arraignment," Phelan said. "How's that, boys?" He started for the door, then moved back to Kleinmutz. "You know about the gerbils, Phil?"

"What about them?"

"The homos been using them, *gerbils*, they're like hamsters, shoving them up their ass for a thrill."

"What kind of thrill's that?" Kleinmutz said.

"They're getting fucked and the gerbil's really getting pounded and he's squirming and that's a thrill." He sucked in smoke, savored it. "Course I only know from what I hear."

Corcoran was smiling. "Cruelty to animals," he said.

"Well, there's two gerbils in a pet store—you hear this one?"

"No," Kleinmutz said.

"Well, this flaming queen comes in, prancing around, looking at the pets. And the one gerbil says to the other, '*Quick, bark like a dog!*'" He laughed his deep, resonant laugh and Corcoran laughed till tears came to his eyes. "What do you think?" Phelan said to Kleinmutz. "Pisser ain't it?"

"You ought to go on T.V., Judge," Kleinmutz said. "On the cable they have these comedy things."

"I've thought about it," Phelan said, starting for the door. "You've got blind Justice? Here you got Justice pissing in her pants." His mind was on other things now. He whispered something to Corcoran. He absently popped his ciggy-butt onto the floor. "See you in court in a few minutes."

He never even so much as glanced at me. He and Corcoran moved quickly down the hall, leaving behind Phil and me and the two cops. They stood against the wall near the door, staring at me. Kleinmutz was quiet for a long time. He moved close to me and said very quietly so that the cops couldn't hear him: "I'm your lawyer and I have to know this—"

"Okay." I waited for him to continue. He remained quiet for a while.

"Did you kill her?" he said at last. He was staring right into my eyes.

"Oh, please."

"I have to ask this."

"Of course not." My voice sounded hollow to me. I was accused, in jail. I *felt* guilty. Now isn't that the goddamndest thing! I wanted to plead my case: It looks bad, I know, but—A desperate, sinking feeling came over me in a wave: Kleinmutz didn't believe me. He thinks I'm guilty. "No, I didn't kill her," I said. My voice was tense and forced. I was pressing to convince him. I laughed and it was tight and empty and seemed particularly stupid and inappropriate.

I suddenly felt an enormous fatigue. It was battle, Plain of Reeds, and we are pinned down. The enemy are all around. They have climbed into the tops of the banana trees, dug 'spider holes' in stands of elephant grass, burrowed into the ground in huge anthill structures that are everywhere. Hour after hour they pound on us. We'll never get out of there.

I was exhausted to the core of my being; I wanted to just rest back and sleep. My head ached; my whole body ached. I thought I might throw up. I felt as though I could sleep a year. "It's just like I told you— her ex-husband came and picked her up." He gazed at me and I couldn't read what he was thinking. "Phil," I said. "You don't believe I killed her?"

"No. No, I don't. But—sometimes people lose it and—it happens."

"I didn't kill her. Look at me. I didn't kill her."

His shoulders slumped. He took a deep breath. "I've been at this too long," he said quietly. "I'm sorry, Paul."

"What about the bail?" I just wanted to get out of there, get out of that town with its ugly sky and grimy air and stench and fire in the desert.

"They don't want to let go of you. You heard Corcoran. Well, let's see what we can do."

There was a knock at the door and a bailiff stuck his head in and told us the Honorable Judge Wilson Xavier Phelan was ready for us.

I glanced at Phil and he looked embarrassed and I was embarrassed for him and—I felt guilty. Of what?

Most of my life was spent feeling uneasy and embarrassed and guilty. It was as though my existence had become a party where I was a guest alone and isolated; the host has introduced me to a stranger and then has gone off; I am left standing there, pained, foolish. That was my whole life these days, with everyone. I guess you hang around long enough, you begin to apologize for your existence.

Chapter Twenty-Five

I don't suppose arraignments are all that interesting; you'd think, though, that your own would grab your attention. But I was so beat up I could barely follow what was going on.

The blood pounded at my temples and the pain was awful and I felt as tired as I've ever been in my life and sick to my stomach.

It was a narrow, cramped, stale-smelling courtroom, dark wood, walls of cream-colored peeling paint, with room for perhaps a dozen spectators. At this godforsaken middle-of-the-night hour there weren't any and the people forced to be there, two court attendants and a stenographer, appeared sleep-deprived and sullen. The stenographer was in a quilted housecoat, her hair in rollers. She wore no make-up and that was not a good thing for anyone who had to look at her.

The arraignment droned on as Phil Kleinmutz and Corcoran and Frog Phelan haggled over procedure, nit-picking arcane aspects of the law, splitting all the hairs of the legal system they could pluck.

I was depressed and fatigued and I made little scribbly drawings on a pad in front of me while in my head I played leap-frog with my life. I was going over events recent and not so recent, trying to figure out how I had come to this point, to this place—accused of murder.

I thought of Travis Wells and I knew things would not go well for me here. Travis was a hometown boy, well liked; jurors would have been disposed to giving him a break. And they convicted him. What would they do with me? He had received life without parole; I figured they'd draw and quarter me and feed me to the pariah dogs I had seen skulking down the town's streets.

Judge Wilson Xavier Phelan addressed the prosecutor: "All right, on this matter of the bail—" and that caught my attention. I listened. "Ron, I'm going to have to turn you down on this bail request here—"

"Frog," Corcoran began, "I mean Judge, in a case of this magnitude—"

Phelan's voice, plumy and sonorous, resonated in the small room. "I realize the seriousness of the case. But *no* bail, with this man here, just seems unduly harsh and unjust. It would be against the American way. Therefore, I am *setting* bail." He shuffled some papers on his desk, scanned a page, conferred with the bailiff.

At last he looked up. He cleared his throat, staring directly at me, his eyes dead agates behind his thick glasses. "I authorize bail in the amount of one million dollars."

I heard the words, but their effect seemed directed toward someone else. There are things that occur in our lives that so are terrible that we regard them as though we were a spectator at the event rather than a participant. This was one of those occasions.

Phelan continued to stare at me. He took a sip of water from a glass on the desk, then rose to leave.

Kleinmutz hurried to the bench. His voice was hushed and strangulated. "Frog—uh—your honor, you can't be serious—"

"Is a heart attack serious?"

"Your honor, if it please, your honor—" Phil was stammering. "Now as to, as to—?"

Phelan's stentorian tones rattled the room: "*Million dollars*? I'd call that *very* serious. Cause what we got here is a serious crime. *Rape. Vicious murder.*" He gestured toward Richie who was standing at the far side of the courtroom: "Officer Richard Bledsoe here found the body. Poor girl was almost unrecognizable. Beaten like that. Shot. We're dealing with a crazed animal—"

"Alleged," Kleinmutz shouted. "*One million dollars!* That's tantamount to holding him with no bail."

"All right," Phelan said. "Now some may regard this as too tough. I am tough. I admit and take pride in it. Tough as a fast food steak, cause that's what it takes. I'm not going to molly-coddle no murderer here. *We got us a heinous crime.* As far as bail goes, one man's ceiling is another man's floor. In this case, floor or ceiling, it's a million bucks."

I was aware that someone had come into the courtroom; the door swung open, then slammed shut. Dazed and disheartened, I didn't bother to turn to see who it was.

They were coming down the aisle now, calling to the judge. I looked over. It was Kelly Wells in a housecoat and slippers. Without make-up, her face looked hard as gun-barrel steel. She was shouting: "No-good son-of-a-bitch! Lying motherfucker!" Phelan banged his gavel and called for order. A bailiff tugged at her arm. She pulled away and continued to the bench. "I'll post bail, you cocksucker!" she yelled. She came to the bench and stood there and her anger was palpable. She may have been drunk, but there was no waver in her. She was hard and cold with anger. Phelan looked down at her, unruffled. "Bail is a million dollars," he said.

She stared at him for a moment and he glared back. "That shouldn't be a problem," she said quietly.

"I'm sure it's not."

"You snake bastard, Phelan. You did in my son. You'll not do it to this man." She spoke so quietly now you had to strain to hear her.

"You got a garbage mouth, you know that?" Phelan said, struggling to maintain his composure.

"Fuck you."

He leaned forward. "I advise you to zip it. *Now.* You say you're going to post bail for this man. So be it. Now get out of my courtroom before I start throwing around some contempt citations." He looked over at Kleinmutz and myself. "See you at trial time." He rose, eyes huge behind his glasses, and stared down at Kelly. "You're not piss water round here no more, Miz Wells. Not piss water." Then he hurried from the bench, followed by Richie and Corcoran.

No one spoke for a time. Kelly lit a cigarette. "How did you know they were arraigning me?" I said.

"I still have friends around this town," she said. "Not many, but a few." She stared down at the end of her cigarette. "I knew someone would eventually do in the little slut. She had it coming to her. But you certainly didn't do it."

"I appreciate this," I said.

"I have respect for you. You're only here because of my son," she said. "I have a lot of respect for you."

Kleinmutz said, "I think we ought to get out of here."

"Okay."

"You'll go back to—?"

"Tehachapi," I said.

"That's good. Yeah, it's best you get out of this godforsaken place."

"Let's go," Kleinmutz said, tugging at me.

"Assholes in high places," she said. "They won't rest. They're going to do everything they can to destroy you—"

"Why?"

"You pissed them off. Don't piss off the Good Humor man—that's gonna give you problems."

"I'm really grateful for this, you know?"

"You'll make it up to me some day."

We kissed. She had her eyes open. She was studying me to see if I felt anything. I didn't. I was just happy to be getting out of Joshua Crest. "Yeah, this town," I said.

"Asshole of the world. I been meaning to get out of here for a long time. I just never seem to make it." She was still staring at me and I could tell she wanted something more from me and I just couldn't find it in me to say anything. She squeezed my hand and I squeezed back, but it was an awkward gesture without any real feeling. She smiled, embarrassed. "You take care, okay?"

"I will," I said and hurried to Phil who was waiting for me at the door.

.

Chapter Twenty-Six

There was heavy fog, but it hadn't descended to the prison yard. I looked up toward my house and you couldn't see it or even the mountains.

The men were waiting for me. A fine drizzle fell and they huddled in their Levi jackets and black watch caps and I hurried across the yard to them. Baker, stomping up and down to keep warm, said: "What the hell happened to you?"

"How does the other guy look?" McMullin said.

"I bumped into a door."

"I know how that goes," Sergeant said.

"How was your week, men?"

"More fun than a barrel full of assholes," Culpepper said.

I entered the guard area. Rita Macklin was on the phone. She didn't look at me, though I was sure she knew I was there. I went to the Mr. Coffee and fixed myself a cup. She got off the phone, but still didn't look at me. "I was out of town," I said.

"You don't owe me anything. Jesus," she said, seeing me for the first time. "What happened?"

"You know what the good ol' boy said? 'I thought I was dancing till someone stepped on my fingers.'"

"What were you trying to do?"

"There was this biker bar."

"Never figure you for that."

"A lot we don't know about each other."

"Okay."

She was staring at me and she looked lovely. She smelled fresh of soap and a hint of White Shoulders. There was concern in her gaze and I was surprised and that felt good: she cared. "How about dinner tonight?" I said.

"All right."

"I have my kids for a couple of days."

"I'd like to meet them," she said.

"Good," I said and it felt fine, her wanting to meet the kids, her looking at me with concern. There was still this distance between us and yet I felt a measure now of connection. Perhaps this can work out, I found myself thinking.

I could see the men through the glass, still huddled on the yard. It was raining harder now. Water streamed down the glass.

Macklin suddenly looked lost; she looked as though she might cry. "I'm sorry," she said. "I just don't want to be stupid in all of this. Okay?"

"Okay," I said. I wanted to reach out and touch her but I realized the men could see us through the glass. I entered the library and opened the door to the yard and the men came in.

"Hey, boss," Baker said, "It's wet out there. I know you want to score some trim, but, hey, a little consideration for your murderers." He laughed that elfin, crinkly, good-natured laugh of his.

The men seated themselves around the large table and the class began. Blast limped into class. He wanted us to deal with his work first. "I... done some re-writing... here. On... you know, my article..."

"Sexual harassment by female guards?" I said.

"Now I'm... zeroing in on something here..."

"Okay. I heard you got shanked. They had everyone down in the mud."

"It were nothing... little scratch... They was some... Jews done it." Crow laughed. "What's so funny?" Blast demanded.

"He was a *carnal* stuck you."

"Jews… put him up to it…"

"Ain't no Jews on this motherfucking yard."

"You… always sticking up… for the… Jews…"

"I just ain't paranoid, my bro."

"You know… I worked for some… Jews a while back. I did some… hauling of concrete block… And it were just before Christmas… and I was broke… and I asked for my pay… And they wouldn't… give it to me…till after Christmas… They hate Christmas… This been going on… for two thousand… years…"

"Let's get back to your sexual harassment article," I said. "The new work you've done."

"I trace it… to the…Jewish… conspiracy…"

"How's that?"

"There's gender exploitation…here… and racial… animus… There's this… Jewish prudence…"

"Jewish prudence?" Culpepper said. His eyes laughed. "You mean, 'jurisprudence.'"

"Jewish prudence…"

"Whoop de whoop, whoop de woo," Crow said and the men all laughed.

Blast, though, was dead serious. He had found a link between the Jewish conspiracy and female guards, sexual harassment and "Jewish prudence" and he was determined to get his point across: "When… they… lookin' at you… in the shower—" He paused, fighting to get the words out. "—they lookin' to see if… your dick—is *cut*!"

"Circumcised," Culpepper said.

"That's it," Blast said. "That's all part of the… International Jewish Conspiracy—"

"How much meds you on?" McMullin said. Blast, peering at him, eyes dark with suspicion, did not answer. "You need 'em upped." The men all laughed and Blast grew angry and his stammering increased and I had to simmer everybody down and go on to the next project.

Travis Wells was watching me. There was a bleakness in his gaze, a wariness there, and I wondered if he had talked to Kelly. Had she told him what had gone on between us?

McMullin brought in a story about his childhood and Culpepper had some poems and Sergeant had some more material about war.

I was feeling uncomfortable under Poet's look. His gaze didn't waver and I couldn't fathom what was behind it. It was difficult concentrating on the men's work. I started to critique it and knew my comments weren't making much sense.

When class was over, Poet came to me on the yard. It was raining hard now and we stood under an overhang that ran alongside the building. "I spoke with my Mom," he said. "And she told me—"

He didn't talk for a moment and I didn't say anything. The rain lashed the yard. I stared at him, wondering what he knew. "She told me that you're trying to help me."

"I got into this thing deeper than I should have," I said. "I made a mistake."

"I understand," he said.

"It's against regulations for me to get involved like this."

"I know."

He looked away. There was sadness in his eyes. "I never wanted anybody to get involved for me," he said. "I just want to thank you." He started off, then turned back to me. "She told me they killed Millie."

"Yes," I said.

He stood there, rain streaming down his face. He had tears in his eyes. "I loved her," he said. "God, how I loved her. She did a bad thing to me, helping them set me up. But I couldn't never stop the good feelings I had for her." He stood for a while without speaking; the rain continued on him, hard. "She was the first girl, the only girl, I ever loved." It was difficult for him to continue. "I'll never have the chance to love another girl. I'll never have kids, a family."

"Prisoners marry," I said.

"No," he said. "I mean a normal life. I wanted a normal life. I wanted to be a father."

"I'm not sure Millie would have been—"

"You don't know. We had something between us. She liked books. We would talk about different books. Dostoyevsky. We used to read Dostoyevsky together." He didn't speak for a while. His voice finally came out like a child's and I was moved. "It hurts, you know? It hurts a lot."

"I understand," I said.

"Things didn't break right for me. Just—nothing broke right." He stood in silence for a moment; water streamed down his face. At last, he hurried off through the rain.

I walked back across the yard and out the gates and through the sally-port and past the front gun tower. I was soaked by the rain and numb. I felt for Poet in a very deep way and there was a disgust in me for what life brought to some. Was there justice anywhere? The innocent were slaughtered, the guilty went free, and even there, the innocent were forced to become the guilty, to take their place behind these walls.

I drove down to Bakersfield and picked up the kids. They wanted to know what had happened to my face and I told them I had been hit by a baseball in the batting cages. "You were keeping your eye on the ball," Kurtie said.

"Exactly," I said.

By the time we arrived back in Tehachapi the rain had stopped. The air was fresh and clean and smelled of pine from the surrounding forests.

I had told Macklin I would meet her at the Sierra Inn, the only restaurant in town that was more than a diner. It was done up in western ranch house style, a lot of wood and ivy. There was a pot-bellied stove in the center of the room and horse shoes and branding irons and quilts hanging on the walls.

We were seated in a booth that was thick, dark hand-hewn wood, the benches, the table. There were hurricane lamps on the table.

Macklin looked more beautiful than I had ever seen her. She was wearing a white cotton dress that was frilly and feminine and there was no toughness to her this evening: the vulnerability I had noticed at the prison in the afternoon still seemed with her, the delicacy, the concern. It was as though she were another woman and I was amazed. I found myself thinking: she could be a wife and mother. And suddenly I was flooded by a rush of tenderness toward her that was as close to love as anything I had felt in a long, long time.

The kids were fascinated that she was a prison guard. "Where's your gun?" Annie said.

"They don't wear guns," I said.

"Why not?" Kurt wanted to know.

"We're on the yard with the men," she said, "and they could always grab our guns and then we'd be in big trouble."

She was enjoying the kids, which surprised me. That hard edge that was always so much of her was gone. The *feel* of her was gentle, shy, even innocent, and the great tenderness within me flooded my whole being and it was extraordinary.

And still—as always, there was a place in her that I knew I could not get to, that I would never reach or understand.

"But how do you keep the bad guys in jail?" Kurt said.

"There are big, high fences and men in towers with rifles."

"Is she your girlfriend, Daddy?" said Kurt.

"I'm a friend," Macklin said.

"Yes, she's a friend."

"Well, she's also a girl," said Kurt. "And if she's a girl and a friend, she's a girl friend."

Macklin laughed at this and looked sidelong at me and took my hand and squeezed it gently. "You're very smart," she said.

"I know," Kurt said.

"I'm smart, too," said Annie.

"I know you are."

"You're pretty," Annie said.

Macklin smiled and it was almost relaxed and I wondered what I had to do to break through the last measure of distrust and reserve. And then, of course, I thought of myself, what I knew of myself, what I knew of myself in the world: there was a barrier always. It even existed between me and my children. And I thought, again, as I did so often, of that line—who had said it? I had first read or heard it in Vietnam. Who, who had said it? *Experience is a lamp which only lights the one who bears it, dim and uncommunicable.*

"Daddy," Annie said, "she's a girl and she's a friend, so she's your girlfriend."

Macklin laughed, but I couldn't tell if the laugh was real.

"What are you doing, Kurtie?" I said. He was digging his fingernail into the table-top.

"Making a heart, for love."

"This is a behave yourself restaurant," Annie said.

"Kurt, don't do that," I said.

"I want to make a heart."

He began to cry. "What are you crying about?" He held up his finger. There was a sliver of wood under the nail. "Splinter," he said.

"See," Annie said.

I took out my Swiss Army knife and removed the tweezers from it and began to pull on the sliver and it wouldn't come out and then something exploded in my head: *The wood under Travis Wells' grandfather's nails!*

It was blood exploding there, thoughts exploding in a great rush, a convergence that happened so quickly that I was stunned and shaken, many things coming together at once and I felt like I might be having some sort of breakdown. I felt crazed. "Yes," I said.

"What?" said Macklin.

"Look, kids, something—I just realized something—" I stood. "Can you take the kids up to the house and stay with them for a while?"

"Where are you going?"

"I have to do something." Kurt was still crying and I handed the tweezers to Macklin and she began to work at the splinter. She got it out and gave the tweezers back to me. By then I had paid the check.

My hands were trembling. I was trembling inside. I could not stop the feeling. Macklin was watching me with concern and I realized how stunned and blasted I must look, and it must be troubling to her and the kids and yet I could not control myself. "Are you all right?" she said.

"Yes. I'm really sorry," I said.

"What is it?"

"I just realized something. Kids, I'm sorry. I'll see you in the middle of the night—"

"I don't understand," Macklin said. "What? What is it?"

"Have to do something. Sorry."

"This is a little goofy," she said. And she was watching me and shaking her head and she was troubled.

"I know. It's something I have to do. I'll be back late. Is it okay?"

"It's okay," she said, but I wasn't sure she meant it. She looked wary and I bit annoyed and I felt stupid and uncomfortable and yet my heart was racing and I could hardly breath. I kissed her and the kids and hurried from the restaurant. And then I was in the truck, speeding back to Joshua Crest.

My brain had been pierced: that was how it felt. There was a wire of extraordinary thinness and strength that cut through the heart of my mind and it was burning bright and hot and I wondered what was happening to me? Was I having some sort of breakdown?

Of this I was sure, though: I had discovered something of great importance.

Chapter Twenty-Seven

It was nearly ten o'clock when I got to Joshua Crest. The furnaces outside of town were going full out, sending eruptions of fire into the night desert sky. Thick black smoke poured out, obliterated the stars.

The mobile home park was quiet. There were a few lights on in individual homes, but much of the place was dark. The old man who had always been out front banging away on some contraption or other was not to be seen.

I moved through the park, past rickety, run-down, scarred homes to the gully's edge and the building where Travis' grandfather had been murdered. I had a flashlight with me and I went around to the back of the place. I got down on my hands and knees and ran the flashlight beam along the wooden trim at ground level.

I heard a pattering sound and then a low growl. I shined the light ahead of me. It was Kelly's Doberman. Teeth bared, he growled louder. I said, "It's me, Jukie. It's me. There, there—"

I put my hand out so that he could sniff me, wondering if he would sniff or bite.

He sniffed and I petted him and he began to prowl around the base of the mobile home. I saw some scratch marks in the trim and I moved the dirt away.

Something had been scratched into the trim, an attempt at words, and I ran my hand over the carving and then I took a notebook out of my pocket and removed a sheet of paper and placed it over the carving and ran a pencil over the paper and made a rubbing of the carving.

It read: "Cute killed me."

My initial reaction was elation: the old man had identified his killer. Then confusion—what did it mean, "Cute?"

I returned to the truck, my mind racing. The old man, dying, had dug into the wood the name of the person who had killed him. That's where the fragments of wood under his fingernail came from. *Cute?* Who was *Cute?*

I arrived back at my house sometime after midnight. The kids were not in their room and I had a momentary stab of anxiety, but I looked into my room and there they were, in bed asleep with Macklin.

I lifted Kurt and noticed that my prison I.D. was clipped to his sleeper. I removed it and placed it next to my bed and took him to his bed and returned for Annie.

I kissed both kids and told them I loved them.

In my bedroom, I lay down next to Macklin. She stirred. I kissed her. Her eyes fluttered open. We kissed and it was passionate and I started to pull at her dress. She began to get undressed. "Did you find what you wanted?" she said.

"Yes."

We made love and it was not good. It felt empty and I wondered if it wasn't my involvement with Kelly that had somehow affected the way I felt for Macklin.

I sensed she knew something, though she didn't say anything. I could tell, though, that she was disappointed. "I'm sorry," I said.

"What for?"

"I didn't seem to be quite in it."

"Me neither. It happens."

"Yes. I guess it's because—well, maybe—"

"What?"

"I made a discovery."

"Discovery?"

"I found out who killed Travis' grandfather."

She looked at me as though I were talking some completely foreign language. "That's where you went?" she said, incredulous.

"Yes."

"And?"

"The old man had scratched the name of his killer into the wall of his mobile home. That's why he had splinters under his nail. When Kurtie got that splinter I suddenly thought—you see the kind of wood was different from that of the baseball bat. That's why."

She was shaking her head as though I was completely off my rocker. "And who did it?"

"That's the problem. The name means nothing to me. 'Cute 'That was the name…"

She was sitting now. She lit a cigarette. She seemed peeved. "You know, you're a very strange man," she said. "Maybe all writers are like this. I don't know. Most of the men I've known can barely write their names. But this is just crazy. This kid was convicted of killing his grandfather. Maybe he did, maybe he didn't—"

"You said you thought he didn't."

"Maybe I did think that. But he was convicted by a jury and I just don't know what you're doing snooping around. It's very weird."

"You're upset—"

"I'm not upset. I don't get upset over things like this."

"Maybe you're upset over what's between you and me."

"What's between you and me? There's damn little, except some fucking, that's between us. We're from different worlds. I got a feeling you're from your own world."

Her words hurt because they were so much like what my wife had said to me at the end of our marriage. *We're from different worlds.* What did that mean? Where was I from?

I had this great feeling of isolation as well as a sense of foolishness, deep, deep, deep within. Fortune's fool.

Why was I here? What had brought me to probe into the death of Travis' grandfather? What was I doing? Where would it lead? I realized that war had cut something deep and terrible into me. I would live forever with a sense of unease over what had gone on there, what had happened to me.

Macklin had finished her cigarette and she lay back and I closed my eyes and fell into an uneasy sleep. Sometime later, I was aware that Macklin had gotten up and was dressing. I could sense her moving around in the dark and then she was out of the room and a few minutes later I heard her car start up and drive off.

Chapter Twenty-Eight

I was awakened early the next morning by the sound of television. The kids were watching cartoons. I came downstairs and started to get breakfast and an argument immediately broke out over what cereal they would have, Fruit Loops or Peanut Butter Captain Crunch. I ended up giving them each the one they had asked for and as soon as I did that, they wanted the one the other had.

I switched bowls. They were still unhappy. At last it was resolved: they each would have a bowl of Fruit Loops and a second bowl of Captain Crunch. What hope was there for mankind when kids could not agree on what cereal to eat? I told them this and it wasn't a thought they were happy with. "We're just brother and sister, Daddy," Annie said. "We're supposed to fight."

"I'm getting tired of it."

"I'm sorry," said Kurt and he came to me and kissed me and Annie kissed me also and said she was sorry and I knew that my kids were the most important thing to me by far and they were my reason for living. I wondered that I had had them and regretted that I hadn't had them earlier. The disaster of my marriage was suddenly all right. I had these two miraculous beings, these bright, slight, touching beings.

"Daddy, are you going to marry Rita?" Annie asked.

"Would you like that?"

"Yes, yes," they both yelled.

"You, Kurtie?" I said.

"Yes."

"Why?"

"Her has big titties," he said. I began to laugh. I tried to put on a stern face, but I couldn't make it. I laughed and laughed and Kurtie sat there smiling, proud of what he had said.

The kids started on their second bowl of cereal and I went to my notebook and looked at the rubbing I had taken from the base of Ray Wells mobile home.

Cute killed me. I took a pencil and began doodling around the rubbing, trying to see if there was some thought there that the dying man hadn't completed. The words had a rough, unfinished look, something that was accomplished with extraordinary effort. Had he intended something else? Something more?

The phone rang and it was Phil Kleinmutz. "I got a call just now from Wild Bill Coty. He's back in Joshua Crest. Wants to see you."

"What for?"

"Says he knows who killed the stripper."

"Where does he want to meet?"

"Are you crazy? You're not going back there. They're cooking something up."

"I have to go—"

"This whole thing is crazy. You'll get back there and they're going to hang something else on you or find some excuse for revoking your bail."

"Wild Bill killed Millie—"

"That's not for you to get involved with."

"Who will? Phelan? Richie? Corcoran?"

"He killed his ex-wife and now he's looking to kill you."

"Tell me where he said to meet him."

There was a long silence on the end of the line. "Out at The Fat Lady's gambling joint. He's waiting there now. Do you have a gun?"

"No."

"War hero, you don't have a gun?"

"I was no hero, believe me."

"I'll meet you at the Mountain Inn Coffee Shop. You'll take my Walther. You know how to handle a Walther?"

"Yes."

I called Macklin. I had awakened her. Her voice sounded dull, indifferent. It was her day off—we had planned to take the kids to Brite Lake, just across the valley. "Something's come up. I have to go back to Joshua Crest. Could you baby sit the kids for the afternoon?"

"I have to pick up my paycheck, then I'll be free…"

"I'll meet you at the prison gate."

"Fine."

I gathered up my wallet and my Swiss Army knife and then I went to find my I.D. It wasn't in the drawer where I usually kept it. I remembered that Kurtie had taken it the night before and I began to look for it but couldn't find it. It was one of those days. I also couldn't find my leather jacket.

"Kurtie, what did you do with my prison badge?" He stared at me. "You had it last night. Where'd you put it?" He just shook his head and I told him not to play with it again and then spent another five minutes trying to find my jacket. I could feel I was getting really angry and then I said to myself, what am I making such a big deal about? The jacket's here somewhere as is the I.D. and let me just get out of there. I wore my canvas windbreaker.

Macklin was waiting on the near side of the gate, which was fortunate: I couldn't have gone through without my I.D. She seemed annoyed and I thanked her profusely, but she didn't really seem to care. I kissed the kids and then drove off to meet Kleinmutz.

"I'd been calling all over trying to find Wild Bill," he told me as he sat down. He looked rushed, sloppy, and severely hungover.

We were in a far booth in the Mountain Inn Coffee Shop. I had arrived before him and had started on my breakfast: bacon and eggs, home fries, biscuits and gravy. He looked at my plate, shocked. "What are you doing?"

"What?"

"You're going to have to stop that, eating like that."

"You're lecturing me?"

"Okay. So?"

"You're seventy pounds overweight."

"Some of us have a set weight, a weight determined by the number of fat cells we have, which cannot be controlled by diet. For some people the only way to beat it is to exercise an hour a day." He went on about his exercise regimen—running a mile in the morning, workout for an hour at night, Nautilus gym he had joined where he did 12 stomach exercises a day, including a great one with a Nautilus machine where—he demonstrated—he turned from side to side, burning up fat at his midsection.

"I've lost 11 pounds."

"Last time we talked you said 2."

"My scale was wrong. It was 11."

"You don't look it."

"It's this jacket." He grew pensive. "I've been thinking about Doug Filiberti. I'm convinced his cancer was caused by his diet. It's all in your shit." The waitress came to the table and Phil ordered bacon and eggs. He shrugged apologetically at me. "When I get anxious I eat the wrong things." He shook his head. "The Cat, Death—I was thinking about the last time I saw Doug. It was in Bakersfield Memorial. The cancer by that time had got to his brain. It was after visiting hours and they didn't want to let me in so I snuck up to the room. He was in a kind of coma, semi-coma. He's dying, you know? I'm emotional, thinking about his family, three kids—"

"Yes, yes."

"Didn't I tell you one day, the Cat, Death, would come for the mouse, us?"

"You have said that."

"I come into the room. He looks up at me, alarmed. 'Who is it?' he says. I can hear the fear in his voice. He thought I was Death coming for him. 'It's Phil Kleinmutz,' I said. 'Oh, Phil.' I could hear the relief in his voice. He calls me 'Phil'—"

"He always called you Kleinmutz."

"Yes. So I knew we were at the end of things here. 'Where are we?' he says."

"He's hallucinating?"

"He's rambling. 'We're in Jack O'Neil's Blarney Bar in San Jose.' 'What are you drinking?' 'Dry Martini.' I tell him. 'Gordon's gin.' 'What am I drinking?' 'A Margarita with Cuervo tequila, salt, and lime.' 'Are we having fun?' 'Yes, we are.' And he closed his eyes and slept. And I left. That night he died."

I shrugged and sighed and he sighed and I was thinking I had to get out of there and out to see Wild Bill Coty.

"The sun-of-bitching Cat, Death," he said. "I want you to be careful. Wild Bill this morning contacts my office. Says he knows who killed his wife." He reached over, took one of my biscuits and stuffed it into his mouth. "Wasn't you, he told me."

"Did he say who it was?"

"Said he'll tell you when he sees you. There's just something wrong, here, Paul. He's looking to do you in."

Kleinmutz reached into his briefcase and drew out a nickle-plated Walther pistol. He demonstrated how it worked, which wasn't really necessary.

I tucked the Walther under my waistband. My windbreaker covered it. "You look good," Phil said. "Be careful."

"Sure."

"I mean it now." He paused for a moment, thinking. "We're too old for this kind of thing. We have to listen to time—"

"Yes."

"We have to find that stillness. All that's good in us comes out of that—"

"I know. You're right."

"Listen to time. It's telling us what it hears." He looked old, tired and bloated and we shook hands and his hand was fat and without strength.

The wind was picking up as I headed east from Tehachapi. By the time I reached the desert on the other side of Mojave, I was in the center of a full-blown dust storm.

Chapter Twenty-Nine

A ferocious sandstorm was blowing, the kind that could peel the paint right off your vehicle and cause your windshield to be pitted in a thousand places. I couldn't see more than twenty feet in front of me and it wasn't the greatest feeling, driving in a sandstorm, but I was determined to get to Wild Bill and hear what he had to say.

The neon lettering of The Desert Flower Motel sign emerged out of the dust, ghost-like. I sped past it.

A distance down the highway I came to the Oasis Poker Parlor. Its neon was not on. The gray hulk of the building suddenly appeared out of the blowing sand; I almost drove on by.

I pulled into the parking lot. There were several cars there, but the place was shut down. I got out of the truck, fighting wind and sand, and made my way to the front door. It was locked. I banged on it.

It opened and The Fat Lady stood before me. She was wearing a muumuu, large as a tent, with a tropical pattern of palm trees and ocean waves. She smelled of some godawful sweetish perfume, a five and dime variety. Her dyed red hair was done up in a mountain of ringlets. Her grotesquely fleshy face was packed with make-up. I wondered what the occasion was. "Well, well," she said. "Look what the cat drug in."

The place was dark save for a small area of light where Wild Bill sat under a single bare bulb. He had a plate of chili in front of him and a water glass filled with some kind of booze and a bottle of Dos Eques Beer.

The Geezer was waiting on him, serving up nacho chips and cheese dip. The Fat Lady led me to the table. "Hey, Bill," she said, "I was forced to lay some muscle on this here lame t'other day. Knowed he was a friend of your might a' kissed him 'stead of whopping him."

"Think he might have preferred the whopping," Bill said, smiling languidly.

The Fat Lady laughed loud and long at that. "Hear that, Geezer?" he said.

"Kiss my bony ass, Bill Coty," the Geezer said.

"Knows how to hurt a girl, for sure." The Fat Lady sat at the far end of the bar and began to stuff her mouth with peanuts from a plastic bowl. A soap opera was playing on the television above the bar, a hospital scene.

The wind rattled the shutters and the reception on the television wavered: the roof satellite was rocking in the wind.

"What's your pleasure," Bill Coty said to me.

"Beer'd be fine."

Something was griping The Fat Lady, something on the television soap opera. "This Lila is such a deadbeat. She done stole Hilary's husband and now Hilary's got amniocentesis—"

"What?" said the Geezer.

"Lou Gehrig's disease, and is in intensive care and Lila has the *gall* to show up at the hospital. What's she going to do here?"

"Goin' to kill Hilary," the Geezer said, lighting a cigarette. He inhaled deeply, then erupted in a ferocious fit of coughing.

"No!" the Fat Lady said.

"Goin' to disconnect that life support system…" He spat behind the bar.

"Goddamn, Monty. Sure knows this horseshit. Skinny little runt's right again. Look at that deadbeat."

The Geezer, a self-satisfied expression on his face, moved around the bar and fetched a beer for me. He returned to his place in front of the television. He and The Fat Lady stared at the screen, deeply involved.

"Richie killed her," Coty said in a quiet voice to me.

"When you left the motel the other night, I saw you beating on her."

Wild Bill did not say anything for a while. He was gazing down at the knuckle of his right hand. There was a scab there. He had a thick ring on his third finger and he twisted it around and around and I could see there was a scab under the ring. He had stubby fingers and skin raw from the weather. He had a scab on his wrist, also. "Was things goin' on," he said at last. "We was arguing about Richie. He sucked her into this whole thing."

"What whole thing?"

"'Bout a half dozen people out here got themselves some sweet racket. I'm talking seven figures here." He continued to twist the ring on his finger. He mimed a needle going into his arm. "Richie got her hooked on the white stuff. Broke up our marriage. I could take the fucking around. Couldn't take that scag thing. What I figure is—Richie began to distrust her. She had been calling me… Was afraid she was telling me things, so he whacked her." He took a long swallow of booze, chased it with beer. "Richie had never met Mr. Defeat," Wild bill said.

"Who's Mr. Defeat?"

"Millie and her mouth. Everything's always gone his way. Suddenly he meets up with Mr. Defeat. Mr. Defeat is a doomsayer, a nihilist. Knocked on Richie's door, then pushed right in—went right into his living room, sat down and ate his cookies. He'll eat your goodies and spit in your face. Mr. Defeat." He remained quiet, exhausted by drink and his spiel. "If your only tool is a hammer," he said after a while, "you treat everything as a nail. That's Richie's problem. Someone's meeting us. Hope you don't mind?"

At the bar, The Fat Lady went ballistic. She slammed her hand down on the bar, leaned back, hollered: "Look at that. Look at that deadbeat. She did it. Done pulled the fucking life support system!"

"Tol' you that's what she'd do," The Geezer said. I looked over at the television. The actress in the hospital bed had fallen to the floor. She lay there, struggling for breath. Organ music swelled behind her, syrupy, ominous. She went limp. "She's dead," The Fat Lady said.

"She ain't dead," said The Geezer.

"She ain't breathing." The Fat Lady got up and moved her ample form with some effort around the bar. She stood on a beer crate and put her face right up to the screen. "No, sir, Monty. She ain't breathing. Dead as a rat's ass in a cat's mouth."

"What about these two?" I said to Coty.

"Oh, they're in it, the whole dope business. Not for long. I'm going to smash it. Bust this town. Phelan, the whole bunch." He was silent for a while. He sat there sipping his beer. He lit up a cigarette. "Millie was good people. Just had a thing for hard guys. When she found out I was human, had no more use for me." He swirled his whiskey around in his glass. He looked infinitely sad.

"When you investigated the old man's death, you ever come across a carving in the wood, rear of the trailer?"

"Carving?"

"He had splinters under his nails. He's dying. So he tries to carve in the wood who did it—"

"Never saw nothing like that. Want another beer?"

I said yes and he got up and went to the bar. I took out the paper with the rubbing on it. I traced my finger over the word "Cute." And then something struck me. The "u" was feeble, the "e" barely readable. I took my ballpoint pen and wrote over the letters and "Cute" became "Coty." *Coty killed me.*

I stared at the letters. They looked proper. There was a rightness to the whole thing. I had completed the dying man's thought: *Coty killed me.*

Wild Bill returned to the table with two beers and I put the slip of paper back in my jacket pocket. "Now what was it you was saying?"

"Ah, just some crazy idea I had. Makes no sense." Both of us remained silent for a while. Coty was studying me with sad, bleak eyes. At the bar, The Geezer and Fat Belle were also watching me, gazing with blank impassivity. I felt uneasy. Something went off inside me, an alarm sounding: I was in danger. It reminded me of the war, when we'd be moving through the brush or across a ricefield, and I'd get this cold feeling that things were not right. And sure as anything that's when all hell would break loose.

I pressed my right hand against the Walther pistol under my windbreaker. "Why did you want to see me?" I said to Coty.

There was a loud knock at the door. "Get that, Monty," the Fat Lady said. "They're coming back from commercials. Gotta see this."

The Geezer hobbled to the front door and opened it. The wind flung the door out of his grasp and he struggled with it as a fierce thrust of air and sand rushed into the room, sending playing cards and poker chips, coasters and place mats flying. The single bare bulb on a cord swung erratically above Coty. The room was suddenly a mess of bouncing shadows, cards, chips.

Richie entered. "Shut that fucking thing!" Fat Belle yelled and Richie and The Geezer struggled with the door and finally got it closed.

"She's blowing out there," The Geezer said, moving back to the bar.

"No shit, Dick Tracy," The Fat Lady said. "Richie, you ever watch this one?"

Richie went up close to the television set. "Who's that? Hilary? What happened?"

"Lila killed her," Fat Belle said.

Richie was genuinely shocked. "No!"

"Pulled the life support system. Goddamn deadbeat!"

"She's no good," Richie said.

"Scumbag," said The Fat Lady.

"I got this here one on tape," Richie said. "I tape 'em all. You can have your PBS, your arty-farty stuff. These are stories about real people…"

He walked back to the table where Bill Coty and I were seated. "What's this fuck-head doin' here?" he said, nodding toward me.

"I figure he's up on a murder charge, he should know how things are developing."

"Developing just fine," Richie said.

"Really?" Wild Bill said. "I drove off with Millie from the motel where she was with him. She told me she had to meet you."

Richie grew very still. He stared down at Wild Bill; his eyes had gone stone cold. "She never met me," he said quietly.

"Rich, give me your gun."

"Don't believe I'm going to do that."

Coty turned to me. "See the arrogance here? Kills the girl, then doesn't even do away with the gun. They run ballistics on that thing, they're goin' to know it was you. Give it to me." Coty raised his hand above the table. He was holding a .45 Colt Single Action long barrel.

"Always were a nutcase, Coty," Richie said. "Cowboy. We all had ourselves a nice thing around here, but you gotta be a hardass."

The Fat Lady, who had moved closer down the bar, suddenly swung out with something large and heavy. It was a wrench of some sort, a plumbers wrench; it caught Wild Bill on the side of the head, knocking him sideways to the floor. The Geezer grabbed his revolver. Richie had his own gun out now, the snub-nosed .32 he had threatened me with. "Don't know why everyone has to kick up a fuss. Billy, we have us a nice thing here. Why're you causing trouble?"

Wild Bill was seated on the floor, dazed. He looked up at me and there was fear in his eyes. "We're going to have to lose a few," Richie said. "Huh, Billy? Going to have to feed the desert, feed them coyotes. You know what the environmental whackos say? Them coyotes got to be fed."

I had my hand over the Walther. It was a question of when to try to get it out. "If he killed Millie," I said to Wild Bill, "who killed the old man and the kids? He didn't do that."

"No, he didn't," Wild Bill said.

"You did," I said. "But why?"

"I know who killed those kids," Richie said. "I know. Travis did them, don't shit me. He fucking did them."

"No," I said.

"Why did you kill Millie?" Wild Bill said to Richie.

Richie spoke softly, reasonably: "You were going to turn her. She told me. She ends up talking to this guy, you. She'd have blown the whole thing. I tried to keep her in control. But you were getting to her. Hey, but Billy, younse are coyote meat now."

In a flash, Wild Bill dove for the Geezer, knocked him down, and grabbed his revolver back. Richie fired; Coty went down. Richie moved to him and put the barrel of his revolver right up to his head.

Coty wheeled around, his revolver booming. Richie fell. Coty rose to one knee. Blood was spreading across his chest, one enormous stain. He spoke and there was blood coming from his mouth. "I'm dead," he said. "Bring these two in." He indicated The Fat Lady and The Geezer. "Call the Sheriff's station. Mojave."

I lifted Richie's gun. "That's the gun killed Millie," Wild Bill said. "I'm dead. Jesus, I'm dead…"

"'Why'd you kill the old man and the kids?" I said. Coty tried to speak. He couldn't. "Why?"

He emitted a gasping sound. His eyes were all whites now: the pupils had rolled back in his head. He was trying to say something. I put my head close to his. I could make out nothing. There was a loud gurgling sound and blood poured from his mouth and he was dead.

I had my gun out and levelled on Fat Belle and The Geezer. Both had gone chalk pale. The Geezer was trembling.

I checked Richie. He was dead. Coty had got him right through the heart.

"How much do you want?" the Fat Lady waved her arm toward the cash drawer. "You can have it all, the goods. This place looks like a rat hole, but we got bucks here. How much we got Geezer?" Geezer squirmed. He did not answer. "It's all right. Tell him. How much we got. Give him a square count."

"Near fourteen thousand dollars," the Geezer said so softly I could barely hear him.

"Fourteen thousand dollars. That's good bucks. That's tax free." I just shook my head. "How much, then? I'm reasonable. Give me a number."

"Naw, you don't buy me on this," I said. I went to the phone on the bar and called the operator and had her put me through to the Sheriff's station in Mojave. The Fat Lady began to blubber. She spoke of her health, the hard life she had lived, how she had worked to bring herself up out of poverty. The Geezer had his arm around her, consoling her. She spoke of the days she had been a prostitute, a common whore, how degrading it had been.

When it became apparent I couldn't be bought, the Fat Lady sloughed off her abused soul act like a snake sheds its skin and sat there glum, grim and hard.

It took nearly an hour for the Sheriff's men to arrive. The Fat Lady, The Geezer, and I watched television. We did not talk.

The coroner's ambulance came out from Joshua Crest. Somehow Kelly Wells had heard what had happened and she was there, also. The sandstorm had died down somewhat, though the wind still blew.

I checked my truck and it was a mess: paint half off, the windshield horribly pitted. Everything was thick with dust.

They loaded the bodies of Wild Bill and Richie on metal gurneys and carted them to the coroners refrigerated truck.

I filled the Sheriff's men in with as much as I knew, emphasizing what Coty had said about Richie and Millie's death and the dope stuff.

They had been trying to make their own case, I was told: they took The Fat Lady and The Geezer into custody.

I didn't say anything about the death of the old man and the carving and Coty's connection to it. I figured I'd talk to Phil Kleinmutz first.

The Fat Lady had been babbling as soon as the Sheriff's crowd arrived. "What do you want to know?" she said to anyone who would listen. "I'll tell you everything."

A Deputy tried to read her her Miranda, but she would have none of it. "Fuck that communist bullshit," she hollered. "I know everything's gone on around here. Let me make a deal. Who do I make a deal with?"

The Geezer, in handcuffs now, trailed pathetically behind her. "Me, too. Just ask me…what do you want to know?"

The Kern County Sheriff, a large, thick-boned man who wore ostrich-skin boots and a large Stetson, talked briefly with the two of them. Then they were unceremoniously shoved into a squad car. It was an effort getting The Fat Lady into the back seat. The car sagged almost to the ground under the her weight.

Kelly Wells was looking at me with this funny expression, almost, but not quite, a smile. "You know what they say," she said.

"What's that?"

"Ain't over till the fat lady sings. Let's have a drink." I got into my truck and followed her back to her house.

Chapter Thirty

We sat in Kelly Wells' living room sipping scotch and water. When we arrived at the house she had gone upstairs and showered. She came down wearing a silk kimono. Her hair was still damp. "That's better," she said. "That goddamn dust."

She had put on music, Bach, I think it was, something slow and gloomy, with trumpets and strings. I had a headache. I felt sick to my stomach. I kept seeing in my mind the blood spreading across Wild Bill's chest.

"What are you going to do?" Kelly said.

"Assuming I'm cleared in this killing of the girl?"

"Oh, you'll be cleared."

I was sitting next to her on the couch. She smelled of perfumed soap. I wanted to take her into my arms and make love to her but I knew there was really nothing between us. I had to admit to myself: Rita Macklin had captured me.

I found myself thinking of how mysterious the women in my life had been. I had never really known any of them, not my wife, no one. When she had come to tell me she was leaving, it was as if a stranger was talking to me. And I felt it with Macklin. And with Kelly Wells.

I was in fog. They were shadows in fog. And I was groping for them. I lived in fog.

She refilled my glass with booze, but I pushed it away. I was feeling tired and a bit drunk and I knew I'd be driving back to Tehachapi that night.

Earlier, I had called the house. No one had answered and that made me nervous. I assumed Macklin had taken the kids out for something to eat and perhaps to the park. "You could move out here. You could make a life," Kelly said.

"Not in this town."

"You don't like me all that much."

"I like you."

"It's not enough."

"No."

"There's someone else."

"Maybe."

"You don't know? That's funny."

"What do I know about anything?" I said and we kissed, but I had no real feeling for her and she knew it. I wanted to make love to her, but I didn't want to stay with her. "I know about Travis, though," I said.

"What?"

"I know who killed your father and the kids. I have the evidence."

She grew weepy. It was the booze. "Sent my poor baby up like that. He loved my father. And my father loved him. From the time he was just a little thing, my son loved him so much. Cute…"

I wasn't sure what she had said. "Cute?" I said.

"That was my father's nickname for Travis. 'Cute.' From the time he was so little. 'Cute,' he would call him. And Travis was *cute*."

Cute! Cute killed me. I got up and moved around the room. I kept moving. *Cute!* Inside me something was falling apart. Graves were opening, women and children spilling out. I was soaked in blood. "What's the matter?" Kelly said.

"His name for your son was—Cute?"

"Yes. Why? What is it?"

I was trembling. I found myself saying over and over, "All wrong. Had it—all wrong. Oh, my God." And I was talking about Travis, but somehow I was talking about the war, too. Would that never leave me? And the death of Millie and Coty and Richie. So much blood. "All wrong."

"Thought it was dope and—had it all wrong."

"What?"

"*Everything.*"

The phone rang. Kelly moved to answer it. I could see she had received bad news, something horrific. "When?" she said. "Yes. Yes. Oh, no." She had put her hand up to her mouth in horror.

She hung up the phone and shook her head over and over. She turned to me. She continued to shake her head. "Travis has escaped," she said. "He somehow got a hold of I.D. and civilian clothes. They think a guard was involved."

And I knew it was Rita Macklin.

Chapter Thirty-One

As I sped back to Tehachapi, the dust storm kicked up again. I couldn't see anything in front of me, but I hurtled through the thick brownish gray. Images of the murder scene rose up in my mind. Travis swinging a baseball bat. Two kids. My kids.

And I was yelling aloud in the car; I could feel myself coming apart. Everything was cold and lost inside and I was yelling, "No. No. *All wrong!*"

My life was wrong. I had figured everything wrong. And now my kids—My hands were trembling violently on the wheel. I hadn't trembled like that since the day we had walked into Moc Hoa and seen the bodies scattered all over the village. Oh, dear God. What have I done?

By the time I reached Tehachapi the dust storm had dissipated, but fog had moved in. The town look eerie, yellow lights moving in and out of fog.

I sped across Cummings Valley. I could see the lights of the prison and they came out of fog and the place looked like an immense ship on an ocean of fog.

I started up the mountain to my house. I was praying. I had never prayed, even in war, but I was praying now. I prayed fervently that my kids were all right. I had no idea what God was, where He was. The words of the dying soldier were a storm in my brain: *God isn't anything we think he is*. All right. All right. Whatever God is, please, please take care of my kids.

I was going so fast that I almost missed a turn. I skidded and came to the edge of the road and then straightened the truck and continued on up.

The house was completely dark. Macklin's car was parked in front. There was not a sound from the house.

I got out of the truck and moved to the front door. I didn't open it, but listened. I could hear nothing, see nothing.

The air was cold. Moisture from the fog had settled over everything. I felt a chill. I realized perspiration was pouring from me and I was trembling. I moved to the rear of the house, tried the back door. It was locked. I took out my keys and fumbled for that key—it was not one that I used very often. At last I found it and inserted it in the lock and swung the door open and went into the house.

I removed the Walther from my waistband and held it in front of me.

Everything was quiet. I moved across the kitchen floor. The house was completely dark; no light, no moonlight. Because of the fog, I couldn't see anything. There was a swinging door between the kitchen and the dining area. I slowly pushed it open and entered the dining area.

It was empty.

The swinging door made a soft creaking sound as it moved back into place.

Holding my breath, I moved through the dining room into the living room. I crossed the living room.

I came to the stairway leading to the loft and the bedrooms. I put my foot on the bottom stair. It creaked.

Then I heard it, Kurt's voice: "Daddy? Daddy?"

I moved to one side, to a book shelf where I kept a flashlight. I picked up the flashlight. At the top of the stairs a figure seemed to be huddled.

There was a night light on the loft and I could make out the figure but was it one of the kids? Or Travis?

I could hear a quiet whimpering sound.

Silently I took a chair from the dining room and placed it below the loft railing. I put the Walther back in my waistband and the flashlight in my rear pocket.

I reached up and grabbed the wooden beam at the edge of the loft and pulled myself up. I eased myself over the railing. I reached into my pocket and took out my keys. I held them tight in my hand and there was no noise. Then I flung them toward the bottom of the stairs. They hit the floor with a loud clatter.

The figure at the top of the stairs rose up. I heard Kurt's voice scream, "Daddy!" Then Annie's voice: "Daddy, Daddy!"

I snapped on the flashlight. At the top of the stairs stood Travis Wells. He had my baseball bat in his hands. Kurt and Annie cowered at his feet.

His face had no expression. He raised the bat and I fired. The force of the shot threw him backward. He hit the wall and slid to the floor.

A loud wail rose from the kid's room. It was Macklin: "Noooooooo!" She ran from the room. In her hand was a revolver.

"Drop it!"

She hesitated, then let the gun fall. She began to weep. Travis was looking at me with that same empty expression. "Why did you do that?" he said. It was as though he was asking me the time.

"You came after my kids," I said. He shook his head. "You killed your brother and sister. Your grandfather."

His breath was coming in short gasps now. His voice was barely audible. He was dying. "Found him with them. He was molesting them. Doing to them what he did to me. Couldn't let them live the life I led. I killed them to save them."

"What were you doing here?"

"Wanted to see—your kids—love—kids. Knew this was your house. She told me. Wanted—to see—how you lived. I—admire—you…"

He sat there breathing heavily. There was almost no blood, just a little in the center of his chest. "Why did you shoot me?" he said. Then he died.

Macklin continued to weep. She was quivering and weeping. My kids had crawled to me and I was holding them. They, too, were shaking. "You did what you did with me to get him out," I said to her. "How long had it been going on with him?"

"Ever since he came to B Unit. I loved him." She looked me and her tear-streaked face had an expression wide and innocent and childlike. "Why did you kill him?" she said.

"My kids."

"He just wanted to see them. He made me bring him back here. He said he wanted to hug them and beg forgiveness for the other thing…"

I didn't speak. We remained quiet for a long time. Travis Wells' eyes were frozen wide and questioning and I leaned over and closed them.

"They'll walk me through the yard," Rita Macklin said. She was talking to herself, really. I didn't say anything. She put her face in her hands and shook her head over and over.

Suddenly, she snatched up her revolver. She pointed it directly at me. I was looking into the cold silver blue of the barrel and the blackness in the center of it. I could sense my own death. And at that moment I was resigned. I said in my head, just take care of my kids.

Her eyes had this terrible anger in them. Was she angry at me? At life? At what she had done with her life? I would never know.

She turned the gun on herself. She bit down on the barrel and fired and fell backwards and did not move again.

I held my kids hard, hard. Quiet the trembling, I was saying to myself. Quiet the trembling.

I never went back to the prison. There's a park at the edge of Cummings Valley. I would take the kids there from time to time. Winter was coming on and snow began to fall.

I would sit there and listen to time.

Great snow clouds would fill the valley and I would think of my prisoners. Would they be waiting in the yard, huddling, slapping their arms, bouncing in place to keep warm? Would they be waiting for me? Would they be writing?

My kids would be on the swings or on a seesaw. They'd ride up and down, laughing. Snow would swirl about us.

I'll write another book, I told myself. And I did.

END

9 780595 147489